ROBYN SCHNEIDER

INVISIBLE GHOSTS

KT KATHERINE TEGEN BOOKS
An Imprint of HarperCollins Publishers

Katherine Tegen Books is an imprint of HarperCollins Publishers.

Invisible Ghosts
Copyright © 2018 by Robyn Schneider
www.epicreads.com

Library of Congress Control Number: 2017943385
ISBN 978-0-06-256808-3

Typography by Carla Weise
18 19 20 21 22 PC/LSCH 10 9 8 7 6 5 4 3 2 1
❖
First Edition

For the girl who secretly hoped she'd get a Hogwarts letter—
For the girl who makes wishes on every 11:11—
For the girl who ran out of space on her bookshelves
and bought this book anyway

The past is never where you think you left it.
—KATHERINE ANNE PORTER, *Ship of Fools*

I LEARNED RECENTLY that the ancient Romans used to interpret even the most ordinary things as signs from the beyond. A spilled drink was a supernatural disaster. A sudden crack in a roof beam would send people into a panic. Things could sour in an instant, going from good luck to bad with a change in the weather or the setting of the sun.

Even though I've never believed in those kinds of auguries, I can't bring myself to dismiss them entirely, because there's always been one specific omen in my life: a good-hair day.

I'm not joking. Whenever my hair goes right, something else goes wrong. I have this theory that the universe expects payment for fixing it, except I never know what form that payment will take.

The first time it happened was the morning the *For Sale* sign appeared in the Aldridges' front yard. It was the summer before sixth grade, and my unruly bangs lay

1

uncharacteristically flat while Jamie and I sat on his front steps, his cheeks splotchy as he mumbled that his parents were getting a divorce and he was moving to Santa Cruz with his mom.

The second time it happened was during the auditions for my middle school's production of *Peter Pan*. My hair was in these awesome braids Claudia had done, and I'd been rehearsing all week. Except I got hiccups right before I went on, and instead of Tiger Lily, I got cast as Pirate #5.

The third time was the day of my brother's funeral, which was already awful. I'd only been able to find two bobby pins for my bun, and then I'd accidentally dropped the deli platter, apologizing uselessly as my mom scraped lox off the kitchen floor in tears. But my bun had stayed put, despite its lack of pins, like it knew *something* needed to hold itself together that day.

All of those disasters happened a long time ago, but there have been other, less devastating good-hair days since: the failed algebra test, Delia's birthday scavenger hunt where I tripped over a patch of poison oak, the time I borrowed my dad's car and hit a pole in the Trader Joe's parking lot.

They were days when I should have taken stock of my appearance and known to stay inside, marathoning Netflix in my pajamas. Except I never did. Each time, I convinced myself that I was imagining it, that good hair days couldn't really be bad omens.

Then I read about the ancient Romans, and everything started to make an odd kind of sense. Because I realized that superstitions don't have to be just one thing for everyone. There's probably a boy somewhere who believes heads-up pennies are unlucky, and a girl who refuses to wish on her birthday candles.

People rarely have the same fears, so it makes sense that we have different omens. We're all haunted by different things, until the day our ghosts finally leave us. Or the day we finally leave them. And maybe that's what we're really afraid of—not being ready to let go.

THE FIRST DAY of my junior year dawned hot and cloudless after a week of gloom. It was the perfect weather for a beach trip, and I couldn't decide whether that was depressing or just inevitable in Southern California.

I stumbled toward the bathroom, already second-guessing the jeans and sweater I'd laid out the night before. That was when I glanced in the mirror. My impossible hair hung in loose waves instead of its usual tangled curls. It looked like those pictures on beauty blogs that explain how to get French Girl Hair, as though switching shampoos can change your nationality.

No matter how much I reassured myself that everything would be fine, I knew how this went. And so I biked the mile between my house and Laguna Canyon High with a sense of impending doom. The whole way, I kept trying to work out what disaster might be waiting for me.

I didn't have any assignments due, other than the summer reading for Mr. Cope (*Wide Sargasso Sea*, which sounded like a euphemism for a vagina, but was actually a novel about postcolonialism). I guessed it could be a pop quiz in English, or some hideous group project in French, or a lemonade spill down the front of my shorts. But somehow I knew it wouldn't be that easy.

My phone vibrated gently as I biked past Canyon's football field. My five-minute warning before the warning bell. I liked to think of it as my antisocial alarm, since it got me to school with just enough time to cut across the parking lot, dock my bike at the rack, and slide into my seat in advisement without having to talk to anyone.

Advisement was the same group of students all four years, and there was literally no point to it. No one stood for the Pledge of Allegiance. No one had any announcements. No one cared.

Plus, Mrs. Yoon taught biology, so we didn't even get desks. Instead, we had to sit at four-top lab stations, on stools. In alphabetical order. Although I'd rather have an assigned seat than be forced to call out "here" at eight o'clock every morning. Especially with a last name like Asher, which usually placed me first on the roll sheet.

At my station were Sean Baker and Colton Barnes, who promptly went to sleep inside their flipped-up water polo hoodies, and Darren Choi, who studied through every advisement with his headphones blasting hip-hop. Which meant I could either pretend to be fascinated by the lab-safety posters or dig out a book of my own.

Despite my good-hair day, the universe remained suspiciously well behaved that morning. Mr. Cope went over the syllabus and begged us to cover our textbooks with paper bags. And then Ms. Dubois, aka Madame of the Perpetual Headache, put on *The Adventures of Tintin*. We'd already watched it last spring, and Darren, who was across the aisle, shot me an eye roll over this. I eye-rolled back.

At lunch, I sat with the same group of girls who'd adopted me out of pity back in middle school. I guessed we were friends, but it didn't really matter what we were, because lunch tables are just another version of assigned seating.

It's like when teachers tell you to partner up for a group activity. Most people pick from whoever's sitting right there, because it's easier than packing your stuff and moving across the room. Eventually, you start choosing the same people out of habit, without even considering the other options.

There were four of us at my lunch table, which sat under the shaded overhang of the math building. *An up-and-coming neighborhood, cool-kids adjacent*, I'd joked one time, and Delia had practically murdered me with her glare.

Some friend groups are defined by a sport everyone plays, or an extracurricular everyone joins, but we were defined by Delia Kelly. We were her subordinates, the adjectives to her noun.

Mrs. Kelly taught at our middle school, and back then,

5

Delia had used her mom's classroom as her private clubhouse. She'd ushered us into the cool air-conditioning and screened episodes of *Pretty Little Liars* at lunch like we should worship her for the honor. By the time we started high school, her power over us was absolute, and she made sure we knew it.

Sometimes, though, I wished I could forget. I imagined drifting away into the sea of students and washing up at another lunch table. One where people seemed happy, instead of just resigned to each other's company. Except I was afraid that if I ever let go of Delia's table, instead of floating away, I'd drown.

The cafeteria line at our school took forever, and only seniors could leave campus, so most of us packed lunch. I nibbled at my buttered bagel, and Emmy very earnestly dug into her tuna sandwich. We were both performing our specialty of staying out of it while Delia was a total bitch to Kate.

This time, the drama was over the rolling backpack Kate had brought to school. It really *was* unfortunate, all pink-and-black checkers, like someone's middle school Vans. And she hadn't even tried to hide it, which I would have done. Instead, she'd parked it next to our table with the handle extended, which only proved what everyone already knew: that as far as groups of junior girls went, we were just a little bit tragic.

"Ugh, it feels like we're in an airport," Delia complained,

rolling her eyes for what must have been the third time.

Kate's cheeks went pink with embarrassment. I tore off another piece of my bagel, wishing we could move on.

"If you want, I can loan you my bag from last year," Emmy offered, trying to help.

Except we all knew a different backpack wouldn't undo the damage. Kate had made us look juvenile, which was unforgivable. And Delia would conveniently bring it up the next time she wasn't invited to someone's party or a cute boy didn't smile back in the hallway.

"I *can't*," Kate said, looking even more embarrassed. "My mom will be offended if I don't use it."

She stared at her backpack like she was already resigned to dragging it around on a yearlong layover. And everyone was being so dramatic over that stupid bag that I couldn't take it anymore.

"What if you told your mom it's too big to fit in the overhead compartment?" I joked, trying to lighten the mood.

No one laughed, and I wondered if there was something about me that neutralized jokes. Or, more likely, something about them.

I sighed, disappointed with my friends, and how they never seemed to have fun, except in photos they'd posed for a million times. And then I glanced across the quad. Over on the slope next to the no-sodas vending machine, Sam Donovan and his crowd looked as cool as ever.

Sam was holding court, his white-blond hair catching

the sun. His theater-trained voice carried over everything, even though I was too far away to make out more than the boom of his laugh. Sam's girlfriend, Claudia Flores, lounged stomach-down on a scarf, using it as a picnic blanket. Her shoes were off, and she was drawing on her wrist with a Sharpie. Darren and Max were there too, the school's cutest couple in their matching sunglasses. Nima and Sam were arguing over something, which must have been hilarious, because Max put his head down on his arms, his whole body shaking with laughter. Nima gave a theatrical little bow, and Sam held up his hands, giving in.

I watched as they laughed and chatted, and it felt like a million years ago that I used to hang out with them. Except it wasn't a million years, just a lifetime ago—my brother's.

We all grew up together in Hidden Canyon. It's the turn off Felicia Parkway that dead-ends at the back of the nature preserve. When we were kids, we'd ride our bikes up and down the cul-de-sac and swim in Sam's pool and eat sour candy in our tree fort.

The group was different then: Jamie still lived two houses down, and Nima constantly had piano lessons, and Darren hung around with those boys who played Yu-Gi-Oh in Chris Keeler's garage. Then Jamie moved away, and Max moved in, and Darren started waving whenever we biked past.

I'd distanced myself from my friends after Logan died. I'd thought it was a good idea, since it's harder to tell what's missing when nothing is familiar. But then I'd learned that running away is the easy part: it's finding your way back that's almost impossible.

By freshman year, my window of opportunity had passed. Their popularity had been bestowed, their ranks had closed, and nobody remembered that I'd stood onstage alongside them in our sixth-grade production of *Peter Pan*.

Now I was as good as not even there. My vibrant former friends raged on, while I'd faded so much that, when people looked through me, I barely even tinted the landscape.

We hardly had classes together anymore, except for Advanced Theater, which I only took because I did costumes. Gardner's class was our third block, right after lunch. The chairs in his room were arranged in a giant U, creating a makeshift stage.

Gardner runs a tight ship—you need to be in Advanced to audition for the plays. Otherwise you get drafted into stage crew or ticket sales. He claimed it was because our class functioned as an extra rehearsal period, but I think he just liked playing favorites.

I sat with Kate and her wheeled backpack, because that's the other rule of friend groups: if you have class together, you sit together. And then you partner together, creating this endless loop of forced sameness.

Kate wasn't much of an actress, but she stuck around so she could design the playbills. Last year, we'd been the only students in Advanced whose names weren't on the audition sheet—well, except for Leo Swanson, who'd broken his leg jousting at the Renaissance Faire, but that doesn't count.

On the far side of the room, my long-ago friends sat in a cluster, giving the impression they'd somehow transported their lunchtime picnic right into our class. They were our school's reigning theater royalty, and this was the seat of their kingdom. They ran the drama club, the class-spirit committee, and the improv team. They ran so many things that I wondered if they ever got tired from all that running.

Mr. Gardner was mostly stomach, which he somehow managed to belt his khakis underneath. It made him look like a human ice-cream cone. I did this thing where I imagined his polo shirts were the flavors: today, he was pistachio.

Gardner droned on, making me want a scoop of Ben & Jerry's. He was just about to announce his selection for the fall play when the door opened.

"Sorry," a boy said, trying to catch his breath. The sun was fierce behind him, and he was nothing but a silhouette framed in the doorway. "I thought Advanced Theater was *in* the theater."

"Well, now you know," Gardner said. "Have a seat."

"Will do. Sorry, again."

He headed for an empty chair, and if I couldn't already tell he was a new student, the way he was clutching his planner clued me in, folded open to the campus map. He was cute, though, with dark messy hair and soft brown eyes that turned down at the corners. His jeans were cuffed short, revealing a flash of ankle, since he was wearing loafers without socks.

It wasn't the kind of thing anyone did at our school, where our mascot probably should have been a flip-flop. He looked exactly like he made the girls in his English class fall in love with him every time he raised his hand, and he also looked like he knew it.

I watched as he sat down on the other side of the room, crossing his bare ankles and glancing around in a way that was almost hopeful. I couldn't figure out what he was looking for. And then his eyes met mine and stayed there just a moment too long, asking a question that I couldn't quite decipher. It was strange, and totally unexpected. I frowned, because I had no idea what he wanted. He glanced away, embarrassed.

I've always been suspicious of attractive boys. I don't know why. It's not like they chose to be born with gorgeous eyebrows or perfect jawlines. But still. Whenever a reasonably cute boy paid attention to me, I assumed he meant it as a joke.

"As you know, the fall play is usually a drama," Gardner said, "and this year's pick is no exception. At the end of the semester, we'll be putting up the chilling, the creepy, the bloodcurdling . . . *Dracula*."

Everyone looked elated. Max and Nima high-fived, and Sam let out an ironic "hip, hip, huzzah!" Some of the seniors rolled their eyes, but everyone else loved it.

Dracula. I couldn't help but think how awesome it would be to do nineteenth-century costumes. I've always been hopelessly in love with Victorian England, even though living there pretty much sucked for everyone who wasn't a rich white guy. Even so, I was slightly giddy at the thought of sourcing corsets and top hats.

"All right, settle down," Gardner scolded. "Auditions won't be for another few weeks. And I still need to take roll."

He opened the manila folder, and I braced myself for the inevitable "Rose Asher?"

"Jamie Aldridge?" he called instead.

The boy who'd walked in late raised his hand, and I'm pretty sure my mouth fell open.

"Here," he said, his voice a deep rumble. But there was no way. Absolutely no way this was the neighbor I'd built pool-noodle floats with in the third grade.

Except the more I stared, the more I could see it. Sure enough, beneath the trendy-somewhere-else clothes and hipster haircut was the boy who used to live two houses down.

Sam's crowd was also eyeing him with interest, and I couldn't blame them. It almost didn't feel real. But then, Laguna Canyon was no stranger to ghosts, both the kind that blew in with the Santa Ana winds and the kind that sat in your classroom looking nothing like you remembered.

Gardner finished taking roll and picked up a thick stack of handouts. A table read, probably. We did those when we weren't running rehearsals. The same students always volunteered to read, and the rest of us followed along silently, which is a perfect metaphor for high school, if you think about it.

"This year we're going to change things up," Gardner said, splitting the handouts into stacks. "I want everyone to choose a monologue from this packet, to be memorized and performed on Friday."

My stomach dropped. That wasn't an assignment, it was a punishment—sudden death by stage performance. Judging from the horrified look on Kate's face, she'd also been expecting the table read.

"Feel free to take these outside to practice," Gardner said. "And before anyone asks: no costumes and no props, please. That means you, Seth."

My classmates laughed. Seth Bostwick, who was wearing a fedora and juggling erasers in his seat, went red.

Everyone grabbed their bags and surged forward, chattering excitedly. They jostled for the handouts like it was a race, passing them back to their friends. I sighed, because of course my classmates would act like *monologues* were a group activity.

By the time Kate and I stepped into the south quad, most of the tables were already claimed. Our usual spot had been taken over by a loud group of sophomore boys.

"Let's sit outside the choir room," Kate suggested.

Without waiting for an answer, she started wheeling her backpack toward the music building. She only wanted to sit there, I knew, because Delia and Emmy took choir.

It struck me as kind of pathetic to station ourselves on the ground outside their classroom, as though we had nothing better to do than follow in Delia's wake like human versions of a rolling backpack. But I didn't say any of that. Instead, I trailed after Kate, twisting around to see how Jamie was doing.

He stood in the doorway, surveying the quad in dismay. He looked slightly shocked, like he couldn't figure out what to do, or how he'd missed the memo about groups.

For a moment, I imagined walking over there and inviting him to join us. Except that would be a disaster. Jamie would ask how I'd been, and I'd freeze up, not wanting to watch his face bloom with sympathy as he found out about Logan. I'd barely survived it the first time, having everyone look at me like that. I didn't think I could stand it again.

No, it was better to leave him alone. Better to follow Kate to the choir room the way she expected. Because we all played a role in high school, and mine was invisible sidekick in an insignificant friend group. The kind of role no one auditions for, but someone gets assigned after reading for a bigger, more exciting part and not being good enough.

Except Jamie was still frozen in the doorway. Alone. I had this awful fear that he was going to sit down right there, all by himself, in front of everyone.

And then I saw Claudia hurrying toward him, her perfect hair swirling around her perfect smile. Claudia, who was a little bit magic.

"Jamie!" she called. "I can't believe it!"

Even her voice was magical, with its high, clear bell of a laugh that was always on the verge of ringing out.

"No freaking way!" he said, brightening instantly.

He wrapped her in an enormous hug, swinging her around so that her feet left the ground. Or maybe she was flying.

"Stop that," she scolded, but she was laughing so hard you knew she didn't mean it.

From over on the grass, Sam cupped his hands around his mouth and bellowed, "Aldridge, get over here!"

Everyone looked up to see what was going on.

"Wait your turn, Donovan!" Jamie called, flashing a grin that made me wonder how I could have thought he needed rescuing.

I watched as Jamie sauntered over to the grass and flung his bag onto the royal pile. It didn't matter that everyone else was in sandals or that he hadn't been able to find our classroom on time. Just like that, he'd gone from confused new kid to rejoining our old friends as though he'd never left.

2

I BIKED HOME from school the way I always did—along the hiking trail, rather than the parkway. The parkway was faster, but I hated how my classmates zoomed past in their new cars, music blasting, so I stuck to the scenic route.

The preserve had seemed magical when I was younger, as though our cul-de-sac were pressed up against a forgotten slice of Narnia. My friends and I used to play there, in our tree fort, inventing secret worlds.

Back then, I actually believed that adventure might be waiting for me just beyond the wall of sandbags. But I knew better now. The only thing beyond the wall was the place where Logan had died.

I searched for it every time, unable to help myself. I'd pause my bike, looking for the familiar cluster of honeysuckle bushes. And when I found them, it was almost too easy to close my eyes and go right back to that day.

Sixth grade had just ended, and Sam, Claudia, Max,

and I were doing junior rep at the Harbor Playhouse, putting on a production of *Annie*. The cast list had gone up that morning.

All of my friends had lead roles, while my name was on a different sheet, for backstage helpers. I'd stared at it in disbelief, unable to figure out what had happened. I'd thought my audition had gone well, but apparently not, since I hadn't even made the ensemble.

I went to talk to our director during lunch. She was an older woman, with breath that always smelled of coffee and the yellow teeth to match. I mustered my courage and asked if anything had been the matter with my audition.

"It's Rose, right?" she said, shuffling through her notes to unearth whatever she'd written about me.

And then she looked me square in the eye and said, in a gust of coffee fumes, "I'm going to be honest here: I just didn't see any real talent in you."

It was as though she'd picked up my dreams and smashed them on the floor. I stared down at the broken shards, quietly devastated. And then I mumbled a thank-you and slunk away.

I couldn't tell you what I ate for lunch that day or what improv games we played that afternoon. All I remember is counting down the minutes until I could go home and cry.

Miraculously, I managed to hold it together, even as my friends were given scripts and told to stay after. Even as I waved good-bye like it was nothing to walk home alone while they all stayed behind for a cast meeting.

I was halfway home before I realized that I'd left my sweater in the theater. And everything might have turned out very differently if I hadn't gone back to get it. But I did, which is how I caught Sam and Claudia kissing behind the water cooler.

In sixth grade, the idea of kissing someone had felt as strange and unreachable as a distant planet. But standing there, watching Sam's mouth pressed hungrily against Claudia's, I felt like I'd missed the shuttle launch. And there was nothing I could do about any of it except clutch my sweater and walk away.

When I got home, Logan was in the living room watching TV. He was supposed to be babysitting me, I guess, except our parents never called it that. "Watch out for each other," they always said, even though Logan was four years older.

He looked up and grinned, pausing the episode.

"I'm only a couple minutes in. Want me to start it over?"

I shook my head, and the tears I'd been so careful not to let out rolled down my cheeks, along with an explosion of snot.

"Rose," Logan said. "What's the matter?"

"All of my friends were cast in the play without me," I admitted.

I didn't tell him what the director had said to me or what I'd seen backstage, but he seemed to guess that I wasn't giving him the whole story.

"You can hang with me instead," Logan promised. "It'll be awesome. We can watch *Doctor Who.*"

He was just trying to make me feel better, but it had the opposite effect.

"You only want to hang out with me because you don't have any friends," I snapped.

It wasn't true, but it was *almost* true, which made it even worse. Logan stared at me like I'd betrayed him, and I was suddenly overwhelmed by my inability to do anything right. I shouldered my backpack and ran out of the house, my eyes burning with tears.

I plunged into the preserve, past the honeysuckle bushes that were buzzing with bees, past the scenic outlook sign, and along the footpath to the tree fort. Sam's dad had built it for us a few summers before. It was nothing elaborate—just a wooden platform with a rope ladder—but it was exactly what I needed: higher ground, to escape my flood of tears.

I curled up on the platform and took a book out of my bag, trying to disappear into it. I must have succeeded, because the sun was low when I finally looked up.

Logan hadn't come looking for me, which felt wrong. The fort should have been the first place he checked. But my shadow was long and slanting, so I started to walk home, past the scrub brush full of feral rabbits, and back toward the trail.

That was when I saw Logan, his body splayed in the dirt.

"Very funny," I called.

We never played games like this, trying to scare each other, and I wondered why he'd decided to start now.

"I get it, I was a brat. You can stop doing that," I pleaded. He still didn't move.

"Logan?"

It was too quiet in the preserve all of a sudden. Too still. My skin prickled, and suddenly I knew it wasn't a prank. Logan was on the ground next to the honeysuckle bush, which was buzzing with bees.

I knew he was allergic, just like I knew that he was supposed to carry an EpiPen in case he got stung. Mom had even shown me how to use it. But Logan was still wearing those shorts he'd been lounging around in, and his ratty hoodie, and I couldn't see anything in the pockets. Not even a phone. Not even his keys.

"Logan?" I whispered, coming closer.

That was when I saw the beestings. One on his arm, another on his leg. They were red and angry against his pale skin.

He was so still, lying there.

Not still. Dead.

Logan had come out to the preserve to find me. Because I'd run off. Because our parents had told us to watch out for each other, and I hadn't listened.

Everyone said Logan died of an insect allergy, but that was only a half-truth. The other half was that he'd died because of me.

It was the truth no one said. The truth that got buried behind sad smiles and condolence casseroles dropped off in dishes we never quite got around to returning. And every day, when I biked past the place where I found my brother's body, it didn't matter how many years had gone by, or how much I'd tried to atone. The guilt of losing him still stung. Except it turns out you can't be allergic to guilt. Bad memories can haunt you, but they can't kill you.

So I adjusted the weight of my backpack and coasted the rest of the way down the trail. My house was at the far end of the street, which meant I had to pass Jamie's old place. I hadn't thought of it that way in a long time—as Jamie's—and it was strange realizing that Max still lived there.

The garage door was open, and Max's mom was unloading the twins from her minivan, yelling for them to run and get changed for softball. She saw me and waved.

"Home early, huh?" she called.

For a moment, I didn't know what she meant. School had ended twenty minutes ago. But of course there was no reason to go straight home, especially today.

"Yeah," I said, embarrassed. I cast around for an excuse that wouldn't sound weird. "I'm studying for the PSATs."

"Max took a great Kaplan course this summer," she said. "It's over at the college, if you're looking for one."

"I'll check it out," I promised, just being polite.

"He can tell you all about it," she called, as though Max Coleman was still in the habit of talking to me. He wasn't. He was in the habit of loudly making sarcastic comments and threatening to run for homecoming queen just to piss off the cheerleaders, because they all knew he'd win.

As I pedaled away, I realized that everyone from school was probably on their way somewhere else. The mall, or Pelican Beach, or the frozen yogurt place with free Wi-Fi.

I was the only one desperate to rush home. I had a reason, though. Well, a theory. And my theory was that just maybe my house wouldn't be empty that afternoon.

"Hello?" I called, pushing open the front door. "Anyone here?"

I dropped my school bag onto the little bench in our entryway. It looked nothing like the pictures my mom had shown me on Pinterest featuring coatracks and galoshes and someone else's perfect life. Mostly, it just looked sad, like it knew it was destined to be forgotten, so I made an effort to use it.

"Hello?" I called again.

My parents were both at work, but it wasn't either of them I was hoping to find. It was the first day of school, and he'd never missed one before.

"Please," I whispered for good measure, in case the universe took requests. *"Please, please, please."*

"Wow, someone's being polite." Logan poked his head around the corner. "Two and a half pleases would have been enough."

"Logan!"

I barely resisted the urge to rush at him in a tackle-hug

like the one Claudia had given Jamie. Except ours wouldn't end with my feet swinging off the ground. It would end with my butt on the floor.

"Boo," Logan said sarcastically. "Did you miss me?"

He was a little smudged around the edges, but nothing too bad. I hadn't seen him for days, and even though that happened sometimes, I'd still worried.

"Never," I lied, grinning.

"You're so full of it," he accused, making my grin stretch wider.

I studied him even though I had him memorized, even though he hadn't changed at all in the past four years. He looked fifteen, like always, but somehow, fifteen wasn't the same anymore.

His face seemed rounder and younger than it used to, his dark curls more unruly. He was wearing the same shorts and unzipped hoodie, the same periodic-table T-shirt, and the same shark-print socks with a giant hole in the toe.

Once, when Mom had narrowly avoided a freeway accident, I'd turned to Logan and joked about how terrible it would be to die wearing dirty, stretched-out underwear. But it turns out there's something even more embarrassing: to come back as a ghost with a giant hole in your sock.

"Where have you been?" I asked.

It wasn't a good question.

"Around," he said vaguely, and then brightened. "Hey, wanna watch *Doctor Who*?"

It was what he'd asked the first time he'd reappeared, and now it was kind of our tradition. If you can have traditions with a ghost.

"Sure," I said, padding into the kitchen to grab a snack.

My stomach had been growling for the past hour, since I hated eating lunch in school. It's pretty depressing to pull a bagel that's been assassinated by a pile of textbooks out of your backpack, and it's even worse at 11:40 in the morning, which was the start of our lunch block.

"First day back?" Logan asked, trailing after me.

"Yeah. I'm a junior now."

The instant I said it, I wished I hadn't. I'd lapped him months ago, and it wasn't something we acknowledged—that we'd switched, and that I was the older one now.

I dug around in the fridge, coming up with some veggies and hummus.

"There's ice cream in the freezer," Logan suggested. He sounded pleased with himself, as though being able to see through the freezer door was some big accomplishment.

"Wow, amazing superpowers," I teased, reaching for the carton. Mint chip. It would have been hilarious if it were pistachio, to match Mr. Gardner's polo shirt, but oh well.

"Thank you." Logan preened, missing my sarcasm. "So how was school?"

That was all the invitation I needed to launch into a full-on rant about my friends. I told him everything, from how Delia had insisted on approving our first-day outfits to how

I'd spent most of lunch trying not to scream in frustration.

"I mean, who freaking *cares* about Kate's backpack?" I finished.

"Ooh, me! I care about her backpack!" Logan stuck his hand in the air for emphasis.

"Believe me, you don't."

"Well, I'd reassure you that high school is survivable, but I *literally* didn't make it past geometry." Logan grinned. "I got a B. Get it? A *bee*?"

"Thanks for hitting me over the head with that," I said, rolling my eyes.

"It's what I'm here for. That, and the Netflix."

Logan drifted into the living room and plopped onto the couch, reaching for the remote. His hand went right through it, and he groaned.

"Do you want me to—" I started to offer.

"—I can do it!" Logan insisted.

"Sure you can," I said, waiting for him to admit defeat.

"Fine," he said after his tenth try. "You can have the remote. But only if I get to pick what we watch."

"You *always* pick."

"Because I'm the oldest."

I didn't correct him. It was so strange, aging out of proportion. But it didn't matter whether Logan was fifteen, or nineteen, the age he should have been. He was still my older brother, and it was amazing that we were hanging out after school, like we used to.

"Wanna watch a new episode?" I asked, scrolling through the latest season.

"Nah, I like the old ones."

"All of time and space and you just want to go back to things you've already seen," I teased.

"Yeah, because the older seasons are the best. Matt Smith's okay, but he's no David Tennant."

Matt Smith hadn't been on *Doctor Who* for years, but I didn't say anything. Instead, I pulled up an earlier season, and Logan chose a silly episode that I'd loved back in elementary school.

Next to me, Logan recited most of the lines from memory. He laughed at them anyway, snorting a little. His mouth was curved into a grin, and his feet were draped over the armrest, and the hole in his sock looked ridiculous.

And suddenly, it didn't matter that school had been depressing, or that my friends were disappointing, or that my hair was full of bad omens. I still had Logan, and that made everything else bearable.

SO IT'S WEIRD, right? The ghost thing.

Of course it's weird. I know, I know. But it's a good, surprising kind of weird, like the soundtrack to *Hamilton*, or maple-bacon doughnuts.

It all started on my first day of seventh grade. Everyone had gaped at me in the halls like dead brother was this horrible outfit they couldn't believe I was wearing. The teachers were just as subtle, pulling me aside during the passing bell to say how sorry they were, while their next period walked in and overheard the whole thing.

Maybe it would have been different if Logan had died of something that's supposed to kill you, like cancer or a car accident. Or maybe it was because I'd been the one to find his body. But somehow, I'd become tainted by association. That first day back, no one asked me about my summer. They were too busy whispering about it instead.

I didn't know how to be a spectacle. And I didn't know how to be an only child. After we finished sitting shiva, my parents never cried in front of me, but I'd hear their shower running at odd hours, and I pretended not to notice when dinner was late or laundry went forgotten. The landmarks we'd used to navigate our lives had vanished without warning. And somehow, we were expected to find new ones.

You mourn and then you move on in the Jewish faith, but it's harder than it sounds to let go of someone so easily. As the months ticked by, I watched my parents gather up their pieces and glue themselves back together. I watched as they got dressed, went back to work, and, at the urging of the family therapist, joined a gym.

When September rolled around, Logan had been gone for nearly three months, and I was the only Asher who was still lost. The only one without a new landmark.

And on that first day of seventh grade, when I came

home to an empty house, it occurred to me that I might never find one.

What I wanted were my old landmarks back. I wanted Mom to wave up at my window from the backyard on Sunday mornings, when she sat in the sunshine doing the crossword puzzle. I wanted Logan to come back from sci-fi club the way he used to, all keyed up and doing goofy impressions. I wanted Dad to make a big production over the arrival of a Netflix DVD, going around the dinner table and making us guess the movie.

Except I didn't have any of that. What I had were whispered rumors about how I'd found my brother's body, and too much math homework, and no idea where to sit at lunch.

So I put my head down on the kitchen table and started to cry. And then, impossibly, Logan was there, asking if I wanted to marathon our favorite show.

I didn't question it. I didn't even think it was weird that he was kind of see-through. I'd just burst out laughing at the hole in his sock, and he'd told me to shut up about it, and it was the first normal thing that had happened in a long time. So I'd wiped away my tears and turned on the TV. It became our routine. And it became my secret, since no one else could see him.

Sometimes, when we were hanging out in the living room, Mom would walk right past him without even realizing. Logan would frown and go sullen, and I'd pretend everything was fine. Which was hard at first, but not as hard as if I'd been sitting on the sofa alone.

I read somewhere that ghosts come back for a reason, and since Logan's probably wasn't to rewatch episodes of *Doctor Who*, I guessed he came back because of me. Because Mom and Dad had told us to look out for each other. And no matter how many times I figured it, I always arrived at the same conclusion: that looking out for a ghost was much better than having to let go of my brother.

3

MY PARENTS AND I ate dinner in a parallel universe, where everyone except me was having a normal day. And I could usually play along, but that night, I was having trouble.

It was Logan's fault. He'd faded away after less than an hour, when I'd been looking forward to an entire afternoon. And while Dad's attention was elsewhere—he kept sneakily checking the baseball score on his phone—Mom definitely sensed something was up.

"Sweetie, is everything okay?" she asked, frowning at me over her salad.

She was still wearing her scrubs. Purple with white piping, to match her nail wraps. I don't know why she bothers, since she has to wear gloves. But if there's any way to glam up a dentist's uniform, you can bet my mom has found it.

"Yeah, of course," I said, wondering what had betrayed me. "Just tired."

I took a huge bite of salad and attempted to look

cheerful, but I probably just looked like one of those bizarre stock photos.

Thankfully, Mom's cell phone rang, sparing me. She dug it out of her pocket and sighed.

"It's work," she apologized, already pushing back her chair.

As she disappeared upstairs, I could hear her asking, "Which patient? No, we ordered those X-rays this afternoon."

This happened a lot. You'd think there was no such thing as a dental emergency, but you'd be wrong. The moment Mom was out of range, Dad immediately went for the remote. He flicked on the ball game and lowered the volume, like that made it more polite.

"Our little secret," he said, winking at me from behind his accidentally hip glasses. He had about five different pairs, since he was an optometrist, but these were the ones I liked best. They were horn rimmed and retro and made him look like a character from an old spy movie.

We sat there watching a slow-motion recap of the last play. Dad glanced at me every so often, smiling like we were coconspirators. He was like that, my dad. Always made you feel like you were getting away with some big heist, even if you were just taking double samples at Costco.

Mom came back downstairs, and Dad fumbled to turn off the TV but didn't make it in time.

"Roger," she scolded.

"Sorry," he said sheepishly. "It's the end of the game."

He flashed a smile, trying to charm his way out of it. Mom sighed, instantly defeated.

"That's no excuse," she said, softening. "We're having a family dinner."

I waited for the wrongness of that statement to land, but it never did. Because *this* was family dinner now. On days when Logan was around, it was hard for me to remember how things were for everyone else. It had only been a few hours since I'd last seen him, but for my parents, it had been more than four years.

"Everything okay at work?" Dad asked, trying to get back into her good graces.

"Fine, fine," Mom said, even though it clearly wasn't. "The new computer system keeps freezing and—"

"Take a deep breath, honey," my dad told her. "It's just your job that's causing you stress, not your life."

She nodded and actually took a couple of deep breaths, centering herself or something.

That was the other alternate-universe thing about my parents. After Logan died, they'd become obsessed with self-help books. An obsession that showed no sign of ending. A few weeks ago, Mom had told me to fold my socks vertically, because it would give me joy, and I'd thought she was joking.

"So, Rose," Dad said excitedly, "how was your first day?"

I rolled my eyes over his enthusiasm, but my parents

looked so hopeful that I knew I couldn't disappoint. So I told them about the disaster of Kate's backpack.

I made it funny, rather than sad, stretching out the situation at lunch until it was practically a comedy routine. Dad laughed at my overhead-compartment line, and Mom grinned at my impression of Delia's displeasure. And then, I don't know why I said it, but I told my parents that Jamie had moved back.

"Really?" Mom looked surprised.

"He showed up in my drama class this afternoon."

Mom frowned. "I thought Angela liked living in Palo Alto—"

"Actually," my dad interrupted, "her husband got transferred to Shanghai for his job at—some bank, I think."

Mom and I both stared at him, wondering where this information had come from.

"Tom Aldridge came by the shop to pick up his new frames today." Dad shrugged. "Said Jamie's living with him down in University Village."

Mom shook her head, murmuring that it had to be tough on all of them. She turned to me, suddenly inspired.

"You should make sure he doesn't have trouble settling in," she said.

"I'm sure that won't be a problem," I said dryly, remembering how easily Sam and Claudia had reclaimed him.

"Just try, Rose," Mom insisted, mistaking my contempt for disinterest. "You adored each other when you were kids.

Remember the Egypt books?"

In case I did not, in fact, remember the Egypt books, my dad helpfully reminded me how Jamie and I had both gotten obsessed with ancient Egypt at the same time. Except he'd beat me to the library and had checked out all the books. We got locked into a full-on war over interlibrary loan until Mom decided enough was enough and marched over to his house to make him share.

"Oh my god, we were *eight*," I said.

"And you were the cutest Cleopatra and King Tut that Halloween." Dad grinned.

"By accident!" I said, but it was no use.

My parents were smiling at each other across the kitchen table, having one of those silent conversations about me like they thought I couldn't tell. Like they thought we lived in the same universe.

By some miracle, I'd convinced them that I was normal and well-adjusted. And maybe I was, on paper: I had a group of friends, and an extracurricular activity, and a place on the honor roll. No one knew the truth—that I spent my afternoons with a ghost, who was either a figment of my imagination or a supernatural condolence card from the great beyond.

"I bet I have a photo of you two somewhere," my dad teased.

"Honey," Mom said, her voice low with warning. "I don't think we *really* need to go through the old albums."

I stabbed at my chicken, wishing we didn't have to tiptoe around so many fragile things, but mostly wishing I knew what to say to fix dinner.

Logan would have known. He would have done some spot-on impression or turned his napkin into a costume or found a weird gif on his phone to show around until we were all laughing.

As for me, I just sat there chewing.

Because only child was a role I'd never auditioned for. A role that was never meant to be in the script. I felt so guilty, and so exhausted, trying to be enough for all of us and constantly falling short. It wasn't easy filling the empty seat at the table along with my own.

And maybe I had been Cleopatra once, but I wasn't anymore. I was a broken potsherd in someone else's funerary urn, and the girl my parents thought I was—the girl Jamie had been looking for across Gardner's classroom—didn't exist.

4

OF COURSE JAMIE sat with our old friends at lunch the next day. And of course it was the topic of conversation at my table.

It's hard to explain, but Sam's crowd wasn't just some collection of popular kids. They weren't even the only theater group in our year. There were other offshoots—the musical-theater kids, the student filmmakers, the boys who made terrible sketches for their YouTube channel—but something about Sam's crowd was magnetic. You'd find yourself watching while they waited in line at a vending machine or opened a locker, drawn to them without quite knowing why.

I'd lost my own charisma that summer before seventh grade. Maybe it had been redistributed among the group the moment I left, making them shine even brighter. Or maybe I'd only lit up in the reflection of everyone else, the way the moon becomes visible when it crosses the path of the sun.

But Jamie's glow was intact. And it definitely wasn't a

reflection. There was something half-remembered about him, and that made him even more interesting.

"I still can't believe that's *Jamie Aldridge*," Kate said, staring shamelessly. "I wonder why he moved back."

I looked down at my bagel, not quite daring to chime in. And then Delia leaned forward, lowering her voice to an excited whisper like she knew everything.

"Well *I* heard he *had* to move back," she said, "because he got kicked out of art school for turning in a *portfolio of nudes.*"

I didn't mean to snort, but it slipped out.

"What?" Delia demanded.

"Nothing," I mumbled.

"God, I'm just saying what I heard." Delia narrowed her eyes. "You don't have to be so savage."

"Sorry," I said. "Forget it."

Except that was the problem with Delia. She wouldn't forget it. I hunched forward, trying to make myself smaller, as though that would undo the damage.

"I bet he starts dating some popular girl in, like, five seconds," Emmy said with her mouth full of pasta. "He's really cute."

"Isn't he, like, half Chinese or something?" Kate asked, frowning.

"I can kind of see it," Delia said.

"If he's Asian, how come his last name is *Aldridge*?" Emmy countered.

"His mom's Filipino," I explained, and then wished I hadn't.

Nothing good ever came from talking around my friends. If anything, it just gave them more ammunition to use against me. And sure enough, Delia's claws were out, and waiting to swipe.

"Wow, Rose, obsessed much?" she purred, sipping her juice.

"Well, we used to be . . ." *Friends*, I'd almost said.

". . . neighbors," I finished. "About a million years ago."

I don't know why I couldn't bring myself to say it. That, a long ago, we used to be friends. Not just Jamie and me, but Sam and Claudia and Nima and Max. That, once upon a time, I'd had real friends, instead of just belonging to a friend group. Except it turned out they all had their own orbits, and without their gravitational pull, I was just drifting uselessly in space.

I HAD AP Art History after lunch, which I was actually looking forward to. I'd signed up in secret after my friends had decided to take sociology. When we'd compared schedules over the summer, they'd freaked. I'd claimed that sociology must have filled up, except that wasn't the truth.

The truth was, I wanted some space. And I liked the idea of becoming someone who could walk through a museum one day and know what I was seeing, and why it was so important.

I took a seat toward the back and glanced around the room, curious who had signed up. I recognized a few people, like Maritza Fernandez and Adam Kwong, the power couple of the Mock Trial crowd. And, annoyingly, Preston Rice. He was a senior, and president of the Anime Guild, and I only knew this because he'd asked me to prom out of nowhere last spring. I was on my way to a French test, and all of a sudden this total stranger was shoving a wilted carnation in my face during the passing bell. I probably could have been nicer about saying no, but I was frantically conjugating the *imparfait* in my head.

Preston stiffened when he saw me, then took out his phone and started typing. A few seconds later, the curly-haired kid next to him also took out his phone, shooting me a look. It wasn't hard to guess what they were texting about.

I brought my phone out too, trying to look busy, even though I was just scrolling Instagram, which is probably the opposite of art history. The wall clock changed from 12:29 to 12:30, and then the door opened one last time.

It was Jamie. He was draining a can of Coke. His head was tipped way back, and he looked so relaxed, like he hadn't almost been late to class. Like being a new old student was the easiest thing in the world.

Yesterday's cuffed jeans and dad shoes were gone. Instead, he had on the same Adidas everyone owned and a plain black tee. He was one of those people, I noticed, who wore a T-shirt like it was an Olympic sport.

He took a seat by the door, and I let out a breath I didn't realize I'd been holding. The seat in front of mine was empty, and I'd hoped he wouldn't choose it.

The bell rang, and Mr. Ferrara shuffled some papers around on his desk. He was older, with graying hair and a funny little bow tie that I couldn't tell if he meant to be ironic. He mostly taught senior history, so I'd never had him before.

"Excellent," he said, surveying the room. "Looks like I can skip the lecture about not coming in late from lunch."

He was holding a sheet of paper with squares on it, and my stomach dropped as I realized what it was. *Please*, I hoped, *not alphabetical order. Not alphabetical order.*

"The dreaded seating chart," Mr. Ferrara joked. "Don't worry, I'll learn your names by the final exam. But until then: Jamie Aldridge, front and center."

I closed my eyes, as though that would help. But the shots had already been fired, and there was nothing to do but triage.

"Next victims: Rose Asher, Michelle Avery, Jacob Bell . . ." It was like a cosmic joke. Except the joke was on me, because I was the one who'd signed up for art history.

I grabbed my bag and moved to the front row, even though I would have given anything to stay where I was, sandwiched between a girl in a color-guard uniform and a boy who was quietly Googling his math homework.

Jamie and I arrived at the same time, and he stepped

back to let me sit first.

"Hey there, stranger," he said, smiling.

He had a great smile, unfortunately. One dimple on the right side, like a punctuation mark. I stared at him, wondering if he knew about Logan, until I realized I'd let the silence stretch on a little too long.

"You came back," I said. It sounded awkward and charmless, and Jamie's smile faltered a little as he sat down.

"Well, yeah, I couldn't let you have the monopoly on the best library books forever," he joked.

I shrugged. It was uncomfortable, being on the spot like this. He was staring at me like he'd been dying of thirst, and now he was drinking me in.

"So what's the excuse?" he went on, plugging the silence. "French Club? Mock Trial?"

"What are you talking about?" I asked, confused.

"Just trying to figure out where you disappeared to," he explained, still smiling.

I wished he wouldn't do that—try to make sense of me. Anyway, he was wrong about my departure from our old group: It wasn't because I'd chosen a new destination. It was because I'd used an emergency exit.

Jamie's eyes danced, as though he'd thought of an amazing joke and couldn't wait to tell me.

"Can I guess?" he asked.

Before he could, a shadow fell across our desks.

"I don't allow food or drinks in my classroom." Mr.

Ferrara frowned down at Jamie's soda can.

"It's just an empty." Jamie shook it to demonstrate. "I was waiting to find a recycle bin."

"There's one in the corner," our teacher said.

Jamie got up and threw away the can. He did it properly, instead of trying to bank it from across the room, like most boys would have done.

I watched as his gaze flickered to our teacher, checking that he'd smoothed the tension, and I realized it had been a calculated move. Just like the change of clothing after he saw that he'd unintentionally stood out on his first day. I didn't get it. If he wanted to blend in, he should have picked a less-visible friend group.

Jamie sat back down and took out a pair of round glasses. He hadn't needed them when we were younger, and they made him look a little like Harry Potter. Mr. Ferrara gazed at us expectantly, and I wondered if he was going to ask for a volunteer to set up the SmartBoard.

Instead, he uncapped a marker.

"Art pushes boundaries. History creates them," he said.

He summarized it on the board like a math equation: History → Boundaries → Art. There was a scramble to copy this down.

"Over the course of this semester, we'll explore how and why that is," Mr. Ferrara continued. "We'll be looking at art, essays, and historical documents, and we'll scrutinize the influence of history on artistic expression. This is a college-level course, and memorizing who painted *Starry Night* isn't enough. In my classroom, we'll ask difficult questions and attempt to answer them."

He paused, letting the full advanced-placementness of his class sink in, the way my other AP teachers had done. And then he smiled.

"But since this is the first day, I guess it won't hurt to have a little fun. Everyone take out your phones."

We stared at him, confused. Most teachers told you to put away your phone, not to do the opposite.

"Now turn them off," he said, once all our phones were out. "I don't want any cheating. The assignment is simple: to fill in this packet with the answers you know, and to make me laugh with the ones you don't."

He handed out a stapled packet thick with pictures of art. The first page featured a cave painting of horses and some classical sculpture. I honestly had no idea about either of them.

Suddenly, my dream of traipsing through a museum and knowing its secrets seemed supremely stupid. And about a million years out of reach.

"You have thirty minutes before I'm collecting these," he said. "You can work alone, or together in pairs."

All around the room, desks scraped the floor as students moved into groups. Before I could even process what was happening, Jamie scooted his desk toward mine.

"Ready to own this?" he asked, grinning at me from

behind those nerdy glasses.

Somehow, I managed a weak smile in return.

The edges of our desks were touching. We weren't just sitting next to each other anymore. We were sitting together. His right knee was inches from mine, and I could practically feel the heat radiating from it.

J. Aldridge / R. Asher he scrawled at the top of his packet, a shorthand that felt impossibly foreign. He was using pen, too. I looked down at my mechanical pencil, which was bright yellow with cartoon eggs all over it. And then I glanced back at the packet, my stomach sinking. I was totally unprepared for a test in a subject I'd never studied.

"Um," I said, staring down at the page. "I have no clue about either of these."

"Don't worry, I've got it," Jamie said absently, scrawling down the answers so fast that I didn't even have time to read them.

He flipped to the second page, which looked just as impossible. A painting of a girl in a scarf and a modern piece with gold stars. Without hesitating, he scribbled down *Girl with a Pearl Earring—Vermeer* and *Jazz—Matisse*.

He went straight on to the third page, totally focused, like we were already taking the advanced placement exam. I sat there feeling like an idiot.

I glanced around the room. At least none of our classmates were racing through the packet. Behind us, Maritza and Adam were arguing in a loud whisper over the cave painting.

"Come on, Cleopatra, jump in." Jamie flashed a grin and slid me the packet.

It was an Egyptian sculpture. One that I actually recognized from those forever-ago library books.

"The bust of Nefertiti," I said, writing it down. And then I added, "You're really good at this."

"Well, my mom's an anthropology professor," he reminded me. "If she heard I couldn't identify the Chauvet cave paintings, she'd probably drop dead."

There it was: the smallest wince, followed by the panic in his eyes that he'd said the absolute wrong thing.

"Sorry," he mumbled, mortified. "Shit, I'm really sorry. I didn't mean to joke about that."

I stared at him, waiting for him to stop. Desperate for him to stop.

"Claudia told me," he went on, "about Logan, I mean. I can't even imagine what that must have been like. She said he died from a beesting?"

He kept going, rambling about how sorry he was, and how great Logan had been. At some point, I must have closed my eyes, as though I could eclipse his words by plunging myself into darkness. The next thing I knew, Jamie was gently touching my shoulder.

"Hey, Cleopatra. You okay?"

"Fine," I snapped, glaring at him. "And for the record?

My name's *not* Cleopatra."

Jamie looked like he was about to say something else, but he swallowed it down.

"I'll finish this," he said, gingerly reaching for the packet as though it had transformed into something fragile just from sitting on my desk.

Before I could stop him, he filled in the rest of the packet like it was an act of charity. Like it was a freezer meal he was generously dropping off on our doorstep, four years too late. It was exactly what I'd been afraid would happen yesterday, in Gardner's class, except somehow it was worse. No matter how many years had passed, and no matter how much had changed, my brother's disaster was still the one thing that defined me.

I stared down at my notebook, at the line I'd copied about history creating boundaries, and I thought about how, sometimes, those boundaries exist for a reason.

5

"YOU SHOULD IMAGINE your audience naked," Logan suggested, snickering. "Naked, and extremely cold."

It was Thursday evening, and he was draped across my bed, watching me practice my monologue. When he stretched out like that, with his feet hanging off the edge, the hole in his sock looked even more ridiculous.

"Yeah, thanks," I told him, rolling my eyes.

He was wrong, though. The trick wasn't to imagine your audience any specific way; it was to forget they were there entirely. Which was a lot easier in front of a nameless crowd, and a lot harder in front of a particular group of classmates.

"You'll be fine," Logan said. "You're a great actress. Remember all those skits you used to put on with your friends?"

I wished he hadn't brought that up.

"Yeah, in elementary school," I said. "And then I was pity-cast in our sixth-grade play as a stupid pirate with one line. But in summer rep, against actual competition? I wasn't even good enough for the ensemble."

"You're the one who keeps taking drama," Logan pointed out.

"To do *costumes*, not monologues," I said with a sigh. "I would have taken theater tech, but it conflicts with French."

I glared at my monologue, wishing it would transform into something else, like a table read other people could do while I watched.

"Do you want me to come?" Logan asked. "For moral support and mockery?"

"That's okay," I said. "Besides, I think those two things are mutually exclusive."

"Hey now, I can be mockingly supportive," Logan insisted. "I am filled with contradictions."

"Oh, you're filled with something all right. Now shut up. I need to memorize this."

Before I had a chance to read it all the way through, I was interrupted again.

"Rose?"

"I told you, not now," I snapped, looking up.

My dad stood in the doorway, wearing his wire-frame glasses and a goofy grin. He'd traded his work clothes for workout clothes, even though he never went to the gym anymore, so they'd basically become pajamas.

"Oh, sorry," I mumbled. "I thought you were . . ."

There was no good explanation, so I didn't even try.

"Dinner?" I asked, putting down my script.

"Yep. And there's a surprise for dessert."

He mouthed the word *cheesecake*.

"Chocolate or plain?" I asked. We both preferred chocolate, but Mom insisted on original.

"Can't tell you." Dad winked. "That would ruin the surprise."

Chocolate. Definitely.

"I'll be right down," I promised, glancing over at my bed.

But Logan had disappeared.

THE THEATER WAS freezing. I'd forgotten how the air-conditioning blasted everyone who wasn't under the hot stage lights. I folded my arms across the paper-thin fabric of my T-shirt, wishing I'd brought a sweater, or worn a thicker bra.

Kate and I were planted strategically in the back row, since Mr. Gardner always started calling people up to perform from the front. Kate was convinced he might run out of time and spare us, but I doubted either of us had that kind of luck.

Sam's crowd was sprawled in the first row, making too much noise. Jamie sat with them, as he had all week, a now-permanent fixture.

I'd ignored him in art history on Thursday, taking notes on Mr. Ferrara's PowerPoint in the neatest version of my handwriting and sighing whenever Jamie tried to get my attention. He'd finally given up halfway through the period.

"All right," Gardner said. "Let's get started. Who's on first?"

"WHAT ARE YOU ASKING ME FOR?" Sam bellowed.

It was a terrible joke, and one he'd made a million times. But Gardner laughed as though he'd never heard it before, going red in the face. Which of course was the real joke, not Sam's lame attempt at an ancient Abbott and Costello bit.

"Very funny." Gardner wheezed, trying to catch his breath. "Sam, get up there."

Sam stood, a strip of neon-blue underwear showing above his jeans. He wasn't even embarrassed by it. Just tugged his shirt down and hopped onto the stage without using the stairs.

The thing with Sam was that he didn't look like he could act. His older brother had been a varsity athlete, and they looked so similar that you half expected Sam to lob a football into the wings or roll his eyes and make a joke of it. But acting was the one thing Sam had always taken seriously.

"Yeah, what's up?" he said, his voice booming across the auditorium as he slated his scene. "I'm Sam Donovan, performing a monologue from *The Foreigner* for Mr. Gardner's Advanced Theater class."

He looked so relaxed up there, under the stage lights, with all of us watching. His gravitational pull made sense in the theater. The moment he started to speak, no one could look away.

The rest of the group went after Sam, all of them in perfect planetary alignment. Their monologues seemed effortless, even though we'd only had a few days to practice, as though they'd played these roles forever.

Jamie was the last of them. He'd chosen one of the Shakespeare pieces, and when he announced it, I wondered if he was going to pull a British accent, which Gardner hated. But someone had warned him, and of course his monologue was fantastic. I hated him a little bit then, for disappearing, and for coming back even better.

I watched as the rest of my classmates went. No one was terrible, not even Seth Bostwick, who attempted the gravedigger speech from *Hamlet* with so much clowning and space work that Gardner probably wished he'd allowed props. The only disaster was Kate. She sped through the lines without pausing for breath, her hands fidgeting in the pockets of her cardigan.

And then it was my turn. I was last, and I could feel everyone's impatience as they realized that I was the only thing standing between them and getting to the parking lot before it jammed.

The lights felt hot and bright in my face, and the stage was scuffed, up close, shabbier than it looked from the audience. There were tape marks everywhere, leftover blocking from a show that had long ended its run. A show that my former friends had starred in while I'd fussed with the costume rack, wishing so many things had turned out differently.

I took a deep breath, steadying my nerves.

"I'm Rose Asher," I said.

It came out too soft, and I frowned. I had no business commanding the attention of an entire theater, but I also had no choice. And I wasn't about to go down in front of everyone. So I tried again, letting my voice carry to the back row the way I hadn't done since my *Annie* audition.

"I'll be performing a monologue from *Hamlet*."

I closed my eyes, taking a moment to ready myself. And when I opened them, I was Ophelia. Broken, tragic Ophelia, quietly going mad.

I'd forgotten what it was like, having words that came easily. Having an audience that wasn't waiting to talk over you or embarrass you for what you'd just said. It was so freeing, becoming someone else, even without a costume. I didn't want it to end.

But it did, and I was me again, standing onstage in a too-thin shirt in front of thirty classmates who were being forced to applaud my homework.

Except Sam and Claudia weren't clapping politely along with everyone else. Instead, they were cheering and wolf-whistling the way they had for their friends.

Gardner dismissed class before I'd even made it back to my seat. The theater emptied out as upperclassmen raced for the parking lot and sophomores hurried toward the drop-off zone.

"Hey, Asher!" someone called while I was zipping my backpack.

I glanced up and inexplicably found Sam loping toward me.

"Nice job today," he said, grinning.

"Thanks."

It came out like a question, because what I really wanted to ask was why he was suddenly talking to me.

"How come you never try out for the shows anymore?" Sam asked, leaning against a theater seat.

"I do costumes," I reminded him, in case he'd forgotten that part.

Maybe he had. He was staring at me like we hadn't been in Gardner's class together for the past two years. Like every time Gardner had forced us to do scenes, he hadn't watched as Kate and I fell flat.

If only theater were like sports—no one ever asked the girls who didn't make frosh-soph volleyball why they hadn't tried out for varsity. But here Sam was, asking me just that, as though our summer rep director had been wrong about me and I'd been left behind by mistake.

I didn't know what to make of it. And then I noticed Sam wasn't wearing a backpack. He didn't have so much as a notebook on him, which couldn't be right. They played it off like they were more artsy than academic, but everyone in Sam's crowd took APs.

"Where's your stuff?" I asked.

Sam grinned sheepishly.

"Stashed my bag in my locker after lunch," he admitted. "Otherwise I'd just read over my monologue all class and obsess."

It was the last thing I expected him to say. Sam always seemed so effortless on stage that it was strange to realize he was just as shaky off script as the rest of us.

"Can I make an observation?" I blurted, unable to stop myself.

"By all means."

"If you're going to all that trouble about your script, doesn't volunteering to go first kind of ruin it?"

"Damn it, Asher." Sam laughed. "Remind me never to tell you my strategy for math tests."

"Is it 'study for the math test'?"

"Solid guess. But no."

"Is it 'sacrifice half-eaten baked goods to the exam gods'?" I blurted, feeling my cheeks go pink.

Sam looked astonished.

"How did you know?" He goggled at me for a moment, as though I'd actually gotten it right, then shrugged off the act as easily as a sweatshirt.

I'd forgotten how we used to joke like this, just subtle enough to be convincing if you didn't know the game. Our friends would jump in, going from audience to performance, while everyone else stared at us, confused.

But there was no one else around. And Sam seemed to realize the same thing. He glanced toward the lobby, where his friends were waiting. And I realized that Kate was waiting for me too, by the sound booth, so we could walk over to the choir room.

"Well, I'll see you," I said, grabbing my bag and hurrying to catch up with her.

THAT NIGHT, I dreamed I was in a play. It was opening night, and I stood in the wings, my heart pounding as I waited for my cue.

Delia was onstage, giving a monologue that seemed to go on forever. Suddenly the play switched, and instead of Delia, the spotlight was trained on Sam. The audience loved him, clapping so loudly that I couldn't even hear his lines over the applause.

"Where's Rose? She's almost on," a techie said, rushing around with his clipboard and headset.

"I'm right here," I called.

He looked straight through me.

"Hello!" I said again, but no one was paying attention.

Sam stood in the spotlight, silent and frozen. He wasn't wearing a costume. None of us were. Sam glanced nervously toward the wings, and I knew it was my cue. But when I tried to walk onstage, I couldn't, because the stage wasn't there. It was on the other side of a mirror.

I was trapped on the wrong side, missing my moment. I pounded against the glass, realizing the only way through was to break it. And then I hauled back and hit it. But when my fist connected, it wasn't the mirror that shattered into a million pieces. It was me.

6

ON TUESDAY, LOGAN was waiting for me on the nature trail after school. He did that sometimes—camped out where he knew I'd turn up.

Once, after the mile run in gym, I'd found him in the girls' locker room, gleefully spying on my undressed classmates. I'd almost bitten my tongue off having to be quiet about it and had made him swear never to do it again. Even if I was the only one who could see him.

Logan waved, and I slowed my bike.

"What are you doing out here?" I asked.

"Cleaning lady." He made a face.

"Still? I thought she was coming this morning."

"Nope. Afternoon. Let's *go* somewhere," he pleaded.

I tried to think. Logan got irritable the farther we were from home, so it needed to be close. There was the strip mall on Main, but a ton of my classmates worked there. And I didn't really want to watch Danny Efshani flex his muscles over the ice-cream scoop at Cold Stone.

"Billz?" I suggested.

"Always." Logan grinned. "Lead the way."

Our dad used to take us there after Hebrew school for hot chocolate. It was just down the parkway, in the shopping center where I'd backed the Camry into a pole after freaking out over a man in a bloodstained coat, who had turned out to be a figment of my imagination.

I wheeled my bike through the gate, wishing I'd brought my earbuds. They had a microphone attachment, and I usually wore them whenever Logan and I went out. That way it looked like I was on the phone, so we could talk without people staring.

"Just ride your bike," he said, exasperated at how slow I was going. "I'll keep up."

"No way," I protested. "You'll do that weird floating thing and creep me out."

"What weird floating thing?" Logan frowned, like he didn't know exactly what I was talking about. And then he collapsed backward in a mock swoon, lifting a hand to his brow. "Rose, dahhhhling. Draw me like one of your French girls."

I couldn't help laughing, even if he *was* four feet off the ground.

"See, you love it," Logan said, encouraged. And then he hovered alongside me, creepy-dementor style, all the way down the canyon.

When I pulled open the door to Billz, a beautiful wave of air-conditioning hit me full blast, followed by the deep, woodsy scent of ground coffee. I took in the faded tiki masks and grass skirts that covered the walls and the armoire that had been there forever, holding a stack of board games that were probably missing pieces. Some places never changed, and this coffee shop was one of them.

"The Beach Boys? Really?" Logan complained, displeased with the music.

It *was* a little bit tragic. But then, Billz wasn't a hipster hangout like Bean & Bond or famous for their Instagram-worthy cups like Alfie's. Most of the tables here were filled with after-school tutoring sessions or chatty moms in active-wear.

And then I heard a familiar peal of laughter. Sam's crowd was gathered around the large table under the window. They were surrounded by board games and iced coffees, and they gave the impression of being regulars here, of all places, at this tacky coffee shop.

"What are you waiting for?" Logan asked.

"None of your business," I hissed, trying not to move my lips.

Coming here had been a stupid idea. Billz was so close by that I should have guessed my old friends would claim it. I stood in the doorway, debating whether or not I should just leave.

"Come on, you can't reserve *all* of the emeralds!" Claudia

protested as Max picked up a chip from a game they were playing.

"But watching you get angry over it is *so* satisfying," he teased.

Jamie glanced up and spotted me. I thought he might wave hello, but instead, his face drained of color, like I was the last person in the world he wanted to see. Like he'd only been friendly in art history because we were stuck next to each other and no one else was around.

My cheeks went red. I couldn't leave now, not without it being painfully obvious. So I mustered my nerve, walked over to the counter, and ordered the first thing I saw on the menu.

Logan followed, trailing me to the barista station and moaning over how he wished he could eat a mint brownie, which Billz was known for.

"I have a mint brownie for Jamie," the barista called, pushing a plate across the counter. "Mint brownie for Jamie."

Jamie slid down in his seat, like he didn't even want to get up and walk over. I wondered what his problem was. It wasn't as though saying hi meant he'd have to invite me to join their table.

The barista called his order again, sounding impatient. Jamie shuffled over. His shoulders were tense, and the smile plastered across his face was absurdly fake.

"Oh, hey," he said, trying to sound casual. "Sorry I ordered the last brownie."

"They brought more out." I motioned toward the case, which featured an entire tray of brownies.

"Right," he said. "Huh."

He reached for his plate, and it clattered a little against the counter as his hands shook.

"You should cut back on the caffeine," I suggested.

"So they tell me," Jamie said, which wasn't a response at all.

Jamie's eyes flickered to my right, where Logan was standing. And for an absurd moment, I wondered if it wasn't caffeine jitters. If maybe Jamie felt Logan's presence.

It wouldn't have been the first time something like that happened. Occasionally, dogs would freak out when they walked past our house. And my grandma always complained she was cold whenever Logan was in the room.

Jamie and I were still standing there in humiliating silence. The Beach Boys blared, cheerful and wrong, like the soundtrack to someone else's afternoon. My drink was grinding away in the blender, and I wished I'd ordered something less complicated.

Logan cleared his throat impatiently.

"Um, I think your friends are waiting," I said, giving Jamie an out.

Relief washed over his face.

"Yeah. I should—yeah." He didn't even finish his sentence before retreating back to their table, with its spread of board games and drinks and phones.

And then Nima caught me staring and waved. Nima, who was the head of our class spirit committee, and the nicest guy on the planet, and would have waved at anybody. It was just a hello. Nothing more.

I waved back, and then I grabbed my drink and ran out of there before anyone else saw me and chose not to invite me over. Logan bobbed silently at my side, for once devoid of chatter. He wasn't usually this quiet, and I wondered if he felt sorry for me.

"Everything okay?" I asked.

"Yeah. Just thinking."

He went quiet again, and I wished he'd just say it. That my ice-blended latte hadn't been the only frosty offering at Billz. That Jamie had been rude and awful and had all but asked me to leave. Except Logan didn't say any of that. Instead, he faded away with a frown, leaving me to my misery and my empty afternoon.

7

MR. GARDNER MADE us play Zip Zap Zop in class on Wednesday. It's one of those improv games where everyone stands in a circle making eye contact and sending each other weird noises. Gardner claimed it was team-building, but mostly it was embarrassing, because my classmates always sent the weird noises to their friends. And if you got skipped long enough, Gardner would intervene.

"Pass to Rose," he'd urge, insinuating that the next person better send over a pity-pass.

Except that day, Sam and Claudia kept sending me zaps and zops. I didn't know which was worse, getting a single pity-pass, or getting *preemptive* ones.

The game stretched on for an eternity. Even Sam's endless enthusiasm was flagging. Just when I thought we'd be yelling "zip!" and "zap!" at each other until the bell rang, Gardner finally put an end to it.

"Scenes!" he called. "Everyone partner up."

We were still standing in a circle, all mixed up since Gardner had made us play the last few rounds exchanging places.

Kate was on the other side of the room. I started to walk over, but Jamie stopped me.

"Rose, what do you say?" he asked. "Partners?"

I stared at him, shocked.

He flashed me a grin, like yesterday at Billz had never happened. His smile should have been against dress code, since it was distracting in the worst possible way.

I suspected he knew what effect it had, which was even worse. Because he had no business using that smile on me. Especially after the way he'd acted, like I should be embarrassed for even existing in his general vicinity when it wasn't on the seating chart.

I wished I could turn him down, but Sam and Claudia were right there, listening, and I didn't want to cause a scene.

"Fine," I relented.

I glanced over at Kate, who was standing alone. She shot me a look like I'd betrayed her by partnering with someone else.

"All right," Gardner said, passing around a stack of scripts. "Rehearse these for the rest of the period. I want to see character choices, blocking, and everyone off script. Performances are next class in the theater. Any questions?"

Kate put up her hand. She looked utterly miserable as she announced that she didn't have a partner.

Gardner frowned at his roll sheet, trying to figure out

who was missing. But he didn't need to bother, because Nima raced in, wearing a neon-green student government T-shirt and holding a late pass. I'd seen the spirit wheel in the quad at lunch but had fled in the opposite direction before anyone could call me over to give it a spin.

"Sorry, Mr. G.," he panted, trying to catch his breath.

"It's fine. You'll be with Kate," Gardner said, giving him the handout.

That was when I realized what had happened. Without Nima, Sam's friends were an odd number. I hadn't noticed while we were all darting around in that dumb improv game. But I was positive Jamie had.

Which meant Jamie hadn't chosen me as a partner. He'd picked me so he wasn't left without one.

And that was so much worse.

I suddenly wished I'd had the guts to reject him after all. To make him announce in front of everyone that he was the one left partnerless, instead of Kate. I stood there seething over the injustice of it all while Gardner calmly answered questions. Abby Shah hadn't been paying attention when Gardner said he wanted our scenes memorized. And then Seth Bostwick wanted to know if we could use props. And then Leo Swanson asked specifically about "peace-tied weapons," which sent Max into a coughing fit.

We all headed outside to practice, and Jamie grinned at me, still pretending he was excited about our forced partnership.

"Shade or sun?" he asked.

"I don't care."

He picked a shaded patch of grass, under a tree. One of the most visible, central spots in the quad. I wished he hadn't done that. But it was too late now to protest.

I sat down, glaring at him.

"Sorry," Jamie said, looking contrite.

"Good," I snapped. "You should be. It isn't the end of the world to be left out."

Jamie frowned at me, confused.

"What are you talking about?"

"When we were picking partners," I went on. "I *always* go with Kate."

"How was *I* supposed to know that?"

Now he sounded annoyed. And with a horrible jolt, I realized he was right—there was no way he would have known about Kate. Not when all we'd done so far were monologues.

From the way Sam and Claudia had passed to me during improv, I could see how he might have thought I was still part of their circle—at least as far as Gardner's class was concerned.

So maybe he *had* genuinely picked me as a partner, instead of as a life vest, but that didn't explain why he'd been so awful at Billz. There was no excuse for the way he'd acted, and I couldn't believe he thought I'd want to work with him after that.

"Then what was the apology for?" I demanded.

"Um. Well . . ." Jamie looked like he didn't want to say. "The grass here is kind of wet."

I snorted incredulously.

"The grass?" I said. *"Really?"*

Jamie chewed his lip, like it had just dawned on him that asking me to be partners was a spectacularly bad idea. Like he'd been hoping I hadn't noticed his rudeness yesterday and he'd get away with pretending it had never happened.

"You have to pick one," I insisted. "Either you're this old friend who actually wants to work with me, or you're a complete jerk who acts repulsed when I show up at the same coffee shop."

Jamie winced.

"That wasn't—" he tried to explain.

"Repulsed," I insisted. "So if you'll excuse me, I think I'll spend the rest of the period doing precalc."

I unzipped my bag and took out my math book and folder. Thankfully, I'd remembered my earbuds. I put them in and made it clear that he better not interrupt me.

When I glanced up, Jamie had taken out his own math homework. He didn't even hesitate as he scrawled Greek letters across the page. Of course he was in calculus. Suddenly, I felt self-conscious of my own labored attempts at domain and range.

I hated Jamie then, for the way everything came so easily to him. Here he was, so much better than me again, this time at doing homework. When the bell rang, I gathered everything into my bag and hurried off before he could inflict any further misery.

I BIKED HOME from school that day fuming. It wasn't fair. Before Jamie showed up, Sam's crowd and I had moved through high school without much interaction, and it wasn't awkward or weird. It was just the way things were.

But not anymore. Now it was like the fence that divided our backyards had blown down, leaving us with a clear view of the other side and the embarrassing knowledge that we'd been standing ten feet away from each other the entire time.

I felt my phone vibrate in my bag, but waited until I got home to check it. And when I did, I had a missed text from Kate:

Tbh can't believe you bailed on me to flirt with nude art boy. A heads up next time would be nice ☺

I almost laughed when I read it. Because there was no way such a bitchy, underhanded text was from Kate, who couldn't even stand up for herself over a stupid backpack. No, that message was pure Delia.

Even the time stamp, ten minutes after class let out, made me certain of it. I could sense them on the other end of the conversation, waiting for my reply, their heads bent over the screen like the three fates.

Delia had come up with the plan, of course. And Emmy had protested that it wasn't nice, but had gone along with it anyway, like she always did. And Kate, so desperate for their approval, believing she'd actually get it if she just handed over her phone.

They were just itching to remind me of where I fit into their group: Rose Asher, the ultimate doormat. But something in me refused to remain in place any longer.

Before I could think better of it, I typed a space, let it sit there for a minute, and deleted it. I tried not to laugh over the thought of them eagerly watching Kate's screen for my response, only to have my little reply bubble disappear.

"What are you doing?" Logan asked, appearing over my shoulder.

I jumped, and Logan laughed, pleased that he'd spooked me.

"Don't sneak up on me like that," I snapped. "And if you must know, I'm enacting a particularly subtle form of subterfuge. I call it 'subtlefuge.'"

I typed another space into the phone. I kept it going for a good five minutes, typing and deleting, typing and deleting, until I finally sent a response I knew would make them scream:

k

"I don't get it," Logan complained, leaning over my shoulder. "Why did it take you so long to write that?"

"Exactly!" I said. "What did I type but decide not to send? They won't be able to stop thinking about it. It's a sub-text message."

I expected Logan to laugh, but he didn't.

"You should get new friends," he said.

"It's *junior year*. You can't just *get* new friends," I tried to explain.

The truth was, it was entirely my fault that I hung around with Delia. I'd waited too long to fix it, the way I always did, and had gotten stuck. I should have forced myself to run track, or do yearbook, or join any activity that came with a built-in friend group. Except none of those things was *me*. It didn't matter how many years had passed since I'd stared at the *Annie* cast sheet, realizing that just because you want something doesn't mean you'll get it. I still loved theater, and I couldn't make myself walk away.

I needed to take my mind off things, so I took out the ingredients for chocolate chip cookies. Baking always calmed me. It was better to focus on doing something tangible instead of obsessing over things I couldn't change.

Sure enough, as I sifted together the flour, salt, and baking soda, I wasn't brooding over my school day anymore. Instead, I was thinking: *Is the butter soft enough, should I add another pinch of salt?*

Logan hovered, getting in the way as he offered unsolicited advice: more chocolate chips, extra vanilla. At least he couldn't eat the dough when my back was turned.

"Want to lick the spoon?" I asked innocently.

Logan glared.

"Want to hear my list of people who aren't funny?" he said. "Rose Asher."

"How is one name a list?"

"Fine," he snapped. "Rose Asher, Rose Asher, Rose Asher. Now it's a list."

I popped the cookies into the oven and glanced at the clock, making a mental note. I baked these so often that I had an internal alarm for when they were ready. Logan crouched down in front of the oven, watching the cookies bake, and I started tackling the mess I'd made of the kitchen.

The doorbell rang while I was rinsing the last of the measuring cups. I frowned, because we weren't expecting anybody. I hoped it wasn't my friends, because I honestly didn't think I could take them right now.

I yanked open the door, and Jamie Aldridge trained his thousand-watt smile in my direction. He was wearing his glasses, and the satchel slung across his chest pulled his fitted T-shirt even tighter. He looked devastatingly bookish, and I was sure he'd done it on purpose, just to annoy me.

"Seriously?" I muttered.

At least he had the good sense to look embarrassed.

"I'm sorry about earlier," he said. "I really *was* rude at the coffee shop. You have every right to be mad."

I folded my arms across my chest, waiting, because no way had he come all the way to my house just to apologize.

"Go on," I said.

"Also, I think you took my calc notes," Jamie finished.

So that was it.

"Oh," I said lamely.

My bag was still on the bench. He watched as I unzipped it, and I sighed, trying to make it clear that I was only going through my stuff under duress. Because there was no way that—crap. I *had* taken his calc notes. They'd gotten mixed in with mine while we were sitting on the grass.

I handed them over, my cheeks burning.

"Sorry," I mumbled. "I'll see you tomorrow."

"Wait," he said as I went to close the door. "When do you want to work on our scene?"

"You memorize your lines, and I'll memorize mine," I said. "Done."

Jamie looked appalled.

"Gardner told us to work on it *together*," he reminded me.

"Despite what the teachers want us to believe, not *everything* is a group activity."

"But this one is. And I wouldn't want to cause a repeat of the Great Art Packet Disaster of Sixth Period."

"Oh my god, you're impossible!" I glared, and Jamie smiled, like he'd scored some great victory.

"You're only saying that because I've bested you with my infallible logic."

"Infallible logic?" I blurted. "Who even talks like that?"

"Professor parents." Jamie shrugged. "My friends used to keep score. They called it the SATs of Shame."

I knew he meant it to be funny, but it came out sad, as though he was remembering a life he hadn't wanted to leave behind. And it struck me that, out of all the annoying things that were his fault, moving back to Laguna Canyon wasn't one of them.

"Fine." I relented. "Since you're here, let's work on the scene."

I opened the front door a little wider, and he hesitated a moment before stepping inside.

"Thanks," he mumbled, setting down his bag.

When he started taking off his shoes, I snorted.

"You don't have to do that," I said.

Our house definitely wasn't that formal. Although I did have a vague memory of Jamie's mom insisting on it when we were kids. And of their home being filled with expensive-looking art and figurines. It occurred to me that some of the things we'd taken out of glass cases to play with had probably been precious antiques.

"Just so you know, the cookies are burning!" Logan called from the kitchen.

"You should get those," Jamie said, wedging his sneaker back on.

I went very still.

"What did you say?" I asked.

"The cookies," Jamie answered, straightening up.

We stared at each other, realizing what had just happened.

"Oh shit," Jamie muttered.

8

JAMIE AND I were still staring at each other in disbelief when Logan drifted into the living room. He was positively vibrating with excitement, which made him even more transparent.

"I knew it!" Logan crowed, pointing at Jamie. "I *knew* he could see me!"

"Since when?" I demanded.

"Since yesterday," Logan said smugly. "At the coffee shop. And I was right. I *love* being right."

I glanced at Jamie. He'd gone pale, and his mouth hung slightly open, as though he couldn't believe what he was seeing. But it wasn't Logan's presence that seemed to throw him. He was acting as though *I* was as fascinating as a ghost in mesh shorts and holey socks.

"How long ha—have *you*—" Jamie spluttered, but he never got to finish, because the smoke alarm in the kitchen went off, pitching everything into chaos.

"Crap! The cookies!" I said.

I raced toward the kitchen, the smoke alarm bleeping out some of my more colorful swears.

The kitchen was filled with smoke and smelled strongly of scorched chocolate. I should have set the stupid timer. But then, I hadn't been expecting company.

I yanked open the sliding door to the backyard, trying to let out some of the smoke. Jamie turned on the ceiling fan, and between the two air currents, the alarm mercifully stopped beeping.

"I warned you that they were burning," Logan whined. "And you *ignored me.*"

"Well, I was kind of busy," I said defensively.

The cookies were charcoal. I grabbed a spatula and scraped them into the trash.

And then Jamie, Logan, and I stood there staring at one another in the dissipating smoke, a million questions hovering between us.

Suddenly, something occurred to me.

"Wait," I said to Jamie. "You can see him."

Jamie nodded, clearly wondering where I was going with this.

"And you could see him yesterday," I continued, "at the coffee shop."

"We've already established that," Logan interjected, sounding bored.

We *had*, except I hadn't realized what it meant. Now I

understood why Jamie had reacted the way he did when I'd walked into Billz. Why he'd slunk over to the counter as though I was the last person he wanted to see. It wasn't *my* presence that had horrified him. It was *Logan's*.

"Um, yeah," Jamie mumbled. "But I didn't know that *you* could."

That stopped me in my tracks.

"What?"

"I thought—well, I thought you didn't know Logan was there," Jamie clarified. "So I panicked. Sorry. I didn't realize until afterward that I must have come off as a complete dick. But there isn't an easy way to explain that, uh . . ."

"You see dead people?" I supplied with a hint of a smile.

It *did* sound ridiculous. Like we were rehearsing a play, and Sam was waiting in the wings, dusted with flour and fake blood.

"I've never told anyone," Jamie admitted.

"Me neither," I said.

"Don't worry, " Logan interjected. "I'm great at keeping secrets. The only thing I can't do is take them to the grave."

Jamie snorted.

"Don't encourage him," I pleaded. "He'll keep making awful jokes for *hours*."

"You mean *awesome* jokes," Logan insisted, floating upward.

I could tell he was trying to be impressive, showing off his supernatural powers or whatever, but mostly it made me nervous how close his head was to the ceiling.

"Get down from there," I said. "You'll go through and screw up the plumbing. Again."

Logan shot me a dark look.

"It was worse for me than it was for you," he muttered, dropping to a more reasonable eye level.

Jamie laughed, and there was something oddly reassuring about that moment. About the three of us standing around the kitchen making jokes. In the past four years, Logan had never felt as real as he did right then.

There'd been a part of me that had worried it was all in my head. That my brother hadn't really come back as a petulant ghost with very particular Netflix demands. That I'd gone crazy, quietly, and it was only a matter of time before my crazy became audible.

But Jamie confirmed it—Logan's ghost wasn't a figment of my imagination. And knowing that, really knowing it, lifted a weight I didn't realize I was tired of carrying.

"So what's the plan?" Logan asked eagerly. "We could have a *Firefly* marathon. Or wait, Jamie, have you ever seen *Sherlock*?"

"Every episode," Jamie said. We exchanged a wry look over Logan's out-of-date pop culture references. And then Jamie winced, massaging his temple. "Ugh, sorry. Do you have any aspirin?"

I told him to check my parents' medicine cabinet. Jamie disappeared upstairs, and the moment he was gone, Logan whirled around, positively vibrating with excitement.

"Can we keep him?" he asked. "Please?"

"He's a person, not a puppy," I pointed out.

"I know. But it's been *forever* since I've had someone else to talk to."

Logan pouted, laying it on thick. Or maybe he wasn't pretending. It had never occurred to me that he might be lonely.

"We'll see," I said.

Logan was starting to fade, which he actually looked upset about. And I realized that, for once, he was going to miss something bigger than sitting on the sofa and getting to pilot my Netflix queue.

"We'll hang out later, okay?" he said. His voice was tinny and far away, like I was hearing it through laptop speakers. I nodded, even though I had a suspicion he meant the three of us.

Jamie came downstairs a few minutes later.

"Where's ghost bro?" he asked, frowning.

"Don't call him that," I said. "And he comes and goes."

"You mean he comes and *ghosts*."

Jamie grinned, pleased with his own joke. And while he did, I was able to fully appreciate two things: that Jamie Aldridge and I were alone in my kitchen, and that, however accidentally, we had just discovered each other's secrets.

"So, about our drama assignment," I began.

Jamie snorted, like that was the last thing in the world on his mind.

"Oh, we'll get there," he promised. "But first, I have questions."

"Well, I have lemonade, and some leftover dough that I swear I can bake into edible cookies this time."

"I'll believe that when I see it," he challenged.

I expected him to take a seat at the table, but he opened the fridge and got out the lemonade. He grabbed some glasses, too, filling them with ice.

It was such a small thing, the way he made himself at home in my kitchen, like the past six years had never happened. He'd made himself at home in Sam's crowd the same way, acting as though he just belonged. It was a good trick, and I wished he'd show me how to do it.

"So how long has Logan been, uh . . ." Jamie asked, handing me a glass of lemonade.

"Coming and ghosting?" I finished, borrowing his phrase. "Four years and nine days."

I put the cookies into the oven and made a big show of setting the timer.

While they baked, I told him everything.

It was a story I'd gone over in my head a million times, but one I never thought I'd tell. Because who would believe it? Except the answer to that question was right in front of me, slouched at my kitchen table in the most expertly fitted jeans and T-shirt I'd ever seen, sipping a mason jar of lemonade.

"Your turn," I said, taking a seat on our kitchen counter.

Jamie scrunched his nose, embarrassed.

"I was afraid of that," he said. "Okay, Cleopatra, here's the deal. I don't know why I can see ghosts. And I'm not sure how long I've been doing it."

He drank the last of his lemonade, crunching some of the ice. My mom would have died, since she'd lectured me enough on how it destroyed your enamel.

"You didn't have some near-death experience?" I asked, because that was how it always went in books.

"Yeah, right after my Hogwarts letter arrived."

Touché.

"You're seriously telling me you don't have any theories?" I pressed.

"Maybe a few," Jamie allowed. "You know about tetrachromacy, right? Some people have a fourth cone in their eyes that allows them to see, like, a hundred times more colors than the rest of us. The thing is, this condition isn't actually that rare. But only a fraction of the people who have it can see anything different, and no one knows why. Maybe there's an extrasensory receptor that makes some people see ghosts."

"Ghostchromacy?" I suggested.

"Exactly. Or maybe we played with some weird artifact of my mom's when we were little and got ourselves cursed. Doesn't matter how it happened. You get Logan back, and I get harassed by dead strangers. End of story."

Jamie went to the fridge and poured himself another glass of lemonade, offering me the carton. I shook my head no. And then something occurred to me.

"Are there a lot of ghosts?" I asked.

"Not so many here," Jamie said. "I've mostly seen them in cities."

"Then it was lucky you came back," I said. "To live with your dad."

Jamie shrugged, even though the answer was clearly yes.

"I'd totally wreck my class rank if I had to go to international school in China," he said, making a face. "Besides, I figured it's better when the ghosts speak a language you can understand."

Jamie tried to look like he hadn't just admitted something so personal, but it was no use. I felt terrible for him.

"That sucks," I said, not bothering to sugarcoat it.

"Completely," he agreed, sounding grateful I hadn't.

It was strange, realizing that Jamie's life had broken apart twice in five years. I understood all too well what that was like. Because Logan's death had been the first thing to wreck me, but walking away from my friends in the aftermath had been entirely my doing.

I'd gone quiet under the weight of it all, crushing myself into a tiny, invisible ball. And Jamie had gone cocky, giving the impression that nothing was wrong. But we were both putting on an act, trying desperately to fit in. And deep down, I could tell he was just as unsure as I was and just as alone in figuring out how to handle it.

"Did you ever think you were going crazy?" I blurted.

"You mean that the ghosts were all in my head?" Jamie

shook his head. "Nah. After the first few times, I looked up local obituaries, and unless I was hallucinating dead people I'd never met, it wasn't likely."

It suddenly occurred to him why I was asking.

"Rose," he said, looking horrified. "You didn't think you were *imagining* it?"

I shrugged.

"No, of course not," I lied. But I could tell he didn't believe me.

"So, uh, time?" Jamie asked.

I was confused for a moment until I realized he meant the cookies.

"Less than a minute," I said. "And this isn't chem lab, you don't have to double-check me."

The corners of his lips twitched slightly.

"If it *were* chem lab, you'd have already blown us up," he accused.

"No, *you* would have been so insufferable to work with that I probably would have stormed out and left you with the whole experiment."

The timer beeped, and I triumphantly pulled a batch of golden cookies out of the oven.

"Told you they'd come out perfect," I said.

And then we were both very quiet while we ate the cookies warm, picking them straight off the tray.

"My mom would die if she saw this," Jamie mumbled with his mouth full.

"Mine too," I agreed.

Jamie hesitated a moment, but I could tell he wanted to say something.

"What?" I prompted.

"I really am sorry about yesterday," he said. "I was scared Logan would realize I could see him. And based on my previous encounters, most ghosts aren't as chill as your brother."

"*Chill* isn't the word I'd use to describe Logan," I said, reaching for another cookie.

"Well, *normal* then," Jamie amended, as though that was a better fit. "I guess it's because he has you to hang out with."

"What are you talking about?" I asked.

Jamie, who had just shoved an entire cookie into his mouth, held up a finger, chewing quickly.

"You've *really* never seen another ghost before?" he asked.

I was about to say no, but something made me remember that afternoon in the Trader Joe's parking lot. The blurry man in the blood-soaked coat, who had appeared in front of my car one moment and disappeared the next. I'd screamed and backed out in such a panic that I'd hit a pole. And then I'd driven home, answered for my sins, and never asked to borrow the car again.

"Oh, god," I said, realizing.

A beat of understanding passed between us.

"If you thought Logan would be like that, then why did

you come over?" I asked.

Jamie grabbed another cookie, his impossible smile returning full force, like I'd just asked the most ridiculous question.

"Well, you *did* take my calc notes," he pointed out.

9

MY PARENTS WERE in rare form at dinner that night. Mom was still worked up from seeing her nightmare patient, Tiny Bladder Lady, who'd insisted she had to pee not once but *twice* during her filling. And Dad kept glancing longingly at the shut-off television as though, if he stared hard enough, it might flicker on and display the baseball score.

I made sympathetic noises over my mom's story, but mostly, I was distracted by everything that had happened with Jamie. I couldn't shake the feeling that there had been this enormous shift in the universe that afternoon, and it shocked me that the rest of the world had carried on undisturbed.

I could barely wrap my mind around it—that Logan's ghost wasn't in my head. That through some twist of fate or science or luck, I was able to see what others couldn't.

I hadn't realized I'd felt so alone until I had someone to share it with. Not just someone—Jamie Aldridge, a boy who, until a few hours ago, I'd been prepared to loathe for all eternity.

"Rose?" Mom said, and I looked up guiltily.

"Huh?"

"I was asking if you'd had a chance to read that Kondo book. I left it in your room weeks ago."

I had a vague memory of this.

"The book about tidying up?" I asked. "I thought it was a hint to stop throwing my clothes all over the floor. I didn't know you actually wanted me to read it."

"Rose." Mom sighed, in no mood.

"I resisted at first, too," Dad told me. "But give it a chance, Rosebud. It'll change the way you think about everything."

I highly doubted that.

"This is the same book that wants me to find joy in refolding my socks?" I asked skeptically.

Mom nodded, her mouth full, and Dad gave me an encouraging look, and more than anything in the world, I wished Logan were there to make fun of them with me.

"You guys are nuts," he'd say. "All this business about socks makes you sound like house elves."

I'd giggle, and he'd do a Dobby impression, mostly for my enjoyment. And my parents would shake their heads, asking each other why they even bothered. But I'd catch them smiling a minute later.

Except there was no Logan to turn to. No one else to

back me up, or to call out Mom and Dad for being ridiculous. I was outvoted, permanently.

"Ugh, fine," I relented. "I'll read your book."

Mom beamed.

"But only so I can better make fun of you," I finished.

THE NEXT DAY, all I could think about was art history, where I'd get to sit next to Jamie for ninety full minutes. But someone must have alerted the universe, because time decided to slow down and see if it could make me scream in frustration.

My first two classes dragged on forever. Mr. Cope bored us halfway to death with out-loud reading, going down the rows. And Ms. Dubois, who was headache-free for once, had us drilling the *subjunctif.*

It almost sounded like a spell, all of us chanting the same phrases over and over, in perfect unison: *I might see, you might see, he or she might see.*

Might see what? I wondered. *Ghosts?*

My friends took Spanish, and unlike Madame Tylenol, their teacher always let them out early. Which meant, more often than not, by the time I arrived at our lunch table they were already midconversation.

That afternoon, they went suddenly quiet when I sat down. For a moment I thought they'd stopped to fill me in, so I wouldn't have to piece together what they were talking about, but then I realized they'd gone quiet because they'd been discussing me.

"Oh hey, Rose," Delia said, sounding strangely cheerful.

Yep, they'd definitely been talking about me. I wondered what offense I'd committed this time.

And then I remembered: the sub-text message. It had completely slipped my mind, after everything else that had happened. And Delia's fury was just about the last thing I wanted to deal with right now.

"Hey," I said, returning Delia's fake smile.

I glanced over at the patch of grass where my former friends were sitting. Someone had brought a box of doughnuts, and they looked like they were having a party rather than enduring a too-early lunch period.

Jamie caught me staring. He grinned and held up his doughnut, as though trying to tempt me to join them. I shook my head, because he was crazy if he thought I was walking over there in front of the whole school.

That was when I realized my friends were all watching our silent exchange. Emmy and Kate were staring at me as though I'd done something endlessly fascinating. And Delia looked like she wished she had claws.

"Yes?" I prompted.

"What's the deal with you and Jamie?" Delia demanded.

She sounded annoyed, and more than a little jealous, as though she was the only one of us who deserved any attention.

"We're madly in love," I said, dripping sarcasm.

"They're working on a class project," Kate interjected.

Delia laughed, glad to see me cut down.

"Oh yeah," she said. "Kate told me *all* about that. How he picked you because his friend was absent."

Delia beamed, and Kate smirked, and Emmy stared at her lap like her silence wasn't just as mean.

I wished I could tell them it wasn't like that. But it was so much easier to let them think what they wanted.

THERE WAS A doughnut on my desk when I sat down in art history.

"Saved it for you," Jamie said, pleased with himself. "It's an apology doughnut."

"It's secondhand," I told him.

"Well, if you don't want it . . ." He reached to take it back, and I slapped his hand away.

"Oh, I want it," I told him.

Mr. Ferrara was giving me a pointed stare, like he was on the verge of walking over and reminding me what his class rules were about food. So I wrapped the doughnut in a napkin and made a big show of putting it into my bag. And then I dutifully took notes on early Cycladic art, my handwriting a messy scrawl, because I kept glancing over at Jamie.

After class ended, he turned toward me, casually dangling his keys.

"Need a ride home?" he asked.

I was so shocked by the offer that I sort of spluttered at him.

"Or we could go to Billz first," he went on, enjoying himself immensely. "For provisions."

"I don't need a ride," I finally got out.

"Yeah, you do," he said. "We still need to work on our scene for drama."

The scene. Of course. It was due tomorrow, and I'd forgotten all about it. But Jamie hadn't.

"You can't bail on me now, Cleopatra. I brought you an apology doughnut. And I offered you a ride. I'd call that a solid attempt at making up for any earlier rudeness."

Damn him. And damn that striped shirt he was wearing, with the sleeves pushed up to his elbows, making him look a little bit like a movie star.

"You sure you want to work at my place?" I asked doubtfully.

"Why?" Jamie teased. "Is there something you're hiding?"

"Just a ghost," I said. "But don't worry, he's super friendly."

Jamie laughed softly.

"Sorry," he apologized. "I just can't believe this is an actual conversation we're having."

"It's weird for me, too," I admitted. Except it didn't feel weird. It felt amazing, like that moment at the end of a long night when you finally unbutton your jeans and slip into something comfortable. Not that I was fantasizing about taking off my pants anytime soon.

"I'd offer my place, but my dad's only teaching two

classes this semester, so he's *always* home." Jamie sighed.

"Well, my parents are never home," I said, following him out of Mr. Ferrara's classroom.

"Yeah, I remember. Logan used to keep an eye on us."

And now it's the other way around, I almost said.

Jamie and I cut through the library quad and stopped outside the social science building. There was no student lot on this side of campus, and I realized we'd made a detour to his locker.

Mine was behind the cafeteria, and I rarely used it, because I had this fear that anything I put in there would smell permanently of maple syrup. It had happened to a girl in my English class freshman year, and this group of asshole boys had started calling her Pancakes.

"Are there still cookies left?" Jamie asked hopefully, swapping out some notebooks.

"You just ate a doughnut," I pointed out. "Like, an hour ago."

"Sadly, I did not," he said. "I gave it away to a cute girl."

For a moment, I didn't think I'd heard him correctly. Claudia was a cute girl. Abby Shah, from our drama class, was a cute girl. When you looked at me, it was easy to make a list of things that could be better: my thighs were too thick, my nose had bad angles, my chin was currently hosting a pop-up exhibit of hormonal acne. Plus I had Hermione hair. From the books, not the movies.

But Jamie was staring at me like I was real-life Emma

Watson. Either he was blind to the truth, or that grin of his had the power to convince anyone they were extraordinary.

The door to one of the classrooms opened, and out walked Delia, Emmy, and Kate. I hoped they wouldn't notice me, but of course they did.

"Rose!" Delia called, waving a little too enthusiastically. My stomach dropped.

"Oh, hi," I called back. For some reason, it came out embarrassed, as though I'd been caught doing something I shouldn't.

"Are those your friends?" Jamie grinned, and then, without waiting for me to answer, executed a perfect impression of Delia's wave.

We'd done that all the time when we were kids, copying people's mannerisms and waiting to see how long before they noticed. Nima's sister used to lose it. Delia, thankfully, didn't notice.

I snorted, and Jamie nudged his shoe against mine, silently acknowledging the joke, like I was in on it, too.

"Hey," he said. "Kate, right? Sorry for kidnapping your drama partner. I swear I didn't know."

"It's fine," Kate mumbled, fiddling nervously with the handle of her rolling backpack.

Delia smiled sweetly, and I knew that whatever was coming next wouldn't be good.

"Oh my god, don't *even* worry about it," she assured him. "I'm sure Kate was *thrilled* not to get stuck with Rose again."

"Why?" Jamie asked, frowning.

"So we were thinking about going to In-N-Out," Emmy cut in, deftly changing the subject. "It's National Cheeseburger Day."

"Doesn't that mean it'll be twice as crowded?" I asked.

"Yeah, but think how many likes our pictures will get," Delia explained.

"That's a solid point," Jamie said. The corners of his mouth twitched, and I knew he was trying not to laugh.

"So do you guys want to come?" Delia asked, sounding a little too enthusiastic.

And I realized all at once what was going on. It was obvious they hadn't been planning to invite me. That I was supposed to find out they'd gotten cheeseburgers together when I was scrolling through Instagram, as some kind of public payback for my text message.

Now Delia had found an even better way to torture me. I could just imagine what she'd say about me as we waited in the never-ending cheeseburger line.

"Sounds dope," Jamie said, and for a horrible moment I thought he was going to tell her yes. "But it's also National Work on a School Assignment Day, and we already made plans."

"It is?" Delia frowned. "Where did you read that?"

Before he could lose his composure, Jamie yanked my arm and steered us toward the parking lot.

"National Work on a School Assignment Day?" I asked, raising an eyebrow, and we both burst out laughing.

IT MADE ME feel so grown up, climbing into a car with a boy, even if we did have to crank down the backseat to fit my bike. Jamie drove a blue Prius, which smelled faintly of coffee, probably from the enormous CSU Laguna thermos in the cup holder. There was a parking pass for the university on his windshield, too.

"My dad made me take summer classes," he explained, pulling a face. "Free tuition for professors' kids."

"Gross," I said, even though it didn't sound that bad.

My summer had been spent volunteering at the library, just to get out of the house. I'd lasted four weeks before I caught someone's bronchitis and was told to please go home and stop coughing all over the children's book cart.

"Well, it could have been worse," Jamie said, his smile tight. "He could have forced us to go on vacation together."

"And called it a family vacation," I added.

A corner of Jamie's mouth hitched up.

"My parents still call it family dinner," I confessed. "And it makes me want to scream."

"I'll bet."

Jamie slipped on a pair of sunglasses and pulled confidently out of the parking space. He did that thing where he turned the wheel with only his palm, like he'd been driving forever. And I wondered when we'd become so adult.

"So how often does Logan turn up?" Jamie asked, turning onto the parkway.

"Most days," I said. "Afternoons are best, since that's when the house is empty."

"Most days," Jamie repeated, surprised. "Wow. I figured it was more like once a week."

"Hey, I thought you were some kind of ghost expert," I teased.

Jamie's expression soured, and I wished I hadn't said anything.

"Reluctant hobbyist," he corrected. "But I mostly encounter them at random. I don't compile information about how frequently they manifest."

I couldn't help it. I burst out laughing.

"Wow, A-plus science speak," I said.

"That bad?" Jamie wrinkled his nose. "Great. I finally meet someone I can talk to about this stuff, and it turns out I'm a terrible conversationalist."

"I wouldn't say terrible," I assured him. "More like . . . intense?"

"Ugh, that's worse!" Jamie leaned his forehead against the steering wheel, his shoulders shaking with laughter.

When we pulled up outside my house, we were both still laughing.

Logan was already there, waiting for us by the front door like a puppy. He immediately started asking Jamie about his favorite television shows.

It was kind of weird, actually, listening to Logan have a conversation with another person. It made him seem younger, somehow, and geekier than I'd remembered. When Logan started ranking his top three shows in the Whedonverse, Jamie finally cut in with an apology.

"Sorry, dude," he said. "But Rose and I have to work on our scene."

Logan sighed, looking pathetic.

"How about we watch an episode of *Firefly* after?" Jamie suggested. "You can pick."

"If I'm even around then," Logan said pitifully, letting out a fake cough. "I might not be long for this world."

"Oh my god," I told him. "You're *already* dead."

"Fine," he sulked. "Go work on your dumb scene. I'll be down here, watching TV by *myself.*"

Logan drifted over to the couch and flopped onto a nest of sequined throw pillows.

"That's gotta hurt," Jamie muttered, wincing.

"Help," Logan moaned, stretching out his arm. "Can't remote."

I put on the episode for him, realizing my mistake too late. Like most of the homes in Hidden Canyon, ours was open plan. The downstairs all flowed together, and with the TV blaring, there was nowhere quiet left to rehearse.

"So, I guess we're working upstairs," Jamie said, trying not to grin.

My cheeks went pink at the thought.

"Shut up, you've seen my room before," I muttered, embarrassed.

"When we were kids," Jamie teased, as though my room

might have suddenly sprouted boobs.

"It's the *same room*," I told him. Except it wasn't. Because your childhood bedroom is what your parents choose for you. It's only when you start growing up that the space becomes yours.

I watched as Jamie surveyed my twinkle lights and the star charts and sea maps I'd found at the flea market. There were props and costume pieces I was saving because they'd been too good to pass up—a jumble of opera glasses, hatboxes, and vintage tennis racquets. The bookshelf, which was crammed to the point of bursting, featured my embarrassingly huge collection of supernatural romance novels.

Jamie glanced around at the limited seating options. And then he winced slightly, massaging his temple.

"Aspirin?" I asked, and he nodded. "Same place as last time."

The second he left, I made a beeline for the pile of discarded clothing on my floor and shoved it all into my closet, hoping he hadn't seen my beige bra poking out of the pile.

"Sorry," Jamie said when he got back. "I swear I'm not coming down with anything."

"Maybe it's the weather?" I suggested.

"Maybe. My mom always gets hiccups right before it rains."

"You're making that up," I accused.

"I tell you that I see ghosts, and you're all, 'cool, whatever.' But my mom's hiccups are the part you have a hard time believing?"

"Now that you mention it, I am starting to doubt the ghost thing," I teased.

Jamie dropped onto the carpet and kicked off just the heels of his shoes. He'd done that when he was little, I remembered suddenly. The two of us coloring illustrations of the Earth's core for a science project in an explosion of scented markers and similarly scented fruit snacks.

I sat in my desk chair, swiveling it around as I dug out my script. I was nervous for Jamie to hear me read, nervous that he'd assumed I was this amazing actress and would regret choosing me as a partner.

We ran through it once, and then I flipped back to the first page.

"Again?" I asked, but Jamie shook his head.

"Not yet," he said. "First, I want to know what you think of the scene. Like, our characters, for instance. What were they doing before they arrived at the train station?"

His question surprised me. It was just a short scene, two strangers who meet on a train platform, and I'd thought it was pretty straightforward. I'd never wondered whether Character A was tired, or hungry, or frustrated. Whether Character B was poor, or lonely, or old. But as we unpacked the dialogue, our characters began to come into focus.

When we tried it again, neither of us was just reading the lines. We were speaking them as the characters we'd created.

After we finished, I waited for Jamie's pronouncement,

dreading what he'd say. And then his face broke into a grin.

"So much better," he said. "I think we're going to nail this."

I breathed a sigh of relief.

"Where did you learn to do that?" I asked.

"Play a lonely old man? It's ea—"

"No," I interrupted. "The questions."

Jamie shrugged, playing it off.

"I did National History Day at my old school," he said. "You research historical topics and put on performances."

"So it's history club for drama nerds?" I asked.

"Pretty much."

"Canyon doesn't have anything like that," I said, stating the obvious.

"Nope."

A muscle feathered in his jaw, and for a moment he looked defeated. But then it was gone, replaced with the cocky expression I was starting to realize he wore like armor.

"Let's read this through a few more times," he said, gesturing to the script.

We did, until we hit a good rhythm with it and had stopped making adjustments. We were just about to pack up when Logan appeared, moaning about how we were taking forever to come downstairs and watch TV.

"I had no idea ghosts were so needy," Jamie whispered as we followed Logan into the living room.

"I can hear you," Logan said.

Jamie went red.

"Just testing," he mumbled.

Jamie and I squished onto opposite ends of the sofa, polishing off the rest of the chocolate chip cookies as Logan hunched forward, enthralled by the crew of the *Serenity*.

Jamie kept glancing at his phone and getting up to refill his drink. Halfway through the episode, he said he had to head out.

"Are you sure?" I asked, and then mentally kicked myself. *Way to seem desperate for someone to keep hanging out with you.*

"Yeah, I have a calc test tomorrow," he explained, as though he would have stayed for hours otherwise.

He stood up, stretching. His shirt lifted along with his arms, revealing a strip of smooth skin and the waistband of his jeans, cinched with a brown leather belt. I glanced away, suddenly finding the scratches in our coffee table fascinating.

"I'll memorize the rest of the scene tonight," I promised.

"You better," Jamie said, picking up his bag. "I'm counting on you to make me look good."

10

DELIA, EMMY, AND Kate were waiting to ambush me at the bike rack the next morning. It wasn't hard to guess why. All night, my phone had been buzzing with Snapchats from Delia, who clearly thought she was being very covert.

What's going on with Jamie? She'd scrawled over her face in pink cursive. And then I can keep a secret ☺. After I still didn't respond, she sent a stream of pouting puppy-filter selfies.

But I knew she was just waiting to screenshot my answer and show it around. So I'd sent her a deliberately blurry snap of my homework, imagining the excited flutter she must have gotten when she saw the alert that I'd replied.

Now, seeing her standing there, my act of snapterfuge seemed like a grand miscalculation. Like the kind of thing you did when you wanted to ruin an enemy rather than keep a friend. I ducked behind a lifted truck and waited until they headed for advisement before docking my bike.

I slid into my seat seconds before the bell rang, and Darren pantomimed applause, his headphones still on. Somehow, the universe was on my side that morning. Which was why, when lunch rolled around, I decided not to chance my window of good luck.

I made for the quiet study section of the library, taking out my script for Gardner's class and reading it over, even though I knew it by heart. It was a convenient enough excuse for sitting there, in case my friends came looking for me.

Mom always said *doing nothing is doing something you'll wind up regretting.* Of course, she was talking about getting regular teeth cleanings, but it also applied to Delia. I'd put up with her terrible behavior for so long that I'd inadvertently made the problem worse. And now I couldn't say anything without it turning into this huge drama.

"The Egyptology books are over in nonfiction," Jamie said.

He was wearing a button-down shirt, and his sunglasses were clipped to the front, like he'd just taken them off to come inside. There were dark circles under his eyes, and I hoped he hadn't stayed up all night studying.

"That line's getting so old it's practically ancient history," I grumbled.

"Wait, was that a 'yo mummy' joke?" he asked.

I couldn't help it. I laughed.

"I went by your table first," Jamie said, enjoying himself immensely. "Did you know it's both National Talk Like a

Pirate Day *and* National Butterscotch Pudding Day?"

"I did not," I said. "And now I'm sorry you do. Matey."

"Interesting friends you have," Jamie said casually.

"Not really my friends," I told him. And somehow, saying it out loud made it true.

"I can see that, since you appear to be dining solo in the library." Jamie nodded toward the contraband bagel on my lap. "What are you doing in here?"

"What does it look like?" I asked, motioning toward my script.

"Staring at something you've already memorized."

Jamie sat down across from me, and I sighed, caught.

"Okay, maybe I'm hiding," I admitted.

"In here, or in general?" he asked, and then winced. "Sorry."

"Don't be. I mean, you're right."

"It's Logan, isn't it?" Jamie went on. "The reason you try so hard to be invisible."

I didn't say anything.

"Just so you know, it isn't working," he said. "At all."

I knew he meant it to be a compliment, but it didn't feel like one. I didn't want him to bring me into focus, the way he'd done with our scene yesterday. I wanted to stay fuzzy and unmemorable.

At least, I thought that was what I wanted. But staring into Jamie's impossibly deep brown eyes, I found myself questioning that decision.

"It was working fine," I huffed. "Before *you* showed up."

"Was it now?" Jamie asked sarcastically. He leaned so far back in his chair that it looked like he was going to tip.

He lost his balance all of a sudden, the chair tilting much too far back. He scrambled to fix it, his cheeks going bright red.

I snorted. Jamie glared at me like it wasn't funny, even though it was hilarious.

"Damn it," I said mock sadly, "now I only have two wishes left."

"That right there," he accused. "Opposite of invisible."

I shrugged. I knew he didn't see it, but keeping to the shadows came with its perks. No one expected me to get a role in the play or a superlative in the yearbook. No one cared if I wore the same leggings two days in a row or wasn't asked to the homecoming dance or got tagged in an unflattering photo.

High school was hard enough without enduring a constant stream of public scrutiny. And that was when you didn't have anything to hide. I didn't know how Jamie stood it. How he could adjust so quickly, or pretend so convincingly to be normal.

The bell rang, and Jamie pushed back his chair, as though he couldn't wait to get to Gardner's class.

"Come on, Cleo," he said excitedly. "Let's show everyone how it's done."

He meant our scene. I felt this bolt of panic stab through me, because it was only just occurring to me that we were about to go onstage together, in front of everyone.

I hesitated, and Jamie grinned.

"Don't tell me you have stage fright," he teased.

"Performance anxiety," I corrected. Jamie saw that I was serious.

"Hey," he said. "Relax. Just do it exactly like we rehearsed and it'll be great."

I managed a smile and nod, even though there was no possible way I could relax.

If our scene wasn't good enough—if *I* wasn't good enough—I'd disappoint everyone. Sam's crowd would go cool toward me, realizing I couldn't keep up with them, and Jamie would see that I wasn't magic after all. That he'd been wrong about me.

It was like this story my sophomore year physics teacher had loved, about Schrodinger's cat. The moment you looked inside the box, you knew the truth about whether the cat was dead or alive. But so long as you didn't look, you didn't know. And I wasn't sure I wanted everyone to know the truth about me. I wasn't even sure *I* wanted to know the truth.

Except somehow, I'd stopped paying attention, just for a moment, and now Jamie was cheerfully opening the box, convinced he knew what was inside. But he didn't, because we can only guess at what we contain. And our guess is just as good as anyone else's.

When I made a move to sit in the back of the theater, Jamie stopped me.

"Hold up," he said. "We've gotta sit close. I'm blind as a bat, remember?"

He was no such thing. When your dad's an optician you know a thing or two about glasses, and Jamie's prescription was slight. But before I had a chance to protest, Jamie had marched us to the front row of the theater.

I could see the backs of Sam's and Claudia's heads, bent together in conversation. Max and Darren were making their way over from the far aisle, chugging bottles of flavored iced tea before they had to put them away.

"After you," Jamie said, gesturing for me to go first.

I'd always pictured it differently, sitting with my old friends again. I'd imagined that they'd all look up in unison, as though my presence was this big interruption. But that couldn't be further from what really happened.

Instead, no one looked over at all. It was a total nonevent, and I felt mildly embarrassed for having built it up so much in my head. I put down my bag, wedging it under my seat, and when I glanced up again, Max and Darren were arriving sans iced tea.

Claudia glanced over first. She looked surprised and then delighted, as though my appearance was exciting instead of completely unprompted.

"Hey, Rose," she said, leaning across Sam. "I love your top!"

I was wearing a cream high-necked lace blouse that had sat in the back of my closet for months, more intimidating at home than it had seemed in the dressing room.

106

"It's from that vintage store—" I started to explain.

"On Ocean?" she asked, and I nodded. "Oh my god, I spend all of my babysitting money there. Did you know they have a student discount?"

"They do?" I asked.

"It's kind of a secret," she said. "You have to ask, and they make you sign up for their mailing list, but you get fifteen percent off."

"That's amazing," I said.

I loved that place, with its antique phonograph in the window and embroidered aprons hanging from the ceiling, like they were about to take flight.

Delia hated it. When I'd wanted us to go in one afternoon, she'd loudly announced that her cousin had gotten HPV from a pair of used jeans, which isn't even possible. So I'd told her never mind, and had spent the next hour watching her and Emmy try on sixty-dollar sweaters in Brandy Melville.

Max joined us, and Sam glanced around, confused.

"Hold on," Sam said. "Where's Nima?"

Max snorted.

"In the back. With that girl."

"No." Sam looked shocked. "*Our* Nima? Sitting with a *girl*?"

Subtlety definitely wasn't Sam's thing. He twisted around, being wildly obvious.

"Stop," Claudia begged, swatting at him. "Everyone can see."

"I don't care," Sam said, but he turned back around, looking dejected. "Nope. They're both staring at their phones. I can't tell if they're covertly texting or ignoring each other."

"Rose knows her," Darren announced. He turned to me. "What's your verdict?"

Suddenly, everyone was staring at me with interest. But I couldn't picture a less likely pair than gloomy Kate and cheerful Nima.

"Ignoring each other. Definitely," I pronounced, and everyone groaned.

Gardner called our class to attention then. He leaned back against the stage, legs crossed beneath a sherbet-colored polo shirt, looking more like an ice-cream cone than ever.

He had his attendance sheet out, and he checked Jamie off immediately, then frowned, glancing up.

"Where's Rose?" he repeated, squinting toward the back row.

"Right here," I said.

Gardner looked surprised to find me sitting up front, and I didn't blame him. It took him even longer to locate Nima.

The theater tech class was already in the sound and lighting booth with their teacher supervising. The lighting suddenly went orange and then slowly turned blue. I realized that we were doing scenes so they could practice. We combined classes occasionally, I just hadn't expected them all to be here, watching.

Sam and Claudia volunteered to go first, setting up the chairs and helping to set the sound and lighting for everyone. They were calm and patient through all of it, cracking jokes with Lara, the stage manager, whose voice crackled over the God Mic.

While they were setting up, I glanced at Sam's seat. No backpack. And a tiny part of me relaxed, knowing that Sam was secretly nervous.

After they finished, Jamie raised his hand, volunteering us. I wasn't expecting that, and I stared at him in shock. Panic washed over me, fast and disorienting. But there was no time for panic, and so I pushed it down.

I took a deep breath and followed him onto the stage, my heart still hammering. I'd sat down with the best actors in our class, and when you did that, you couldn't screw up. I couldn't screw up.

Jamie gave me a slight nod and then delivered the first line. There was a stillness to the air, punctuated by the occasional crackle from an overhead mic.

So many people were watching. Expecting. Waiting. But somehow, I knew what to do. It was like Jamie and I were passing a bolt of electricity back and forth between us, building it bigger and bigger with each line, until it escaped all at once in a thunderclap of applause.

When we climbed down from the stage, Jamie grinned at me.

"Well done, partner," he whispered, and I didn't know whether to be flattered or relieved.

"You too," I whispered back.

We watched the rest of our classmates perform, all of it blending into a sea of flubbed lines and applause and Seth in a flaming orange hat, improbably doing an old-school gangster accent while Abby murdered him with her glare.

Nima and Kate went last. Part of me hoped it wouldn't be as bad as I thought. Instead, it was worse. She dropped half her cues and recited her lines like she was reading a textbook. Without anything to play off, Nima fell flat, the way that I always had. I'd just never wondered how much of that was Kate.

I could see Nima straining to salvage it, but nothing helped. They both looked relieved when it was over. He didn't even bother going back to his seat, just slumped into the front row with us and slid down in his chair until he was practically horizontal.

"What a face-plant," he muttered.

"Don't worry about it," Darren said.

Max rolled his eyes, obviously of a different opinion.

And I thought about how lucky I was that I hadn't tanked my scene with Jamie. That he wasn't slouched in his seat, trying to forget the horror. But just because I hadn't face-planted the assignment didn't mean anything. The universe was in my favor today, but my luck could change in an instant.

Gardner let us go a few minutes early. Everyone started to pack up, but Jamie turned toward me, his shoulders shaking with silent laughter.

"What?" I accused.

"Kate," he said. "You made me feel terrible for stealing you away."

"It's not like that," I said, and explained my theory about the rule of friend groups, and mandatory partnership, and how it creates this endless loop of forced sameness.

I didn't realize I had an audience until Claudia started giggling.

"Challenge accepted," she said.

"Thanks a lot, Rose," Sam deadpanned. "Now she'll ignore me for a week just to prove a point."

"Not a *whole* week," Claudia countered.

"Well, count me out from this escape-your-comfort-zone bullshit," Max said drily. "You see how well it turned out for Nima."

"Yeah, but what about Jamie and Rose?" Claudia countered. "Who were awesome, by the way."

"Good scene chemistry," Sam added innocently. Claudia whacked him.

"We worked on it outside of class," I admitted. I meant it as an explanation for why I hadn't sucked, but Sam took it completely the wrong way.

"Did you?" he asked, grinning.

"Shut up, we did, too," Claudia reminded him.

I glanced toward the back of the theater, looking for Kate, in case she was still hanging around. But she'd left without me. And somehow, I'd known she would. "Okay, so, Billz?" Nima asked.

"Definitely," Claudia said. "Max owes me a Splendor rematch."

Max grumbled, and I stiffened, waiting to see if they'd invite me along.

"Rose, do you need a ride?" Sam offered, as though there was no question I was invited.

"She can ride with me," Jamie said.

"Great." Claudia grinned. "We'll meet you there."

I could feel myself lighting up again, and whether it was because of my proximity to everyone else's charisma or whether I'd found a hidden reserve of my own, I couldn't say. All I knew was, for the first time since Logan's death, a piece of the darkness had receded, and just like that, I was glowing.

II

THE SUN WAS setting by the time we abandoned the back
table at Billz. We spilled into the parking lot, arguing over
some silly game point of Gloom. Max and Nima had their
phones out, each of them determined to prove the other one
wrong, and somehow, their absurd argument had become a
joke in its own right.

I didn't even remember what was funny about it, but we
were laughing in ragged gasps because the joke was bigger
than the sum of its parts.

And that was the magic of it all, I realized. There had
been so many times when, from the other end of the quad,
I'd wished I could know what they were laughing about.
Except now I knew: the joke didn't matter. Sometimes you
didn't even know what you were laughing about, just who
you were laughing *with*.

I looked around, at this group of friends who only last
week had seemed impossibly distant. I'd slunk out of this

same coffee shop mortified because only Nima had waved at me.

I realized now that everyone would have been friendly if I'd walked over and said hello. That no one would have minded if I'd pulled up a chair and joined in. Jamie had figured this out on the first day of school, but it had taken me an embarrassingly long time to realize that popular kids are intimidating but fundamentally nice.

"You should ride home with us," Sam said. It took a moment to register that he was talking to me.

"Um, are you sure?" I asked, wondering where the offer had come from.

"I don't mind dropping her off," Jamie said.

Sam snorted.

"Whatever, University Village," he teased, since unlike the rest of us, Jamie lived south of the parkway. "I've got this. Rose, hop into my party bus."

Sam's "party bus," it turned out, was a secondhand Suburban. The seats were covered with Navajo blankets, either as a decoration or as courtesy, and the whole thing smelled faintly of stale fast-food grease. There was a Chick-fil-A bag crumpled under the driver's seat, canoodling with a flock of half-empty water bottles.

I climbed into the back, and Claudia sat up front.

"Didn't we used to carpool in this thing?" I asked.

"We still do," Claudia said. "Just without parents."

She fiddled with the radio hookup, plugging in her

phone. The opening bars of a *Hamilton* song spilled through the speakers, and Sam groaned, theatrically banging his head against the back of his seat.

"Not this," he moaned. "Not again."

"I'll make you like it," Claudia insisted.

Sam made a face at her. But his protest was only for show, because he turned up the volume and sang along with us until he pulled into my driveway.

I was still singing when I opened the front door.

"Who's Alexander Hamilton?" Logan asked. He was slouched on the sofa, glaring at me.

"Oh, um. One of America's founding fathers?" I said.

"Whatever," Logan said. "I thought you were going to come home after school. *Both* of you."

"Sorry." I dropped my bag onto the bench. "A bunch of us went to Billz."

Logan stared at me accusingly.

"I thought you said you were *never* going back there."

"Things changed," I explained.

"You mean Jamie," Logan said. "Jamie with his own car and his awesome, cool friends."

It wasn't a question, so I didn't even try to answer it.

"Whatever," Logan snapped. "Go out with your *new friends* to your *favorite coffee shop* and leave me here all afternoon with nothing to do. I don't care."

But he clearly did, because the front door slammed shut behind me. Logan flew upward, his arms folded, his mouth set in a thin, angry line. He was a storm of resentment, all temper and gloom. And I had half a notion of what he was planning.

"Don't you dare!" I warned.

"Oops," Logan said, dripping sarcasm. And then, with surprising force, he rocketed through the ceiling.

Somewhere deep in the walls, the pipes gurgled ominously.

THANKS TO LOGAN'S temper tantrum, our plumbing was erratic over the next few days. My bathroom sink kept whistling like a teakettle, and on more than one occasion, I heard my mom swear from the shower. My dad got out his toolbox, insisting he could fix it himself. But all he succeeded in doing was messing up the water pressure and forcing my mom to call in a professional.

While my mom hovered over the handyman, I spent the weekend agonizing over where to sit at lunch on Monday. But it turned out I didn't need to worry, because I'd forgotten Darren was in my French class.

"Hey, Rose," he said, leaning across the aisle when the bell rang. "Want to do Swap-Tarts?"

I told him I had no idea what that was, and he grinned.

"Claudia made it up," he said, and explained that all you did was get a packet of Pop-Tarts from the vending machine. Except you needed another person to get a different flavor so you could trade. That way you wound up with one of each.

It was actually a pretty genius idea.

"Okay," I said, "but I hate the cinnamon ones."

"Yeah, those are gross." Darren made a face. "Like if someone's car accidentally ran over a Cinnabon."

I laughed.

"I bet that's how the flavor got invented," I said. "Some poor taste engineer had a really bad morning on his way into the office."

Darren let out a surprisingly high-pitched giggle at that one. I glanced over at him, with his oversized denim jacket and black skinny jeans. His hipster art-kid vibe was a total contrast to Max's old-man cardigans and fifties haircut. The two of them were perfectly mismatched, personalities included.

It was strange to realize he'd been there all along, just across the aisle, my partner in eye-rolling. I'd overlooked him, somehow, because he was quiet and used our advisement period to study. Because I hadn't known him very well before I left the group. And I had a feeling he'd done the same thing to me.

"Ooh, are you guys doing Swap-Tarts?" Claudia asked when we got to the table.

"That isn't a thing," Sam complained.

"Shut up, yes it is," Claudia said, throwing a piece of her sandwich crust at him. "You're just mad because I came up with a cleverer name for it than you."

Sam picked up the piece of sandwich crust and ate it.

"If I make you really mad, will you throw the whole

sandwich at me?" he asked hopefully.

Jamie arrived at our spot then, looking thrilled when he saw me.

"Hey there, Cleo," he said. "What's for lunch?"

"Sarcasm, apparently. And squabbling," I said, nodding at Sam and Claudia.

Jamie laughed.

"Ignore them, they just want an audience," he told me.

"We do not," Sam protested.

"Correction: you want a full house, standing room only." Jamie's grin stretched wider, and this time, the sandwich crust was thrown in his direction.

Some music started up over by the SGA building, where a group of kids in neon orange shirts were setting up a spirit wheel, and everyone sighed.

"What?" I asked.

"He could have run for anything," Max said, rolling his eyes. "But it *had* to be the *spirit* committee."

"What's wrong with the spirit committee?" Jamie asked, frowning.

There was a collective snort. And then Sam explained, filling Jamie in on how our school's cheer team was an actual competitive sport and refused to waste their time selling dance tickets or taking orders for class sweatshirts. Which meant that kind of drudgery fell to the student government association. Specifically, to the spirit committee.

It was a thankless job, and no one particularly wanted

it. Last year, we'd had Meghan Watts as our spirit chair. Meghan, who had a huge Kate Middleton obsession, had cheerfully attempted to murder us with charity teas and croquet lawn parties. It was so dire that Nima had stepped in to make sure she didn't run unopposed.

"It was a noble but very annoying sacrifice," Max added.

"So now we're stuck having to step up our class spirit out of support." Sam sighed. "Which means we're going over there. To spin that stupid prize wheel and win a class keychain."

"Go Juniors," Claudia said, sounding completely bored. She stood up, brushing grass off her dress. "Shall we get it over with?"

Everyone agreed that, yeah, it was probably best. And so I found myself crossing the quad with the five of them, heading toward the same spirit wheel that I'd avoided almost two weeks earlier.

I could feel our classmates' eyes watching, questioning why I was there. At least Jamie was an unknown quantity, but I wasn't any puzzle worth solving: I'd already proven myself to be insignificant. Nima was thrilled when we came over.

Rescue me, he pleaded silently.

Sam pushed up his sleeves and swaggered over to the SGA booth, acting like it was the cool thing to do, instead of something corny and vaguely embarrassing. He spun the spirit wheel with aplomb.

"A keychain!" he exclaimed loudly, overselling it. "Just what I've always wanted!"

Max snorted. Jamie looked like he didn't know whether to roll his eyes or laugh. Darren gave a halfhearted cheer, laughing at his own ridiculousness halfway through.

But it worked, because, before long, there was a line of students waiting to spin the wheel.

Nima mouthed a thank-you.

"These are the memories we'll treasure forever," Max said dryly, as Kayla Ashby enthusiastically bounced over to spin the spirit wheel, her dress riding up to reveal a significant flash of butt cheek.

"And the moments nightmares are made of," Darren added.

"Maybe for you," Sam said. "But I'll sleep well tonight, knowing I did my part in making this school a greater place."

"Has anyone ever told you that sarcasm is a crutch, not a cure?" Jamie asked.

Everyone cracked up except for Sam, who shot us a mutinous glare.

"Unfunny," he grumbled.

I glanced across the quad, toward the math building. Delia, Kate, and Emmy were there, at the table under the overhang, staring back at me. And I wasn't sure who I recognized less: them, or myself.

12

I SAT WITH Sam's crowd for the rest of the week, although I made excuses about hanging out with them after school. I felt bad for ditching Logan, and I wanted to make it up to him. He finally turned up on Wednesday afternoon, acting as though our squabble had never happened.

"We should have a *Buffy* marathon," he announced while I toasted bread for a sandwich. "Season three."

And I agreed, since I was so relieved to see him. Except I'd forgotten what season three was about—in it, Buffy struggles to accept her fate as a vampire slayer after a new slayer comes to town.

By Friday evening, we'd made it to the part where the new slayer turned out to be kind of evil when my dad came home, carrying bags of Chinese takeout.

"Rose, quick," he said. "Set the table with chopsticks and hide all the forks."

"Not again," I groaned.

Dad was on an endless quest to force Mom to use chopsticks, and her resistance was impressive. She was of the "ask for a fork when we sit down" camp at Jade Palace. And no dirty looks we sent her direction could shame her out of doing it.

Unfortunately, the restaurant knew our order, so they'd added plastic utensils to the bag. Which only proves that the more you try to change someone against their will, the more the universe helps them resist.

LOGAN TURNED UP again the next morning, climbing expectantly onto the sofa and chanting, "Episode ten, episode ten," until I sat down next to him and turned on the TV.

Dad was out hiking with some nature group he'd joined, but Mom, who was hanging around in her yoga pants and working her way through the pile up of laundry, kept popping in to check on me. I could tell she thought I was fifty shades of pathetic for spending Saturday on the couch. But I couldn't exactly point to Logan, who was sprawled next to me, as an excuse.

"Get dressed," she said, somewhere around episode thirteen. "We're having a girls' day."

I glanced up at her. She looked so hopeful and so eager to spend time with me that I couldn't say no.

"Give me, like, ten minutes," I said.

I reached to switch off the TV, and Logan glared at me.

"I was watching that!" he complained, and I shrugged. I

couldn't leave it on. And I couldn't exactly refuse to go with Mom. Logan knew that, just like he knew that our parents couldn't suspect there was anything going on with me.

For years, I'd been terrified that they'd send me back to the family therapist and she'd figure out I was seeing my brother's ghost. I imagined her trotting out some long clinical term for it, and off I'd go, down a white, astringent corridor, toward a room where I wasn't allowed to wear shoelaces or blow-dry my hair.

It didn't matter that Logan's ghost was real. If anything, that only made it worse, because at least mental illnesses can be managed and treated. I wasn't so sure about paranormal abilities.

So I twisted my hair into a side braid, threw on what I'd worn to school yesterday, and pretended to be psyched for an afternoon with Mom.

She drove us over to Plaza Island, where we got milk shakes from the fancy gelato place and watched the koi swim around in their huge pond.

"I always wanted koi," Mom said wistfully.

"Where would we put them?" I asked, trying to picture owning a fleet of puppy-sized fish.

"I know." Mom bit her straw. "We'd have to take out most of the grass in the backyard. Which we should do anyway, because of the drought. But I'd get so worried about wild animals eating them."

She seemed defeated when she said that. As though the

stress of potentially losing a pet made it too risky to consider getting one. When Logan's guinea pig had died a few years back, it had practically given Mom hysterics.

"You could get them a cover," I suggested. "Raccoon-proof and everything."

"Maybe," Mom said, but I could tell she'd made up her mind already. "Come on, let's see if there's anything good in Sephora."

We poked around for a while, testing out makeup until our hands and lips were so stained that we couldn't even tell if we liked the colors.

"This is nice," Mom said as we waited in line to pay for some lip crayons.

"The nicest line I've waited in," I joked, fiddling with a travel-sized perfume.

"I mean it," she insisted. "I feel like we're all so caught up in our own things, we never just spend time together."

"If only we liked baseball more," I said.

She laughed darkly.

"If only your father liked it a little less."

And then she treated me to the lip crayon and let me cash out all her points on samples from behind the glass case, like we were getting prizes in an arcade.

"Shoes?" Mom asked, smiling mischievously.

"We already did back-to-school shopping," I reminded her.

"There's no harm in looking," she said, and then fell

silent for a second, staring at me. "I can't believe how fast you're growing up. I better get in all of my Rose time before you're off at college."

"Mom," I said. "That's, like, a million years away."

Except it wasn't. All of a sudden, high school wasn't about high school anymore. It was about The Future, and being prepared for it, like college was an incoming storm, and we needed to sandbag the roads.

Max had finished a PSAT prep course. Jamie was already taking college classes. Meanwhile, I was terrified to think what my options were: live at home and attend notoriously shitty CSU Laguna or move away and abandon Logan.

"Okaaayyyy," Mom said. "I get it. I'm embarrassing you with all of this growing-up talk."

"I'm humiliated," I deadpanned. "The only way to make it up to me is a new pair of boots."

"Nice try. And we're browsing, not buying," Mom reminded me, holding open the glass door to Bloomingdale's.

I followed her inside. Since there was a sale going on, the store was crowded. I poked around a display of ankle boots that were sold out in most sizes and watched as Mom perused a selection of practical work shoes with a fierce intensity.

"These?" she asked, holding up a silver clog.

I made a face.

"Very Ziggy Stardust," someone said.

I turned around, and there was Claudia, wearing a

floppy hat and one of those floaty bohemian dresses that I could never pull off. Meanwhile, I was in the same thing I'd worn to school yesterday, plus a ridiculous amount of sample makeup.

"Hey, Rose. Hi, Mrs. Asher," Claudia said. And my mom, who hadn't seen Claudia in ages, lit up.

"Claudiaaaa," a little girl whined, looking up from a video game console. She was about six, and was wearing a pink tutu with a Wonder Woman T-shirt. A miniature version of Claudia, with the same brown skin and ridiculously long eyelashes. She was nothing like the screeching toddler I remembered who used to fling Cheerios at me in the carpool.

"We're getting ice cream in a minute, I promise," Claudia said, unfazed.

"Is that Sophia?" my mom said. "She's so grown up!"

Sophia had gone back to her game, making it clear she was on strike until she got ice cream. My mom exclaimed some more over how big Sophia had gotten and then started asking Claudia a million questions about school.

I'd forgotten how nosy my mom could be, and I felt my cheeks heat up with embarrassment. Did she *really* need to know what level math class Claudia was taking, and if she'd also found the first precalc exam challenging? Claudia, thank god, took it all in stride, chatting politely.

"Mom," I whispered.

But my mom just flapped her hand at me like I was interrupting her while she was on the phone.

"Claudiaaa," Sophia whined, looking up from her video game. "You said we could have ice cream. You promised."

"We will. After you finish that level," Claudia said. Then, as an afterthought, she added, "Oh, Rose, did Jamie ask you to that new Wes Anderson movie tonight?"

"Um, no," I said, wondering why she would think that.

"Hmmm." Claudia chewed her lip. "He said he would. A bunch of us are going."

"What time?" I asked.

"Sam and I got our tickets this morning, and it was almost sold out," Claudia said, making it sound like an apology.

"That's okay."

I wasn't sure whether I meant the fact that Jamie hadn't asked me, or that I wouldn't have been able to get a ticket anyway.

"Done!" Sophia interrupted. "*Now* can we go?"

"I think I better get this munchkin some ice cream," Claudia said, rolling her eyes. "See you."

The moment they were gone, my mom turned toward me, eyebrows raised, not saying a word.

"What?" I asked.

"Is that why you were hanging around the house? Because you were waiting for a boy to call?"

I almost burst out laughing at her theory. I mean, had she forgotten about texting? But it was also a convenient excuse for any future afternoons I might spend seemingly alone on the sofa watching Netflix.

"Maybe," I lied.

Mom lit up, pleased that she'd solved it. Or maybe just happy to have an explanation that didn't point to my being an antisocial couch potato.

"Let's pick up a pizza on the way home," she said. "Giordano's, I think."

"Okay," I said, confused why she was offering me pizza instead of giving me the third degree about Jamie. "Should I call it in?"

Giordano's took forever if you didn't call in your order. But Mom shook her head.

"Don't bother," she said triumphantly. "You can catch me up on *everything* while we wait."

IT WASN'T UNTIL late that night that I saw the messages. Nine of them, sent via Facebook Messenger, of all things. It turned out Jamie *had* invited me to the movie. He'd even offered to get my ticket before they sold out.

I stared at the stack of unanswered messages, feeling horrible.

And then I typed back a response: Omg. No one uses this app. No one. Unless you're secretly a dad?

The reply came immediately: Such a dad.

Just saw your messages this second, I wrote. Was your popcorn very lonely?

The loneliest popcorn in the movie theater.

128

I snorted when I read that. And then I messaged him my phone number, because the ridiculous app kept trying to get me to send a sticker of a weird cartoon dog.

"Facebook. Messenger," I told him, picking up on the first ring.

"In retrospect, not my finest idea," he said. "Everyone used it at my old school. Our teachers figured out how to block literally everything else. I swear to god, there were cell service dampeners hidden in our clock tower."

"You had a clock tower," I told him, "which leads me to believe that your old school was like Hogwarts."

Jamie laughed.

"You've figured it out. I'm secretly a wizard."

"Knew it," I teased. "It's the glasses. They give you away."

I climbed into bed, snuggling under the covers with my phone and trying to imagine Jamie in his room, wearing his pajamas. Or maybe just his boxers.

"Sorry about the movie, by the way," Jamie said. "No one had your number, so I said I'd handle it. But apparently not."

"Hey look, you failed at something," I teased.

"The world may never be the same," Jamie said. His mouth sounded full.

"What are you eating?" I asked.

"Ugh, you can tell?" he asked. "It's pad thai. Again. Because it turns out my dad doesn't cook. Meanwhile, I bet you got a delicious homemade dinner."

"We had pizza," I said.

Jamie snorted.

"At least you know I'm not psychic," he pointed out.

"Wait, are there any other superpowers I should be worried about?" I teased.

A plate clattered on the other end, and I heard a sink turn on.

"My only frequency is ghost," he promised. "How about you, Cleo?"

"Well, it's not a superpower so much as a superstition," I said.

"Doesn't matter. Lay it on me."

"Whenever I'm having a really good hair day, I know something bad's going to happen."

Jamie snorted.

"That's not a superstition, it's a spurious correlation," he accused.

"A what?"

"It's a false mathematical conclusion. You're assuming that one thing causes another just because you can graph them together," he explained. "But you can graph lots of things and claim they're related. Say there's been an increase in ice-cream consumption over the past few years. And the rate of people being struck by lightning has also gone up. You can chart that and be like, 'See? Eating ice cream causes you to be struck by lightning!'"

I couldn't help it. I laughed.

"A spurious correlation," I said, trying out the phrase.

"There's a bunch of really funny ones on the internet," Jamie went on, encouraged. "I'll text them to you."

And then I spent the next twenty minutes giggling over ridiculous graphs.

A decrease in pirates causes an increase in lawyers. The correlation between people eating cheese and people who died getting tangled in their bedsheets. The last graph was one he'd made himself:

Reading books about ancient Egypt causes ability to see ghosts.

I laughed.

I refuse to believe that one isn't real, I typed back.

By the time I went to sleep, it was very late. The soft thrum of the TV in my parents' bedroom had long since been replaced by the rattle of my dad's snores.

I'd heard them talking earlier, whispering about me. While Mom held me pizza-hostage, I'd told her it was nothing. That he hadn't invited me to the movies after all. That we were just friends who had worked together on a class project, and Claudia was mistaken, and to please, please forget about it and also to order extra garlic knots.

Jamie had said it was a group thing. That no one had my number, and he'd volunteered to invite me. It wasn't like he'd asked me on a date. Or that he'd ever said anything about being more than friends. Even if I wished he would.

Because I had such a crush on that boy. Such a stupid,

giddy, heart-racing crush—on Jamie Aldridge, of all people. On glasses-wearing Jamie, who cuffed his jeans and called me Cleopatra and knew the answer to every question in our art history packet. Jamie, who saw ghosts but didn't know why and sprawled on my bedroom carpet like we were still eight years old and obsessed with the Valley of the Kings.

And I had no idea what to do about it or if he felt the same way. All I knew was, the vaguely flirty texts we were sending back and forth from our bedrooms weren't like anything I'd experienced before. They were electric, and I was pretty sure the glow of my phone screen wasn't some connection made of pixels and microchips. That it was us, lighting up the darkness, together.

13

WE KEPT TEXTING all weekend, and by the time Monday morning rolled around, I felt horribly nervous about seeing Jamie in school. I was worried that whatever it was between us was limited to text messages and late-night phone bravery, and that, when we saw each other in person, our connection would drop.

Except I shouldn't have worried. Jamie broke into a grin when he spotted me walking over at lunch. He raised his hand in a wave, and my heart sped up. *Stop that*, I scolded it. *Calm down.*

Before I could join him, Claudia bounded over, dragging me off to buy iced tea.

"So the ice-cream expedition was a disaster," she said as we waited in line at the snack window. "But that's what I get for wearing pink suede boots to babysit a six-year-old."

"Not your boots!"

"Thirty-one flavors of stained," she said with a sigh.

The boys in front of us let two of their friends cut, making the wait even longer. Claudia rolled her eyes.

"Do me a favor," she said. "Please, please keep sitting with us. You don't even know what it's like, holding down the fort by myself. I'm Wendy with the Lost Boys."

I laughed at her description.

"I'm serious," she said. "Picture going to the movies with *five* boys."

Okay, she had a point.

"Funny story about that," I said, explaining the texting mishap.

"Jamie told me," she said. "We have bio together."

"Oh, right." I remembered how he'd said Claudia had been the one to tell him about Logan.

"He gave me your number. I hope you don't mind. I said it was for shopping purposes."

"Those are excellent purposes," I replied.

"Yes, well, it was a lie." Claudia smiled wide and ordered her iced tea, handing two dollars to the lunch lady. "I was really checking to see whether you'd given it to him yet."

When we got back to the slope of grass, I saw what Claudia meant about Wendy and the Lost Boys. It really was a *lot* of boys, all together like that. And left to their own devices, they'd started a heated and hugely embarrassing debate over the director who'd just been announced for the latest Marvel movie.

Claudia made a disgusted noise and unwound the scarf

from around her neck, spreading it out like a picnic blanket.

"Step into my tiny patch of civilization," she said with a sweep of her arm.

I bit into my bagel, and Claudia took out her phone, scrolling the hashtag for Paris Fashion Week and showing me her favorites. The way she chattered about all the designers and their collections reminded me of Mr. Ferrara in art history, unable to contain his enthusiasm for vases.

"Hi," Jamie interrupted, flopping down next to me on the grass.

I felt a little thrill run through me as he did that. And I realized just how intimate it was, sitting on the grass instead of at a lunch table.

"You must think I'm a terrible nerd," he said.

Actually, I thought he was terribly adorable, with his shoes off and his sunglasses on, and the way his smile sharpened the soft curve of his jaw.

"How do you say 'yes' in Elvish?" I asked, frowning.

Jamie opened his mouth to tell me, before getting the joke.

"Ugh," he complained. "No fair."

THAT AFTERNOON IN drama, I didn't even hesitate as I passed the empty seat next to Kate. She glanced up at me, her face a storm of resentment, and I had this sudden realization that she didn't like me. She'd only liked having me around so she got the occasional day off from Delia's wrath.

Delia had blocked me on all her social media that morning, and when I'd checked again during passing, so had Emmy. Kate had actually unfriended me, like she was secretly hoping I'd send her a request, and she could run and show Delia.

I wished I cared, but I really didn't. Sometimes you outgrow your friends, and sometimes you just outgrow the version of yourself that's willing to put up with them.

I took a seat next to Jamie, and this time Gardner knew exactly where to find me when he took attendance. He put on an old movie version of *Dracula*, and we sat there in the dark, a horror movie on the projector screen. On my right, I saw Darren reach for Max's hand during a particularly scary part, and I wished I could do that with Jamie. Except it seemed silly for a girl who saw ghosts to act scared of a movie vampire.

Instead, I watched Darren and Max, the way they swirled their fingers around each other's palms, and I imagined what it would feel like if a boy were doing it to me.

After the movie, Gardner passed out copies of the play, telling us to take them home and give them a read. I stashed my script in my backpack, but my friends all kept theirs out, scribbling notes on the backs as Gardner started walking us through the protocol for Friday's auditions.

"We should all read this tonight," Sam said as we were packing up. "That way we can strategize tomorrow."

"I'm calling Dracula right now, no apologies," Max said.

"Slow your roll," Claudia told him.

"Yeah dude, it isn't shotgun," Nima said, whacking at Max with his script.

In about two seconds, all the boys had rolled their scripts and were using them in a ridiculous swordfight.

Claudia sighed.

"You'd think Gardner could have chosen a play with more girls' roles, so we wouldn't have to deal with these idiots," she said. I must have looked blank, because she added, "You know, at rehearsal?"

"Oh, right," I said weakly, because that was when it hit me. I wasn't sitting in the back of the theater with Kate anymore. I was front and center with Sam's crowd, and now everyone assumed that I was auditioning for the play, too.

THE *DRACULA* AUDITIONS became the only thing my friends could talk about. And every time they came up, I felt my stomach twist at the prospect. I was afraid I'd be rejected while the rest of my friends were cast. And if I wasn't good enough for the play, I had no business sitting with everyone who starred in it.

It wasn't like the girls who'd been cut during cheer tryouts sat with the cheerleaders. Or the kids who'd lost the student government elections hung around the spirit wheel with the SGA.

"Picture this," Max said at lunch on Wednesday, leaning back with an evil grin. "Seth Bostwick as Dracula."

Everyone cracked up.

"He wouldn't make a bad Renfield," Sam said.

"Actually," Claudia said, glancing up from her bio homework, "he'd make the perfect Renfield. Now I hate to ask, but does anyone know anything about mast cells?"

"Jamie," Sam and Nima said in unison.

"When I said I'd donate my brain to science, this wasn't what I meant," Jamie announced, scooting across the grass to see what Claudia wanted.

I watched them for a while, dark heads bent together over the textbook, both of them lying on their stomachs. It was like they didn't even notice that we were sitting on a small grassy island in the middle of the school quad, surrounded by metal lunch tables. Like it never occurred to them that people were staring, or that they were worth staring at.

Suddenly, I couldn't help but imagine rolling around in the grass with Jamie, our mouths and bodies pressed together, my hands in his hair, his shirt riding up above his belt, my legs wrapped around his. I'd never had a thought like that before, and it shocked me. I felt my cheeks heat up, and I only belatedly realized someone was calling my name.

It was Sam.

"What part are you trying out for?" he asked.

"Um, I'm not sure yet," I said, which seemed safe. I'd never said I was auditioning, but everyone just seemed to assume. And I hadn't corrected them. And now the auditions were two days away. Which meant that every time someone said *"Dracula,"* I pretty much wanted to crawl into bed and hide.

"We could be Lucy and Mina!" Claudia said, glancing up from her homework. "It would be like a reunion from our days as pirates in *Peter Pan.*"

Sam snorted.

"By far your best role," he said, and Claudia stuck out her tongue.

"At least I wasn't *the crocodile*," she retorted.

"Hey! Max was Nana the dog!" Sam accused.

Max shrugged.

"I *worked* that dog costume," he said.

The bell rang then, and we all went to class, only to have Gardner turn us loose in the quad to "work on our auditions."

Claudia held up her script, her mouth in a fierce line.

"Mina and Lucy," she demanded, making me read through the scenes with her, even the ones that weren't part of the audition sides, in case Gardner surprised us with a cold reading.

I'd forgotten so much about how it had been with Claudia, when we were little. From afar, she seemed so intimidating that it was hard to think of her as the same girl who had fishtail-braided my hair and dared me to play Bloody Mary at sleepovers.

From afar, her life had looked so perfect, but from

up close, it was obvious how much she wished there was another girl around.

Until the end of freshman year, I'd seen her with Reyna Washington, who'd been dating Max when he came out. Reyna had started hanging around with the musical-theater crowd after that.

It had never occurred to me that, maybe, Claudia was lonely, too. That things really could go back to the way they used to between us, with carpools and board games and swapping clothes.

"You'd make the perfect Lucy," Claudia said as we put away our scripts.

"So would half the girls in our class," I pointed out.

Claudia shrugged, which meant that I was right.

"All you need's a little luck and a lot of red lipstick," she said. "Trust me."

I used to think the same thing—that if you wanted something badly enough, the universe would come through. And maybe it did, for Claudia. But I was intimately familiar with what it was like to have the things you love taken from you.

Still I couldn't help but wonder if maybe this time, things would be different. If I could borrow Jamie's questions trick and Claudia's lipstick and land a role.

I biked home that afternoon thinking I'd go for it after all. I didn't need to try out for a lead. There were a few small parts. I even let myself get excited about the idea of it.

Logan wasn't around, so I sprawled on the sofa, reading my *Dracula* script aloud and imagining myself being part of it all instead of hovering in the shadows watching.

LOGAN TURNED UP on Thursday night, while I was trying on outfits to wear to my audition. I hadn't seen him since Tuesday, and I wasn't expecting him to pop in while I was half-dressed.

"Agh!" I yelped, crossing my hands in front of my chest. "Eyes closed. Now."

"Rose?" my mom called from the other room. "Everything okay?"

"Yep. Just stubbed my toe," I called back, and then turned up my music to mask our conversation.

Logan flopped onto the bed, which was piled with rejected audition outfits. I zipped my dress and glared at him.

"Thanks for dropping in while Mom and Dad are home," I whispered.

"I came earlier," he snipped back. "But you weren't around."

A bunch of us had gone to Billz, where we'd reviewed our audition sides one last time together. I said as much, and Logan frowned.

"Sides for what?" he asked, and then he took in my outfit, a blue shift dress that Mom had bought me for a cousin's bar mitzvah.

"I'm trying out for the play," I said.

Logan looked thoughtful. I thought he wasn't going to say anything, until very softly he did.

"So this play must have a lot of after-school rehearsals." My stomach sank as I realized what he was implying.

"I hadn't thought of that," I said.

I mean, I *had*, but I hadn't put it together, realizing what it would mean for us. How little time I'd have to see Logan.

"You didn't even mention it," he said, his voice small. "You were just going to *do* it, weren't you?"

"Gardner won't even cast me," I said, trying to be reassuring. Except now I didn't know which was worse, if I got a role or if I didn't.

"Then why bother?" Logan asked.

I didn't say anything, but he seemed to guess.

"What about Jamie?" he demanded. "Is *he* trying out for the play, too?"

I nodded.

"Oh," Logan said, sounding strained. "I see."

"Logan," I pleaded.

"No! Go try out for the play with your cool theater friends," he shot back.

"You're the one who *said* I needed new friends," I pointed out.

"Yeah, to sit with at lunch. Not to hang out with every freaking afternoon!"

"That's what you *do* at sixteen!" I snapped, and then stopped myself, appalled.

"I wouldn't know," Logan said coolly. "Do whatever you want about the stupid play. I'll be here if you don't make it. Just like I always am."

"That's not fair," I said, but he disappeared before I could finish.

I stared at myself in the mirror, at the dress and the red lipstick, at my hair pinned back in a way that made me look shockingly grown-up. And then I glanced at the spot where Logan had been only moments earlier, realizing that I was going to have to choose.

14

I'D THOUGHT MY friends would bring their audition clothes to school with them, but instead they showed up wearing them. All the boys were in button-down shirts, except for Max, who was in head-to-toe black. Claudia had on a lace dress and character shoes, her hair smoothed back into an elegant twist.

They looked so different dressed up. Like they really were characters from a play. And I looked like a techie who'd accidentally wandered into their scene.

I'd left the dress at home. Instead, I'd worn my favorite leggings and a black oversized sweater. Clothes I couldn't audition in. Clothes that made me disappear.

I'd slept badly, and even after my alarm went off, the nightmares stuck around, half-remembered and strange. They thrummed together in the back of my head, all whispering the same thing: *Don't try out.*

So I'd left my dress on the back of my chair.

Logan would be thrilled. Whatever it was that had begun to strain between us would snap back into place. Instead of feeling the shame of being passed over for a role, I could sign up for costumes, just like I always did.

"Hey, Rose," Sam said when I joined them. "I'm having a kickback at my place tonight. Hot tub, pizza, maybe even both at the same time."

"Hot tub full of pizza," I said, trying to sound like it wasn't a big deal that he'd invited me. "Check."

I'd never been to a kickback before. I'd heard my classmates talk about them, and I'd seen Delia scrolling angrily through other people's photos, her lips thin with jealousy.

"Pick you up at eight?" Jamie asked.

I couldn't tell if he was joking.

"We could just meet there," I said, since Sam lived approximately nine doors down.

"We could," Jamie agreed. "But how will I ever find you in the crowd?"

I rolled my eyes over his terrible sense of humor.

"'Life finds a way,'" Max said, doing a surprisingly good Jeff Goldblum impression.

And then the boys devolved into a debate over the relative merits of the *Jurassic Park* movies.

"God," Claudia said, making a face. "If someone says *Steven Spielberg* loud enough, it could cause a riot."

"Is that a dare?" I asked.

"No!" Claudia giggled. And then she took in what I was

wearing. "Are you *really* auditioning in that?"

"Um," I said. And then I took a deep breath and admitted, "Actually, I'm not trying out."

"You have to!" Claudia insisted.

"My parents are really on me about my grades right now," I lied. "I have three APs and I just got a seventy-eight on my precalc test."

Claudia winced.

"So that's why your mom kept asking me about my math class," she mumbled.

Actually, my mom was just nosy. But I didn't say that.

And I certainly wasn't proud of my score on the precalc. But I knew what had happened. I'd studied the wrong things, assuming Mrs. Ortiz would test us on the homework sheets. But she'd pulled all of her questions from the textbook, screwing over everyone who hadn't read the chapter forwards.

"That sucks," Claudia said, and then she got a mischievous look on her face. "Although, I bet I can think of a math tutor. . . ."

I swatted at her.

"So you're really not trying out for the play?" she asked.

"I can't," I lied. "If I get another C, my mom said she'd make me drop out."

"Ugh, fine," Claudia moaned. "I get it. But that doesn't mean I can't be completely depressed over it."

"Over what?" Jamie asked, breaking away from the *Jurassic Park* discussion and joining us.

Claudia filled him in.

"You could have asked me about the precalc," he accused.

"I know," I muttered. "It's just—I'm going to do costumes again. It's less of a commitment."

"Costumes are boring," Sam interrupted.

"Shut up, or I'll make yours assless," I threatened.

Jamie made a strangled noise.

"All hail Rose, keeper of our nonboring and extremely tasteful costumes," Sam said, giving me a sweeping bow.

"Now that's more like it," I said.

I BIKED HOME right after Gardner's class, so I didn't have to watch everyone rush toward the theater, clutching their audition sides. I tried not to think about how crestfallen Claudia had seemed or the lines I'd memorized to try out.

But I still thought about them, because bike rides are traitorous things, where you assume you'll be distracted by the scenery, but really, you're left alone with your own thoughts. And my thoughts were kind of depressing.

You wouldn't have gotten a role anyway, I told myself. Not over Abby, or Christina, or Amanda. Not over Lauren Meyer, who'd been an extra on Disney Channel, or Reyna Washington, who'd starred in a Kohl's commercial.

I dropped my schoolbag on the bench with a sigh.

"There you are," Logan said, startling me. "How'd it go?"

"I decided not to try out," I told Logan.

"That's awesome," he said, beaming. "I knew you wouldn't bail on our tradition."

I squirmed, trying not to let on that I almost had.

"Besides," he went on. "We didn't even get halfway through our *Buffy* marathon."

He looked so pleased at the thought of more quiet afternoons on the sofa that I forced myself to smile back.

Maybe a mindless rewatch was what I needed, I told myself. So I settled onto the sofa, taking in the bad nineties fashion and terrible special effects and listening to Logan yell at the screen every time Buffy did something dumb.

After the episode ended, I went into the kitchen, claiming I wanted a snack. But really, I needed a break. Hanging out with Logan wasn't having the effect I'd hoped. If anything, backing out of the audition had made me feel even more stuck in the same place.

I'd thrown away my shot, and now, I was starting to realize what that really meant. My friends were going to spend all their time together, at rehearsal, while I was left behind to watch TV with Logan, just like I'd been doing for the past four years.

15

I'D ALMOST FORGOTTEN about Sam's party, but Jamie texted me a bunch of swimsuit emojis and a car, and with a start, I remembered that he was picking me up at eight. It was already six thirty, and my mom was in the kitchen, stirring a pot of pasta while she hummed along to Joni Mitchell.

"Dinner's in fifteen," she said. "Want to set the table?"

I opened the cabinet and got down a stack of plates.

"So a bunch of us are going swimming tonight," I said, trying to make it sound like no big deal.

I was hoping she'd be sufficiently distracted by the pasta that she wouldn't ask me a million questions. Except of course that didn't happen.

"Swimming? Where?"

"At Sam's," I said innocently. "He's lifeguard certified and everything."

Actually, I had no idea if he was, but it seemed like the

thing to say. And it seemed to reassure my mom, whose frown softened a bit.

"Does this have something to do with a certain boy who was supposed to ask you to the movies?" she asked.

I'd been hoping she wouldn't make the connection. But that's the worst part about being an only child—your parents never miss a thing. Unless that thing is the presence of your brother's ghost, in which case mine were blissfully oblivious.

"If it does, can I go?" I asked hopefully.

Mom laughed and took the pasta over to the sink. I watched the steam billow around her as she drained it, and when she looked up, her bangs had frizzed.

"Will Claudia be there?" Mom asked.

"Obviously," I said.

"Okay, I'll allow it," she said. "I like that girl much more than Delia."

"Thank you!" I said.

"Not so fast." Mom gave the pepper grinder a savage twist. "I want texts every hour. And you need to be home by eleven."

I was hoping for twelve, but I knew better than to argue. If I tried it now, she'd just ask what we were doing that I needed to stay out so late. Which she practically asked anyway, since I spent the entirety of dinner answering a million questions about Sam's crowd, and what they were all up to, until I was ready to scream.

When I went upstairs to get changed, Logan was in my room.

"Hey," he said. "What was for dinner?"

"The Spanish Inquisition," I muttered.

"'No one expects the Spanish Inquisition!'" Logan said, quoting Monty Python.

I couldn't help it. I laughed.

Logan went on, encouraged, doing bits of the sketch as I dug out my collection of bathing suits.

I tossed them onto my bed, trying not to despair. They were all terrible. Every single bathing suit looked cheap and generic, like I'd pulled them from the sale rack at Target. Which I had, but still.

"Why do you need a bathing suit?" Logan asked.

"Because Sam's having a party."

"Ooh, can I come?"

"No way."

"Pleaseeee," Logan begged. "I want to see Claudia in a bikini!"

"First of all, ewww, you perv. And second of all, too bad, because you're not coming. End of discussion."

I grabbed the least offensive bikini—black-and-white gingham with bows on the sides—and went into the bathroom to change.

"Did you forget that I can see through walls?" Logan called.

◄◄◄-►►

I WAS STILL fussing with my waterproof mascara when the doorbell rang.

"Jamie!" my mom said, using her terrifyingly upbeat telephone voice. "It's been forever! Come in, have a seat in the living room. Rose is still getting ready. How's your dad?"

Oh no, my mom.

I pulled on a tank top, jammed on a pair of flip-flops, and grabbed a towel.

"Okay, hi, I'm here," I said, racing down the stairs. "All ready to go."

Jamie and my mom were sitting awkwardly in the living room. He was wearing swim trunks and a T-shirt, and there was a hideous striped towel around his neck. He grinned when he saw me, as though he found my mom amusing.

I remembered what I'd thought when I first saw Jamie, how he probably made all the girls in his English class swoon. *Add mothers to that list,* I told myself. And fathers, since even my dad was hovering in the doorway, holding a mug of tea and his iPad, shamelessly spying.

"Hi, Mr. Asher," Jamie said, calling him out.

My dad shuffled into the living room.

"Oh, hello," he said, pretending to be surprised. "Didn't realize we were having company."

It took another five minutes to get my parents to tone it down and let us out the front door. When we were finally at the sidewalk, I let out a sigh of relief.

And then the door opened again.

"Text every hour!" Mom shouted after me. "Emojis don't count!"

"Oh my god," I muttered.

Jamie's shoulders shook with laughter.

"Don't worry," he said. "My mom and stepdad are the same."

Which of course made me worry even more, because I couldn't tell whether he meant in general or whenever he went on a date. Not that we were on a date. We were just walking over to Sam's place together, because Jamie had to park somewhere, and in front of my house was as good as in front of the Donovans'.

All of a sudden, I was hyperaware of the fact that we were alone. Together. On a Friday night. And then I was hyperaware of the fact that my bathing suit bottoms had gone so far up my butt crack that they were practically flossing my teeth. I tried to pull at them discretely under my shorts, but it was no use; they'd taken root.

"How was the audition?" I asked.

Jamie shrugged.

"Okay, I think. I'll know for sure on Monday." He glanced over at me. "We missed you."

He paused a moment, as though debating asking me something.

"You're so obvious when you do that," I pointed out, and he laughed.

"Okay, Sherlock," he said. "Why did you *really* bail on the play? Because I don't buy that precalc excuse you gave Claudia."

I shot him a look, hating that he'd guessed.

"Logan," I said. "I can't— I mean, it's impossible when my parents are home, so the only time we have together is in the afternoons, which is—"

"—the same time as rehearsal," Jamie finished.

"Well aren't you just a clever little cleverness," I told him.

"Thank you, I am," he said. But then he went suddenly serious.

"Rose?" he asked.

"Yeah?"

"You know that it doesn't matter whether you try out for the play, or sign up to be an usher, or say screw it and go out for the Debate Team. We're all friends no matter what."

I didn't realize that was exactly what I needed to hear until Jamie said it.

"Thank you," I said softly.

"But please don't join the Debate Team," he said, making a face. "They're so pretentious."

"Ugh, says the boy who wears loafers without socks," I teased.

Jamie lifted an eyebrow.

"Take that back," he insisted. "Or I'll toss you in the pool."

"Don't you dare," I warned.

Jamie menaced toward me, and I twisted away, laughing.

His brown eyes were endless pools in the lamplight, and I felt a flutter of expectation, because somehow we'd sky-rocketed miles closer to a kiss in just a few seconds.

Even though Sam was only having a kickback, I still expected to see a crush of cars and plastic cups outside the Donovans' place. For there to be some evidence of the clichéd high school parties Logan had rolled his eyes over while sorting his Magic deck.

But everything looked neat and orderly. I could hear music coming from the backyard, though, and splashes from the pool.

"Thanks for coming with," Jamie said. "I hate showing up at parties alone."

I gave him a weak grin, wondering what he'd meant by that. If it was his way of letting me know we weren't on a date or his way of asking if we were.

Jamie pushed open the gate, and I felt this thrill go through me. I was at my first real party. And I was here with Jamie Aldridge. If you'd told me on the first day of school that I'd show up at Sam's pool party with a boy, I would have laughed in disbelief. But now, it seemed just as impossible that I'd ever gone over to Delia's house for manicure night.

Sam's backyard was strung with twinkle lights, which cast a warm glow over everything. An old Kendrick Lamar song was playing, and at least a dozen flip-flops were dis-carded throughout the yard, turning the patio into an obstacle course.

Reyna and her musical-theater friends were crowded around the fire pit, toasting marshmallows and recording it with their phones. Some theater seniors had a game of flip cup going on the patio furniture. Lara and a few other techies were sitting along the edge of the pool, dipping their feet into the deep end. Over in the shallows, Sam and Nima were aggressively tossing a foam football. And Claudia was in the hot tub with Abby Shah, whose enormous boobs were on full display in the world's tiniest gold bikini.

"Yo!" Sam called, waving. "Perfect timing."

He hoisted himself out of the pool, dripping wet. I glanced away, embarrassed, since his swim trunks were clinging. Sam didn't even notice. He just dug through a cooler, opened two beers, and passed them over.

"Thanks," I said, trying to look nonchalant.

"How'd you swing these?" Jamie asked, examining the label. He sounded like he was used to this kind of thing—to parties, beer—or maybe he was just better than me at pretending.

"Used my brother's old ID," Sam said. "Pizza's on its way. Claudia insisted on Hawaiian, but I got a couple of supremes."

"I like Hawaiian," I said, and Jamie gave me a disgusted look.

"Fruit," he informed me, "does not belong on a pizza."

"Google 'is a tomato a fruit' and then talk to me again when you're ready to apologize," I told him.

Sam cracked up.

"Aww, you two," he said, pinching Jamie's cheek. And then he cannonballed back into the pool.

The water splashed everywhere, and Abby shrieked, shielding her hair with her hands. But Claudia just laughed. She looked flawless as always, in a crochet bikini. Her hair was knotted into a perfect version of the loopy bun I'd been aiming for, and she wasn't even sweating from the steam.

"Hey," she called, waving.

"Guess we should go in," Jamie said, pulling his shirt off like it was nothing. He kicked off his flip-flops and stood there, wearing just his swim trunks.

I glanced away, embarrassed at the sight of his nipples, his belly button, his hip bones.

It had never before occurred to me how much bathing suits were like underwear. But it certainly occurred to me then. I swallowed nervously, looking down at my own tank top and shorts. Oh my god. I was actually going to have to unbutton my shorts in front of him. To take off my top.

I decided the best strategy was Operation Band-Aid. I ripped my shorts off as fast as possible, practically tripping over them. And then I was down to my bathing suit, which was actually smaller than my underwear. And strapless.

"Oww-woww! Rose!" Claudia cheered, like I'd done a seductive striptease instead of an embarrassed locker-room strip.

"Shut up," I grumbled, making a beeline for the hot tub.

Max and Darren arrived just after us. And suddenly, everyone was talking about the auditions. Apparently a ton of freshman had shown up, which made it drag on forever.

"Thankfully a bunch of people from our class didn't try out," Darren said. "Medieval Times is hiring, so the Ren Faire crowd is doing that."

Max snorted.

"And Rose is doing costumes," Claudia pointed out.

"Actually, that was a lie so I could work at Medieval Times," I deadpanned.

"Wait, really?" Abby asked, as everyone else died laughing.

The pizza showed up a few minutes later. Sam lined the boxes up along the edges of the pool like sandbags, and even dragged the cooler over.

"So no one has to get out and freeze," he said, shivering as he joined us in the hot tub.

Then Nima started complaining about being left out, and somehow he wound up on Abby's lap, with his head against her chest and his feet sticking up in the air.

"Can I join?" Seth asked, padding over from the flip cup game.

"No!" everyone shouted.

There really wasn't room. Already, with eight of us, the hot tub was so crowded that water had started spilling over the sides, soaking through the empty pizza boxes.

Over by the folding table, there was a loud cheer as

someone flipped their Solo cup in one try. Suddenly, it seemed hilarious how cramped we all were, or maybe that was just my second beer. All I knew was, the lights strung in the trees had gone soft around the edges, and the music was good, and I could feel Jamie's leg against mine, warm and smooth from the chlorine.

I leaned back, watching the heat from the hot tub drift toward the stars. I didn't care anymore that my butt looked massive in my bikini bottoms or that the hot tub was making my hair frizz.

Suddenly, I felt Jamie's hand on my thigh. I stiffened, unsure what he was doing. Then he nudged me, very gently, in the side. And I realized he was trying to get my attention without anyone else realizing.

Logan had shown up at the party. He hovered by the beer cooler, looking unsure.

When he saw that we'd noticed him, he waved.

"Hey," he called. "I thought this was a house party. Where *is* everyone?"

I shook my head, hoping he'd get the message.

He didn't.

Go away! I mouthed, making a shooing motion with my hands.

"You okay, Rose?" Claudia asked, frowning.

"Yeah," I said. "It's just, someone has a very familiar foot."

"Oh my god, are those s'mores?" Logan moaned. He

drifted toward the fire pit, fascinated, as Reyna and her friends took marshmallow-toasting selfies. Suddenly, the flames shot upward with a dangerous crackle, nearly tripling in height.

The girls shrieked, knocking over their chairs as they backed away.

"Oops," Logan said, backing up guiltily. He drifted over to the hot tub. "Wait, you guys have pizza? And is that beer? Rose, are you *drinking beer*?"

The jacuzzi jets let out a tremendous blast, then turned off entirely.

Everyone groaned.

"What the hell?" Sam muttered, hoisting himself out of the water to take a look at the timer. "Must be some kind of power surge."

"Yeah, supernatural powers," Logan said, looking smug. He took over Sam's spot, dangling his gross, sock-covered feet into the hot tub. He looked pleased with himself, as though he'd found something he could participate in.

"It's kind of crowded here, isn't it?" Jamie said meaningfully.

"A little bit," I agreed.

"Okay, whoever is doing the foot thing, stop," Claudia insisted.

"It's not me!" Sam called, fiddling with the control panel.

"WE KNOW!" everyone yelled back.

I glanced over at Jamie again. He didn't look so great. There was sweat on his brow, and his breathing was labored. If I didn't know better, I'd say he was having some kind of allergic reaction.

"I'll be right back," Jamie said, hoisting himself out of the hot tub like it was an ordeal.

"Me too," I said, following.

We padded into the kitchen, shivering, even wrapped in our towels. Except I didn't think Jamie's shivering was from the cold.

"Are you okay?" I whispered.

Jamie was leaning against the counter like he needed it to stand.

"I just need a minute," he gasped. "It must have been the water."

"No one's allergic to water," I accused. And then I realized what had been in the water. Not what. Who.

"Jamie," I said, my voice low. "Are you, by any chance, allergic to ghosts?"

"I was going to tell you," he mumbled. And then his knees buckled.

"You should sit down," I said, grabbing his arm.

"I'm fine," he insisted, twisting away. "I just need an aspirin."

He staggered toward the bathroom, and as I watched him go, my concern gave way to anger.

It was so obvious now that he'd been hiding something.

The way he always got headaches when Logan was around. Why he'd asked how often Logan showed up and how long he stayed. How he kept escaping to the kitchen when we'd been watching TV.

I'd thought it was just a spurious correlation, but it wasn't. Being around ghosts made Jamie sick. And Logan showing up at this party was entirely my fault.

"Rose?"

I turned around, expecting it to be Jamie.

"There you are," Logan said, looking pleased. "Sam got the hot tub working again."

"What are you even doing at this party?" I demanded, trying to sound stern. "I told you not to come."

"Well I got bored, sitting at home," he said. "Mom and Dad are watching Anthony Bourdain."

But that wasn't an excuse. I'd told him not to come, and he hadn't listened. He couldn't just trail me everywhere. Especially now that I knew what was going on with Jamie.

Oh my god, Jamie. He still hadn't come back from the bathroom.

"Logan," I said. *"Go home. Now."*

"Fine," Logan retorted. "Kick me out of this stupid party. I don't care. I've been to better ones."

Except he hadn't. This was his first, I realized. But it was also mine. My first high school party. My first maybe-date with a boy. And Logan had turned it into a disaster.

After Logan disappeared, I let out a sigh of frustration,

and then I went to check on Jamie.

"Hi," I said, knocking softly on the door to the bathroom.

There wasn't an answer.

I tried the handle, but it was locked.

"Jamie?" I called, trying not to panic.

There was a long pause, when I thought no one would answer. Finally, the door opened.

Jamie looked like he had the flu. He couldn't stop shivering, and there were dark circles under his eyes.

"I told you, Cleo," he said, attempting a grin. "Nothing to worry about. I'm better already."

His knees buckled, and I grabbed his arm, catching him. His skin was hot to the touch, like he was running a fever.

"No, you're not," I said sternly. "Sit down."

Jamie did, easing himself onto the floor. His shivering had gotten worse. I pulled some towels off the rack and draped them around his shoulders.

"Thanks," he mumbled. "God, this is so embarrassing."

"You need to see a doctor," I said, sitting down next to him.

"And say what? Hey, doc, I think I've got ghost flu?"

"Okay, maybe not," I conceded. "But you should have told me."

"Yeah, I know," he said. "Sorry."

"It's fine," I muttered, since he didn't owe me an explanation. It wasn't as though I was his girlfriend.

"I was going to tell you," Jamie promised. "It just seemed

so stupid to bring up. 'Oh, by the way, I kind of get migraines if I'm around ghosts for too long.'"

When he put it like that, it did sound like I was making a big deal out of nothing. Except this wasn't nothing.

"This isn't a migraine," I pointed out.

"Nope." Jamie pulled a towel tighter around his shoulders.

"So what was different this time?" I asked.

"The hot tub must have amplified it," Jamie said. "Water's a conductor, you know?"

I winced. I hadn't realized.

"Either that, or I'm allergic to pineapple pizza," he teased.

"Don't even joke," I warned.

"Hey, *lots* of people are allergic to pizza," Jamie pointed out. "All that dairy and gluten. Watch out!"

"So I guess it's a good thing it's just ghosts," I said.

"Well, ghosts and penicillin." Jamie closed his eyes, and I realized he was exhausted. "Let's stay here another minute, okay?"

I leaned my head against Jamie's shoulder. Somehow, I fit perfectly there.

We stayed like that for a while, just sitting silently on the floor of Sam's bathroom in our wet bathing suits. And I realized I wasn't mad anymore. Not at Jamie. Mostly, I was angry that Logan had ruined everything. He'd never gotten in the way before. But then, there'd never been anything for him to get in the way of.

"Okay," Jamie said, struggling to his feet. "I think I'm

good to go back out there."

"You're kidding, right?" I asked.

"I don't want anyone to think there's something wrong with me."

He bent over the sink, splashing some water on his face and finger-combing it through his hair.

"You're not seriously going—" I began.

"Yes, I am," Jamie insisted, daring me to argue.

I stood there in disbelief for a moment, wondering why he was so determined to prove that he was fine, and then I followed after him.

Everyone was in the living room, trying to choose a movie.

"*Rocky Horror!*" Max shouted, and Sam gave him a withering look.

"Must we parody ourselves?" he asked gravely.

"In this case, yes," Max insisted. "I demand the Time Warp, and I demand it now."

We went with *The Princess Bride*. Except I had to leave halfway through to be home before eleven, and no amount of texting photos of us watching a PG movie would change that.

"I'll walk you," Jamie said, putting on his flip-flops.

He was still a little unsteady, but he was doing a good job of hiding it.

It was surprisingly warm out, and strangely still. A Santa Ana wind was coming, and I wondered if Jamie felt it, too.

The Santa Anas were eerie; they made the ocean lie flat

as they howled through our canyon. There were superstitions about this type of wind. They inspired chaos, everyone said. Drove people to commit crimes and start fights. I glanced at Jamie, who was scrubbing a hand through his hair, mussing it. He didn't look like he wanted to start a fight. He looked like he'd lost one. Badly.

"I can't believe you went back out to the party," I said.

"What was I supposed to do?" Jamie demanded. "Go home sick?"

"Yes," I said.

Jamie shook his head.

"It's funny," he went on. "Tiny, quiet Laguna Canyon. I assumed I'd have a shot at being normal here."

Jamie sighed and stared up at the sky. It was orange where it met the walls of the canyon, another sign of the incoming wind.

"And then I messed it up," I said, feeling terrible.

I'd never considered the possibility that Jamie didn't want to deal with any of this. That just because he saw ghosts didn't mean he wanted to hang around with one.

"How could you mess it up?" Jamie asked. "You're the first person I've been able to talk to about this stuff."

"Same," I said softly.

"So I guess it's lucky I didn't move to Shanghai," Jamie said, half to himself. "For a lot of reasons."

We were outside my house. My parents had turned off the porch light, and standing there, staring at Jamie in the dark, I could hear the distant rumble of cars down on the parkway.

"Hey, Cleo? I had a good time tonight."

"No, you didn't," I said.

"Okay, fine, tonight kind of sucked," he amended. "Plus now Sam's convinced we hooked up in his bathroom."

"Crap," I moaned. "I'd forgotten about that."

"Well, maybe that's what happened in a different timeline," Jamie suggested, going quiet, as though he was imagining it.

I tried to picture it, too. My first real party, where Jamie and I had eaten pizza in the hot tub, and kissed passionately in Sam's downstairs bathroom, and everything had been perfect and normal. I imagined myself floating home with swollen lips and agonizing what to text as I scrolled through his Instagram.

"I like that timeline," I said.

"So do I." Jamie grinned. "A lot."

"It's not too late," I said, shocking myself.

"Actually, it is," Jamie said. There was this awful moment where I thought he was going to say he could never like me in that way. And then he whispered, "Your parents are spying on us from the upstairs window."

16

Dracula Cast List

MINA: Claudia Flores

LUCY: Abby Shah

DRACULA: Max Coleman

HARKER: Sam Donovan

VAN HELSING: Jamie Aldridge

DR. SEWARD: Nima Shirazi

RENFIELD: Leo Swanson

ATTENDANTS: Darren Choi, Seth Bostwick

VIXENS: Reyna Washington, Lauren Meyer

Gardner posted the cast list after school on Monday. My friends gleefully congratulated each other, and Max passed Sam a five-dollar bill without comment, having lost a bet over whether or not our teacher would cast Seth.

I quietly wrote my name on the sign-up sheet for crew, under costumes assistant. A couple of my classmates had already put their names forward as dressers or stagehands, after finding out they hadn't made it into the play. Crew was a consolation prize for them, a second choice. If they'd really wanted to work behind the scenes, they would have taken theater tech. But then, if I'd really wanted to work behind the scenes, I would have, too.

"I can't believe it," Claudia kept saying, over all of them being cast, and then throwing sympathetic glances in my direction.

I'm fine, I kept trying to tell her with my face, but I had a suspicion she didn't speak eyebrow.

"We *have* to go to Duke's," Sam proclaimed. "To celebrate."

So we all walked toward the parking lot, squeezing into Sam's Suburban. He rolled the windows down, cranked the stereo, and executed the most terrifying left turn in the history of our student lot.

Duke's was on the pier, in the ritzier part of Laguna, the one they always show on TV. As Sam maneuvered the Suburban down Ocean, the air turned sharp, with a salt tang, and the street names changed to numbers. I watched as they counted down, marking the blocks left until there was nothing but the water.

Up in the canyon, where we lived, the homes were bright and Spanish-style, but down here, everything was modern and glass. Even the boats bobbing in the marina felt like they belonged to a different world, one where people golfed on the weekends at their fancy country clubs.

Being in this part of town brought back so many memories: Duke's used to be the venue of choice for birthday parties back when we were kids. They had an old-school arcade with Skee-Ball and Dance Dance Revolution, and a counter where you could trade in your tickets for cheap plastic prizes.

"Wow," Jamie said as we climbed out of Sam's car. "What happened?"

When we were kids, the boardwalk had been an endless stretch of seafood shacks and souvenir shops. Now it was a parade of designer boutiques and artisanal gelato bars.

"Gentrification," Claudia said, twisting her hair into a bun. "Isn't it vile?"

We passed a salon that advertised a fifty-dollar blowout special and a pilates studio that also served pressed juice.

Darren made a face.

"Who would pay ten bucks for a green juice?" he wondered aloud.

"Abby Shah," Max supplied, trying not to laugh.

"Duke's never changes," Sam promised.

And he was right. Even better, Duke's was practically empty when we got there. It turned out Nima knew the guy working behind the counter, so he went up to chat. And when he came back, he was carrying an enormous drink cup full of free game tokens, which he upended on the table.

"Boom!" Nima said. "You're welcome."

"No, *you're* welcome for all of those times we just *had* to go spin that spirit wheel," Max said, raking up a pile of tokens.

By the time the burgers arrived, we were all starving. Jamie and I were splitting fries, and I thought he'd dump them out onto the tray and divide them in half, but he just left them in the carton. We kept reaching in at the same time, and finally I gave him a look.

"You're doing that on purpose," I accused.

"Doing what?" he asked innocently. "Eating?"

I made a disgusted noise and dragged my fry through our puddle of ketchup. But I was secretly smiling.

After we ate, we all took handfuls of tokens and hit the arcade. Nima and Max quickly got into a Skee-Ball battle, while Claudia and Darren faced off at Dance Dance Revolution. Sam was over at the pinball machines, swearing he'd finally land himself on the high-score board.

"This is so fourth grade," I said, smiling.

Jamie and I were watching the DDR battle.

"You're going down!" Darren kept insisting, and Claudia would just laugh, her hair swinging. They looked ridiculous stomping on those light-up arrows, arms hanging. Except neither of them was missing a beat.

"Remember when I had my ninth birthday here?" Jamie asked.

"Barely," I said, since everyone had had their birthdays at Duke's that year.

He shook his head, a muscle feathering in his jaw.

"What?" I asked.

"Nothing," he said. "Bad memory. My parents fought that whole day."

"Then we'll have to make a good memory here to replace it," I said.

Jamie grinned.

"It's a deal," he said. "Air hockey?"

"Always."

We played until our fingers were battered from the plastic puck and we couldn't stop laughing. Afterward, Jamie got us some ice from the soda fountain and wrapped it in napkins, and we took it onto the patio to soothe our hands.

The sun was still high overhead, but the day had turned cool, finally giving way to fall. The air was chilly, with a salt tang, and out on the horizon, a line of sailboats bobbed, seeming to shimmer.

Seagulls pecked at our feet, nibbling on stray French fries that someone had left before us. Jamie and I sat on a bench, our legs touching, but neither of us wanting to be the first to pull away.

"Do you ever think about how if you were to draw a map of America, we'd be outside of it?" I asked. "Right now, we're an outlying plot point, hanging off the side of the continent."

"You're so weird," Jamie teased.

"You're just figuring that out now?" I raised an eyebrow.

Jamie laughed. He had a nice laugh, a deep rumble, like a science-fair volcano. And his eyelashes looked so long, catching the fading sunlight, that I couldn't help but stare.

He was the kind of beautiful that made me wonder how everyone else stood it, how they talked to him on the street or sat next to him in class without wanting to reach out and trace their fingers against the sharp lines of his jaw, just to make sure he was real.

"I think I know what I want to spend my last tokens on," Jamie said.

"What?" I asked.

"You'll see."

Jamie reached for my hand and led me back into the arcade. He twisted around, smiling at me, like it was going to be the greatest surprise ever which game he chose, and I almost believed it. Because his eyes were shining and his hand was warm, and he was a boy who could see things that were invisible to everyone else, the only living person in the world who knew my secrets.

The electricity was back between us, crackling more than ever, and I knew he sensed it too.

He led me to a funny old photo booth in the back of the arcade, the kind with a little curtain strung across the entrance and lights on top. Jamie slotted his last few coins into the booth and then pulled aside the curtain.

"Step into my office," he instructed with a flourish.

It was cramped inside the booth, with just a little bench

in the back, and the dark, expectant camera lens pointing at us. We were squeezed closer together than we'd ever been before, even in the hot tub, or maybe the aloneness was what made it feel that way.

"Ready?" he asked, leaning forward to push the button that would start the countdown for our photo strip.

I nodded, and the booth came to life with a rattle, the flashbulb pulsing as it counted down the timer.

"What are we doing in the photo?" I asked, realizing we hadn't planned anything.

"This," Jamie said.

And then he kissed me. It was sweet and warm and caught me completely off guard, because it turned out he had planned something for the photo after all.

The kiss was over in an instant, and when he pulled away, I couldn't tell if I was dazed from the flashbulbs or his lips.

"Aren't you supposed to kiss on the last one?" I asked, breathless.

"Whoops," Jamie said. "Guess we'll have to do it again."

This time, when he kissed me, I was ready to kiss him back. And it was a different kind of kiss, long and deep and full of verses. It was a ballad poem of a kiss, the kind where your tongue goes off on great adventures and returns home different than before.

We didn't stop kissing until all the flashbulbs were spent, all the photos were taken, and the booth had gone dark. When we pulled apart, I could hear the gears whirling inside the wall, preparing our pictures.

Claudia was waiting for us when we stepped out of the booth. She was holding our picture strips, and she looked very smug.

"You *do* know this is a photo booth, not a kissing booth, right?" she teased, grinning.

"Give me those," I said, grabbing for them.

I was expecting a disaster, because I never photographed well. But our pictures were perfect. They were black-and-white, like an image of something that had happened a long time ago. Like the kind of photos you find at a flea market or see printed in an old book.

I looked so surprised in the first frame that I had to laugh. But the next three were so intimate that I hardly recognized myself. Was that girl really me, that black-and-white girl in the photo booth, kissing that beautiful boy, with her hand cupped around his face and her hair trailing in loose waves?

Hair. Oh my god.

"I'll be right back," I said, dashing to the bathroom.

The salt air on the boardwalk had done something to my hair. My cheeks were flushed, and my lips were swollen, and my hair was a perfect cascade of soft brown waves.

It's just a spurious correlation, I told myself, taking a couple of deep, steadying breaths. *It isn't real.* But part of me worried that it wasn't nonsense. That it was only a matter of time before my personal superstition would prove itself true.

WHEN SAM DROPPED me off at home, Jamie's kiss already felt like something I'd imagined. I kept touching the photo strip in my pocket, reassuring myself that it was real.

I went upstairs, humming one of the songs that had been playing on Sam's stereo, this upbeat hipster thing. I put the song on my iPad and then flopped onto my bed, staring at the photos of Jamie and me.

"Hellooooo," Logan called. "You can stop ignoring me now."

"I'm not ignoring you," I snapped. "I'm busy."

I twisted around.

But I didn't see him.

"Where are you?" I asked, frowning.

"Right here," Logan said. "Why?"

"Right where?" I asked, trying not to panic.

"I'm literally right in front of you," Logan said.

I couldn't see my brother.

Oh god.

I felt my heart speed up, because I didn't know what to do.

"Um, right," I lied. "Of course."

Logan had gone almost totally transparent before, but it was never like this. There was always an outline. But this time, he just . . . wasn't there.

What if he was never there again?

"You're lying!" Logan accused, frantic. "What's wrong? Why can't you see me?"

"I don't know!"

"Well, do something!" Logan insisted.

"Like what?" I asked.

"I DON'T KNOW! SOMETHING!"

The lamp on my bedside table flickered ominously.

"Logan!" I scolded. "Calm down!"

Except I wasn't exactly calm myself.

"We'll figure this out!" I promised.

"How?!" Logan shouted.

"I'm calling Jamie," I said, searching for my phone. It was the only thing I could think to do.

"We don't need him!" Logan insisted.

"Yes, we do!" I said.

My phone was at the bottom of my bag, and I dug it out, dialing Jamie. But the call went instantly to voice mail. I hung up before leaving one.

"Logan?" I tried.

But he didn't answer.

"Are you still here?" I asked.

Nothing.

"I'm sorry. Logan, please," I begged. "Move something. Go through the pipes. Do anything."

I waited, but the lights stayed on, and the papers on my desk stayed still, and the plumbing didn't so much as rattle.

I didn't know if he'd come back in an hour, or tomorrow,

or never again. And the not knowing terrified me. He'd shown up irregularly before, but never like this. Something was wrong, and I was terrified we wouldn't be able to fix it. Terrified that he'd disappear on me again, forever, before I was ready. Before I had a chance to say good-bye.

I curled into a ball, clutching a pillow to my chest. My eyes burned with tears, and I could feel eyeliner sliding down my face, but I didn't care.

"Please come back," I whispered. "Logan, please."

17

I WAS A wreck the next day, and Jamie could tell something was wrong. At lunch, he kept shooting me worried glances and nodding toward the quad like he'd follow if I made an excuse to leave.

So I said I was going to study precalc in the library.

"Want some help?" Jamie asked, the picture of innocence.

"Sure," I said. "Thanks."

Claudia winked at us when we left, like she thought we were sneaking off somewhere to cuddle.

"What's wrong?" Jamie asked. "You didn't reply to any of my texts last night."

I glanced at him guiltily. My phone was . . . somewhere. Still on my desk, probably. I hadn't even checked it.

"Sorry," I mumbled.

"Is it me?" he asked quietly. He looked so nervous, and so prepared for the answer to be yes.

179

"No," I said. "It's Logan."

Jamie seemed to sag with relief. But then he saw the look on my face.

"What's going on?" he asked.

"Is there somewhere private we can talk?"

"My car?" Jamie suggested.

We hung a left toward the parking lot and climbed into his Prius. There was a stack of library books on the seat, which would have charmed me any other day, but I chucked them into the back without comment. Jamie turned the radio on low, which helped dilute the silence.

"When I came home from the pier last night, I couldn't see Logan," I said. "He told me to stop ignoring him, but I hadn't even realized he was there."

Jamie frowned.

"You couldn't see him at all?"

I shook my head.

"But I heard him just fine," I said. "It's never happened before. He's always been there. Never half there."

"I'm no ghost expert, but do you want me to come over after school and check on him?"

"Are you sure?" I asked. "Because last time, at Sam's—"

"I'll be fine," Jamie said firmly.

He flashed me a reassuring smile, but then something awful occurred to me.

"What if Logan isn't the problem?" I asked. "What if it's me?"

I could barely bring myself to think it. To imagine what it would be like if Logan was still there but I couldn't see him.

"Then we'll figure it out, okay?" Jamie promised.

"Okay," I agreed.

"I have the world's worst timing, don't I?" Jamie asked.

He was talking about the kiss. His hand was still on top of mine. It was such a small thing, but for some reason, having that physical connection between us was strangely comforting. I remembered that first day in art history class when Jamie had scooted his desk over until it was touching mine, and how invasive that had felt. Funny how much could change in a few short weeks. How much I had changed.

"It could have been worse," I said. "You could have tried to kiss me *right now*."

"That would have been terrible," Jamie said seriously.

"Catastrophic," I said.

His fingers were tracing designs on my palm now, and it was making me shiver.

"Good thing I didn't," Jamie said. "Kiss you right now, in this car, I mean."

He leaned toward me, a mischievous smile on his lips, and before I knew it, we were kissing over the cup holder. The seat-belt clasp was digging into my side, and it felt totally inappropriate, but neither of us pulled away. If anything, we leaned even closer, like the answers were waiting at the bottom of our kiss, and if we only kissed deeply enough, we'd find them.

"HELLO?" I CALLED, pushing open the front door. "Logan?"

I put my bag down on the bench. Next to me, Jamie started taking off his shoes and then grinned.

"Just kidding," he promised. "Logan, bud. You here?"

But there was no response.

My stomach clenched.

Please, I thought. *Please please please please pl—*

"Maybe." Logan drifted into the room, pouting. "How many fingers am I holding up?"

I let out a breath.

"Oh, thank god," I said, and then I turned to Jamie. "You can see him too, right?"

Jamie nodded.

"Logan, don't you ever disappear on me again," I scolded.

"Jeez, *fine*," Logan said. "I'll hang around all the time. I'll even watch you sleep."

I shot him a look.

"Joking," he promised.

Jamie laughed.

"Jamie! What's your favorite *Star Trek*?" Logan asked, drifting toward the living room.

"Jamie can't stay, he just stopped by—" I began.

"I can stay a little while," Jamie insisted, his chin jutting stubbornly.

So we spent the next hour parked in front of the television, watching the *Enterprise* get overrun by tribbles. Logan and I sat on the couch, and Jamie took my dad's favorite armchair.

I knew he was doing it to put some distance between himself and Logan, but I was still disappointed. Not that we were going to snuggle on the sofa in front of my brother's ghost, but still.

Logan was riveted to the TV, and I kept glancing at him and smiling. He looked reasonably solid, too. Whatever had happened last night was probably nothing to worry about. Maybe it was like a dropped connection, like when you're driving through this one part of the canyon and the GPS on your phone stops working.

Logan started to fade partway through the second episode. "Noooo," he moaned.

The overhead light flickered, and then he was gone.

Jamie frowned, staring at the light.

"Weird," he said, shaking his head. "I don't think Logan should be able to do that."

And then he winced and massaged his temple.

"Aspirin?" I asked.

"Got it covered," Jamie said, digging into his backpack and removing an arsenal of supplies. "Told you I could take it. That was, what, an hour?"

I crossed my arms, watching as Jamie swallowed the pills and typed a note into his phone.

"You're conducting an experiment," I accused.

"Field research," Jamie amended. "Just in case I wind up at a college that's loaded with ghosts."

Jamie leaned forward to place his water bottle on our coffee table. And then he let out a little *oof* and stayed like that, bent over, with his head in his hands.

"I'm sorry," I apologized, since it was my fault he felt like crap.

"I'll live," Jamie said with a shrug. "Besides, don't you ever wonder if there's a reason?"

"A reason?"

"That we can . . . you know. See ghosts?"

I hadn't, because until a few weeks ago, I hadn't thought there was anything special about me. Whenever I'd added up the sum of my parts, I'd always come up with a lesser number than the ones I gave to everyone else.

"The universe doesn't work like that," I said finally. "It isn't neat, or rational, or anything you can understand. Because it's a place where fifteen-year-olds die from a bee-sting, and where parents bury their children, and—"

"—married professors sleep with their TAs," Jamie supplied, offering me a thin smile along with the terse summary of his parents' divorce.

"This world doesn't make heroes," I said. "It just creates more and more victims."

"And more and more ghosts," Jamie pointed out.

"You've seen a lot of them," I said. It wasn't a question.

Jamie didn't answer right away, like he was mentally debating how much he wanted to tell me.

"A few," he allowed. "Palo Alto wasn't terrible, but San Francisco is seriously haunted. Whenever my friends went up on the weekends for concerts or movies or whatever, I'd have to make an excuse."

Jamie scrubbed a hand through his hair, and I realized that was why he'd insisted on staying at Sam's party. Because he was sick of sitting things out. Of conjuring excuses.

And so was I. But at least when I bailed on people, I got to hang out with Logan. Jamie had just stayed home alone.

"Pro tip," I said. "You might want to avoid the Trader Joe's parking lot."

"There's also a camping area my dad likes out by Laguna Beach. Very no bueno."

"I'll make a note," I promised.

"So," Jamie said, glancing over through his criminally long eyelashes. "Now that we're all alone, what do you think we should do?"

"Well," I said, pretending to consider it. "Isn't the PSAT coming up? Shouldn't we start studying for that?"

I reached for my backpack, somehow keeping a straight face. And then I couldn't stand it. I burst out laughing.

"You suck," Jamie complained, grabbing me around the waist and pulling me forward until I was straddling his legs with mine.

"Hey, I can't help being an extremely gifted actress," I joked.

"Well, I can't help being an extremely gifted kisser," he said, grinning, as he leaned in to prove it.

OUR FRIENDS COULD definitely tell that we'd become a thing. Sam kept staring at us during lunch on Wednesday. He was lying on his stomach in the grass, his chin propped in his hands, grinning.

"You two," he guffawed, shaking his head. "And here I was hoping Jamie had come back for me."

"Well, I did," Jamie said, blowing Sam a sarcastic kiss. "But you were already taken, so Rosie here is the next best thing."

"That's honestly what he said to me," I confirmed. "He asked me to be his runner-up to Sam."

Jamie rolled his eyes. And then he glanced over at Claudia.

"Hey, Claude, when you're done with him, you just let me know," he teased, winking at Sam.

"Oh, I'm done," Claudia joked. "Take him away, please."

I lay back in the grass and closed my eyes, feeling the sun warming my face. I was dimly aware that we were in the middle of our crowded quad, that we were sitting on a thin peninsula of grass that jutted out between the lunch line and the tables, that people were probably staring at us, but in that moment, I didn't care.

I felt Jamie lie down next to me. Heard the rustle of the grass as he settled in. I knew without opening my eyes that he was on his stomach, that he'd kicked off the heels of his shoes but not the toes. And maybe it was some paranormal ability, sensing that, or maybe it was just knowing someone.

"Can I photosynthesize with you?" he asked.

"What about Sam?" I teased, opening one eye.

"Eh." Jamie shrugged. "He got fat."

Sam let out a roar of frustration, and Claudia cackled.

"Thank god someone else said it," Max drawled, and then made an *oof* noise, presumably because Darren had elbowed him.

I sat up, squinting as my eyes readjusted to the sunlight.

"Shouldn't we head over to help Nima with the spirit wheel?" I asked.

Everyone stared at me as though I'd betrayed them.

"Great," Max said. "Five more minutes and we could have gotten away with it."

We all started to gather our things, and I realized what had happened. Somehow, without my knowing it, instead of orbiting someone else, I'd regained my own center of gravity.

18

REHEARSALS FOR THE play began Wednesday after school, but Gardner got started on the table read during class. I'd always enjoyed them before, watching from the other side of the room as Sam's crowd tried on their parts for the first time. Except now, I felt conspicuously left out.

I sat there with my friends, following along silently as they read aloud. From across the room, Abby Shah called out her lines as Lucy. Abby Shah, who kept her notebooks in a Louis Vuitton bag and had perfect boobs and Disney princess hair.

As I listened to her read with Claudia, I tried not to resent it or wonder if I would have beaten her out for the role. It had been my choice not to try out, but that didn't make it sting any less to be left out of the main thing that was happening in my friends' lives.

Logan and I went back to hanging out just the two of us. But it wasn't the same. Something had changed between us, or maybe a lot of things had. I felt restless, sitting there in front of the television, as though I was wasting my time. As though there was so much more I should be doing.

By Friday, I couldn't take it anymore, so instead of going straight home, I biked over to Billz. Just because my friends had play rehearsal every day for the conceivable future didn't mean *I* had to sit at home.

So I ordered a mint brownie and a blended chai and worked my way through the PSAT practice booklet my advisor had handed out that morning. It actually felt nice, sitting somewhere quiet and answering the different sections, like maybe I'd be able to handle the real thing in a few weeks.

"What are you doing here?" someone asked.

I looked up from the reading comprehension page. Logan was glowering down at me. Seeing him in the coffee shop was pretty unnerving, and for a moment I understood how Jamie had felt.

There was something more comfortable about Logan at home. More fitting. Here, in public, surrounded by strangers who couldn't see him, he stood out, and not in a good way. It was one of his more transparent days, and I could see right through him to where some old guy was scrolling Facebook on his phone.

"What? I'm studying," I whispered.

Logan plopped down across from me.

"Boring," he said, shaking his head in disapproval. "So boring."

"Then leave," I whispered back.

"I came all the way here. I'm not just leaving."

"So did I," I shot back.

He started to whistle, tuneless and annoying. From the faint smirk on his face, I could tell he was doing it to torture me. Immediately, I felt self-conscious. I didn't want anyone to look over and see me chatting with an empty chair. So I sent him a glare and packed up my things.

When we were outside, I glanced around, making sure we were alone.

"What the heck?" I asked.

"You were avoiding me," Logan accused.

"I was not. I just wanted a brownie."

"Then why didn't you wait for me?" Logan asked. "What were you working on that you didn't want me to see?"

"Nothing!" I said. And then I amended, "I wanted somewhere I could concentrate on studying for the PSAT."

Logan stared at me like I'd betrayed him. Like I'd announced I was moving out next week and going clear across the country, just to spite him.

"What do you expect me to do? Live at home forever?" I shot back.

"I don't know!" Logan said. "Maybe!"

"Logan," I said. "Come on."

"You come on," he said pitifully. "How come you want to leave all of a sudden? What's wrong with CSU?"

There were about a million things wrong with CSU. It

was just down the street, for one. And it was so mediocre—everyone called it "C-Student University." If you got on the 405 and drove north to Los Angeles, you'd hit half a dozen better schools along the way.

"Nothing," I said. "I don't know."

"Exactly." Logan looked pleased, but I didn't have the heart to explain.

So I didn't. Instead, I just rode my bike home with Logan floating by my side, listening to him chatter about which episode of *Star Trek* we should watch when we got there.

MY FRIENDS AND I went to the movies on Saturday night, and my parents were relatively chill about it, even if they did make Jamie come inside "just to say hello." Mom was so chatty that by the time we got to the theater the previews had already started, and we didn't have time to get snacks.

But even without the prospect of our fingers accidentally brushing in the bucket of popcorn, everything turned out okay. Our friends had saved us decent seats, and Jamie's hand still found mine under the armrest.

All of us went out for burgers afterward, dragging extra chairs over to the biggest booth In-N-Out had until we'd managed to fit seven of us around the same table. Inexplicably, Max and I got chairs, while Sam wound up squished in the middle of the booth between Claudia and Darren, looking like a giant.

Sam made a comment about it that I didn't understand,

but it sent everyone into hysterics.

"It's from rehearsal," Jamie whispered, and tried to explain, but everyone had moved on to something else that happened at play rehearsal, so there wasn't much point.

The conversation was a cascade of anecdotes, all of them funny to everyone else. I smiled along at all of it, pretending to follow. It had only been three days of rehearsal, and already, they had so many things to laugh about.

There was that thing Seth did with his hat. And Abby showing up in ridiculous stiletto heels. And Gardner eating that giant sub sandwich with the lettuce falling onto his shirt—Nima and Sam competed to see who could do a better impression of it.

"You guys have to vote for your favorite," Sam insisted.

When it turned out to be a tie, everyone groaned. And I realized that, if I'd tried out for the play after all, mine could have been the deciding vote. That I could have been laughing along with them at Gardner eating the sandwich, or Seth and his hat flip, or Abby being such a diva.

"Sorry everyone talked about rehearsal so much," Jamie said on the car ride home.

"That's okay."

"I swear to god, I kept trying to make them switch to something else," he promised.

I laughed.

"Yeah, I noticed," I said. "All it did was make you sound a little too obsessed with the PSAT."

"Standardized tests are important!" Jamie protested, and then laughed at himself. "Wow. Nerd is not a good look on me."

"Nerd is the only look on you," I joked.

"Thanks a lot, Cleopatra," he said.

We drove in silence for another block, both of us smiling. The song on the radio was somehow both sad and upbeat at the same time, and I didn't know how I felt about it.

"I love this song," Jamie said, turning it up. "It reminds me of you."

I must have made a face, because he made one back, teasing.

"Why?" I asked.

"Well, it's beautiful," he said. "And it makes me happy when I hear it, even though it's about saying good-bye."

"You think I'm beautiful?" I asked, surprised.

"Of course," Jamie said, glancing at me sideways. And I could tell that he meant it.

We'd taken the scenic route, through the narrow canyon pass, instead of the direct shot down Ocean. We were stopped at the red light outside the old general store, and there was no one else on the road. The store was closed, and the parking lot was empty, and I could almost believe it was just us, alone in the darkness, even though I knew our friends could pull up beside us at any moment in their own cars.

"You know I had a crush on you back in fifth grade,

right?" Jamie went on. "I had this idea of you, in my head, after I moved away. But I never let myself look you up on Instagram or anything, because I didn't want to ruin the picture."

"Your loss. You would have gotten over that crush in about two seconds," I joked.

"Nope," Jamie said. "Because when I saw you again, on the first day of class, you were even prettier than I imagined."

"I bet you use that line on all of the girls in your English class," I teased.

"Oh, I do," Jamie promised. "So it's lucky you're not in my English class."

"Hey," I said in mock outrage, swatting at him.

A song came on the radio from our childhood, one of those instantly recognizable things.

"No way!" he said, turning it up. "Come on, Cleo, let's see your dance moves."

"I'm a terrible car dancer," I protested, but it was no use. Jamie only cranked the radio up even higher, goading me.

The music seemed to reverberate off the walls of the canyon. It was pitch-black everywhere, except for the narrow path illuminated by Jamie's high beams, and it seemed too quiet and too still for us to be dancing in our seats to an ancient One Direction tune, but we did it anyway, belting the lyrics across the gear shift. Jamie drummed the steering wheel, and I tapped my feet, and the canyon walls rose up high and dark around us, making the sky look like a distant river of stars.

Another song came on after that was even better, and Jamie stared at me in shock.

"That's it," he said. "We're parking."

He pulled off the road, onto one of the narrow ledges on the side of the canyon, and opened the door to his car, turning his stereo up all the way.

"Come on," he said, unbuckling his seat belt.

"Where?" I asked.

"When the universe gives you a moment this good, you don't waste it," he said, stepping out of the car.

I followed him, and we danced in the glow of his high beams, to perfect song after perfect song, whirling along the edge of the canyon.

When we pulled up outside my house, my throat felt raw from singing, and my heart was hammering in my chest, not from fear or stress, but because I was alive and laughing and sitting in the dark with the cutest boy I'd ever seen.

"And you said you didn't dance," Jamie pointed out.

19

OVER THE NEXT few weeks, I watched as my friends disappeared into the play. At lunch, they'd reel off whole paragraphs of dialogue, testing each other so they could get off book. And then, every day after school, they stayed behind for rehearsal.

Costumes had never been much of a commitment—between what we already had in the wardrobe closet and what we could rent from Harbor Playhouse, it was mostly just some steaming and pinning—but it felt like even less of a job once I saw how involved my friends had become.

I had nothing to do during Gardner's class, which now functioned as an extra rehearsal period. But even worse, I had no one to do nothing with. I'd grab a seat at one of the empty lunch tables in the quad and take out my homework. And whenever I looked up from my French or my precalc, I'd see Claudia and Abby, their heads bent close, running lines.

They looked great together, with their matching swirls of perfect dark hair, Claudia in her bohemian dresses and boots, and Abby in her tight skirts and platforms. They were #goals, while I was that mediocre selfie you delete an hour after posting.

"Rose!" someone called, startling me. It was Leah, one of the Renaissance Faire girls in my class. She was sitting at a table with a bunch of other classmates who hadn't been cast in the play.

"Hey," I called, waving.

"Come join us," she insisted. "We're playing Heads Up!"

"Yeah, come join!" her friends echoed.

I'd never really talked to them much, but I went over anyway and joined their game. I'd seen people play it before, holding their phones to their foreheads and looking ridiculous, but it actually turned out to be fun. Everyone was laughing and making fools of themselves, and that was the point.

I was so into the game that I didn't even notice Jamie sneak up behind me. He wrapped his arms around me, and I jumped, startled.

Jamie laughed.

"Wow, you're an easy scare," he teased.

"You're just that scary," I shot back.

"You wound me," he said, putting a hand to his heart.

Leah and her friends were staring at us like we were *that* couple—like we were Sam and Claudia.

"Gardner says everyone can go a few minutes early," Jamie said.

"Everyone?" I asked hopefully.

"Everyone else," he amended, sighing. "Just wanted to pass on the message in case anyone's parked in the lot."

"Oh, crap, I am," one of the girls said, scrambling for her bag.

"Walk me back to the theater?" Jamie asked, so I did.

It was a short walk, but he held my hand anyway, smiling. He looked so happy, like being in the play and hanging around with our old friends and kissing in his car whenever we had a moment together was so much more than he'd hoped for.

"What?" I finally asked.

"Nothing," he said, and then amended, "You weren't sitting alone."

"No," I agreed. "I wasn't. Stop looking so smug about it."

"Who's smug?" Jamie asked innocently. "That's just my face. My unbearable, smirky face."

"Ugh!" I said, pummeling him.

LOGAN WAS WAITING by the door when I got home. I was later than usual—Claudia and I had gotten caught up in chatting about costumes, and our stage manager had assumed I was staying for rehearsal.

"I waited for you on the trail," he said accusingly.

"I took the parkway. It was faster."

"You never take the parkway," he said.

"I do sometimes," I protested, even though it wasn't true.

"Well, you're here now," Logan said. "And I know exactly what we're watching."

He raced over to the sofa, looking so excited that I couldn't help but grin. He insisted on an episode from the first season of *Star Trek: TNG*, and at first I wasn't sure why he'd chosen it, since we both preferred the later seasons. But then I figured it out.

On the screen, I watched as Wesley studied for the Starfleet entrance exam. It looked like he was going to score high, but at the last moment, he failed the psychological test and didn't get into the academy.

"Logan," I said, pausing the TV. "Why did you want to watch this?"

"No reason," he said, smirking.

I waited, making no move to unpause the TV.

"Maybe I put it on so you'd see that it's not the worst thing in the world to stay behind with people who care about you," Logan explained, in a rush.

"You're unbelievable," I told him. "I can't deal with this right now."

"Okay, fine, we can turn it off and watch *Buffy*," Logan said, as though that was the issue.

My eyes narrowed.

"Season four?" I guessed. "Where Buffy and everyone

stay behind in Sunnydale to go to college?"

"Maybe."

"Logan," I said warningly.

"What?" he asked. "It's a good season."

"Buffy *had* to live on the Hellmouth to fight vampires. It was a burden to her, not some amazing option."

"I'm not a burden!" Logan said, losing his temper.

"I never said you were!" I shouted back. "I said being a VAMPIRE SLAYER IS A BURDEN, OH MY GOD, WHY ARE WE FIGHTING OVER THIS?"

"Stop yelling at me!" Logan screamed. The TV remote, which had been sitting on the coffee table, flew across the room and slammed into the wall. It dropped to the ground, leaving a dent.

Logan stared at it in shock, and then disappeared.

"Great," I muttered.

LOGAN SEEMED TO take my banishment to heart, since he didn't show up for the next few days. It was just as well, since they passed in a panicked blur of test prep. The PSAT was on Thursday, and our advisement teachers marched us into the gym, where hundreds of desks had been lined up in a neat grid. Mr. Thompson, the guidance counselor, seated all of us alphabetically down the rows.

Jamie slid into the seat in front of mine. He was wearing an ancient San Francisco State hoodie I hadn't seen before, which looked like the softest thing in the world.

He turned around and grinned.

"Bet I can beat your score," he teased.

"On the nonexistent art history section?" I shot back.

"How's that math coming along?" he asked innocently.

I kicked the back of his chair in response.

I'd thought I would be more nervous, but I was strangely calm as I filled in the answers on my test. There was something reassuring about having Jamie there. About the way his shoulders curved forward in his sweatshirt as he hunched over his exam booklet. About Sam, two rows over, all six-foot-two of him crammed into a desk meant for someone much smaller.

We were outgrowing this place, I realized. One day soon, we were going to look down and realize it no longer fit. I'd seen a picture on the internet once of this bicycle that someone had locked to a tree and left behind. The tree kept growing, lifting the bicycle off the ground and enveloping it so that, even if someone did come back to unlock it, the bicycle was irreparably stuck.

WHEN I GOT home, Logan was flopped on my bed, glowering.

"What?" I said. "It's a required test. It's not like I could have skipped it."

I bent down to unlace my sneakers, expecting Logan to reply, but he didn't say anything.

"Are you seriously sulking over the PSAT?" I asked, straightening up.

Except he wasn't sulking. His mouth was moving, and his arms were flapping, but all I heard was silence.

"I can't hear you," I said.

I took a deep breath, trying not to freak out.

It was happening again.

My chest felt tight, and the panic was rising in my throat.

Logan looked horrified. Worst of all was his mouth, open in a silent scream.

"Logan," I said again. "Stop screaming. Calm down. Nod once if you can hear me."

His mouth closed. He nodded.

And I let out a breath I didn't know I'd been holding.

"Good," I said. "Okay."

Logan said something again, his lip curling with disdain.

"I don't know what you're saying," I told him.

Logan shook his head, as though it should have been obvious. And then he turned around, bent over, and mooned me.

"Real nice," I said, since Logan had floated upward until his butt was level with my face. He waggled it some more, and I sighed.

"Grow up," I snapped.

It was the wrong thing to say.

Logan whirled around, leveled me with a glare, and disappeared.

WHEN JAMIE CALLED that night, something kept me from telling him about the problems I was having with Logan.

202

So we chatted about this weird reading comprehension part of the exam and how someone had vandalized our school's security buggy.

The Santa Ana winds had started up again, making the windows rattle. Every once in a while, this palm tree in our backyard would scrape against the glass, making it sound like someone was trying to get in.

"Got any more weird superstitions for me, Cleo?" Jamie asked.

"Always," I said, trying to pick. "Um, do you know about sneeze prophesies?"

"Sneeze prophesies?" Jamie repeated, as though he hadn't heard me correctly.

"They're a thing," I insisted. "If someone sneezes in the middle of a conversation, whatever was said right before it will come true."

Jamie laughed.

"That would make such a good spurious correlation," he said. "Allergy season causes an increase in prophesies."

"You're such a cynic," I teased.

"Hey now, I used to jump every New Year's Eve when the clock struck midnight," he said. "Although it never made me grow taller."

"Wait, what?"

"Aha!" Jamie accused. "A superstition you *don't* know!"

"It can't be better than prophesneezes," I said.

Jamie snorted at the portmanteau.

"No, prophesneezes take the lead for most ridiculous

thing ever," he agreed.

"I don't know," I said. "It's a way of controlling the uncontrollable. I mean, the second a prophesneeze happens, you know what the future holds."

"True," Jamie said, "but then you start living your life by this arbitrary set of rules, and you become scared to break them."

"Yeah, but we do that anyway," I pointed out. "High school is full of unspoken rules that no one wants to break. Like where you sit at lunch or who you choose as a partner."

"Except we broke those rules," Jamie reminded me. "And nothing bad happened."

"There's still time," I said. I meant it as a joke, but I had no idea how right I was about to become.

20

"HEY, CLEO, WHAT'S your Halloween costume?" Jamie asked.

It was the next week, and Jamie and I were sitting back-stage during Gardner's class in a pile of flashlights, blue gels, and tape. Abby and Claudia were onstage, rehearsing Act I. They were supposed to be off book, but Abby kept dropping her lines, and Gardner didn't sound pleased.

"You'll see it at Sam's party," I said, and Jamie groaned.

"One hint?"

"*No,*" I said.

Jamie angled a flashlight up against his chin, casting his face into blue shadows.

"Is it spooky?" he asked, making such a terrible spooky face that I couldn't help but laugh.

"Shhh," he scolded, putting a finger to my lips. "You're interrupting the rehearsal."

I glared at him, and he grinned back at me, pleased,

mashing my lips around with his finger.

I don't know how we wound up lying down backstage, making out in a pile of flashlights, but suddenly we were. It was the sexiest thing that had ever happened to me. His hands were on my back, and my hands were in his hair, and I was covered in goose bumps all of a sudden, even though I wasn't cold.

Someone cleared his throat, and I looked up, mortified.

It was Max, carrying his phone charger and trying not to laugh. His newly hemmed Dracula cape swished around his ankles.

"Don't stop on my behalf," he drawled.

He bent down and plugged in his charger.

"Photo to remember this by?" he asked, holding up his phone.

"Get out of here," Jamie snapped, shooing him off.

Max left, cackling, but the spell was kind of broken.

I sat up and went back to loading batteries into flashlights.

"So, Cleo," Jamie said. "My dad's got this dinner with a guest speaker at the university tomorrow. We'd have the whole place to ourselves."

I could hardly believe it. Between play rehearsals, our parents, and our friends always wanting to do things as a group, we never had any privacy. Which was probably how we'd wound up making out in a flashlight pit.

"What would we do at your place?" I asked, teasing.

Jamie shrugged, the picture of innocence.

"Well, I do have some pretty great books about ancient Egypt."

I TOLD MY parents I was staying for rehearsal and getting dinner after with my friends. It was an easy lie, and one they bought completely. And it wasn't entirely untrue. I did stay for rehearsal, where I sat in the audience, watching Max flap around in his cape, having way too much fun being evil.

We all split up at the lot, and I noticed that Abby went with Nima, climbing into his Mercedes as though it was routine. Most of the cars were already gone; it was really just the athletes who stayed this late.

Jamie and I drove down the parkway, which felt strange without the usual crush of after-school traffic. It felt even stranger when he turned south, toward the CSU campus, instead of north into the canyon.

The homes were smaller here, attached townhouses with numbered carports instead of backyard pools and three-car garages.

I was nervous, all of a sudden, and I didn't know why. Maybe it was because of the lie I'd told my parents, or the empty house waiting for us, or the three little words that fluttered in my rib cage every time we kissed.

Either way, my heart was beating louder than I'd

thought possible, and a couple of times, I was sure that Jamie heard it.

I glanced over at Jamie. He was wearing his glasses, which always killed me, and he was smiling in a way that made his lips look impossibly full. He drummed his palms against a steering wheel, waiting for the traffic to clear. I smoothed my hair, trying to calm my nerves.

Jamie's house was smaller than I'd expected, but oddly familiar. I stared at his living room, trying to figure out where I'd seen it before.

"My dad kept the furniture," he explained, making a face.

I could tell he hated it, seeing his old living room transported here, the pieces much too big for the space, and I didn't blame him.

"Please tell me you don't want a tour," Jamie said, looking embarrassed.

"Well, I do now."

So he led me around, making up absurd names for the rooms.

"The underwear disco," he said, waving in the direction of the laundry room.

"Meditation chamber" was the bathroom.

"Homework processing plant," he said as we walked into his bedroom.

His room was surprisingly ordinary. Just a guest room with a plain white duvet, a dusty treadmill in the corner,

and an outdated television. Even the bookshelf was someone else's, crammed with reference books and old Zagat
guides.

"It's terrible, I know," Jamie mumbled, staring at the
carpet.

I started laughing. Somehow, since Jamie's room was
such a disappointment, I wasn't so nervous anymore. It
didn't feel like a boy's room, and it certainly didn't feel like
Jamie's.

"It's so bad," I said. "Wow."

"The Zagat guides are the worst part," Jamie said. "It's
like, here are descriptions of amazing restaurants, but just
kidding, because all we eat is Panda Express."

My stomach growled at the mention of amazing restaurants, and I felt my cheeks heat up.

"Um, are you hungry?" he asked.

"Starving," I said.

Jamie led me to the kitchen and got out some leftover
cartons of Chinese food, apologizing.

"I see you weren't kidding about the Panda Express," I
teased.

"We could order from somewhere else if you want," he
said.

"No, this is great," I said, and then I tried to help, opening drawers in search of silverware, until he made me sit
down.

"Hold on," he said, disappearing into the living room.

After a moment, there was a scratching noise, and jazz drifted into the kitchen.

It wasn't anything like the jazz my dad played, the soft, inoffensive background music to his optical shop. This was a warmer, deeper music, the kind that made you pay attention.

"Josephine Baker," Jamie said. "I did this History Day presentation on Paris in the 1920s. The record was just supposed to be a prop, but I liked it so much I kept it."

"Nerd," I teased.

"Obviously," Jamie agreed, pressing his lips to mine.

It was the boldest kiss we'd ever had, our bodies sliding together like magnets. I went slightly dizzy from the force of it, and when I opened my eyes, I was surprised to hear my stomach growl, because I'd forgotten I could want something that wasn't Jamie.

"Dinner is served," Jamie said, passing me a plate of orange chicken and rice.

As we ate, Jamie kept glancing over at me. He looked happy, and a little shy, and I realized this was new for him, too. That we were charting new territory together, stepping into an unexplored universe and mapping the stars.

We talked about our friends, and about the play—Jamie had been cast as Van Helsing, the vampire hunter, which was deeply ironic.

"What's it called when you try to become the character you're playing?" he said. "Method acting? It's like I'm doing the opposite. Method living."

"I think Max is method acting," I told him.

Jamie grinned and did a spot-on impression of Max's Dracula voice.

I laughed.

In the other room, the record went quiet, and Jamie got up to flip it. When he came back in, he didn't sit down. Instead, he put his hands on my hips and pressed his lips to mine.

My mouth was greasy from the takeout, and so was his, but it didn't matter. We tangled our way to the bedroom, the old record crackling through the air like electricity.

It was the kind of music that you heard in old movies where Audrey Hepburn twirls in a pair of elegant ballet flats. The kind of music that plays in romantic scenes where two people hold hands in the moonlight.

We melted backward onto the duvet. We kissed the way we'd started to back in that pile of flashlights, and there was no reason to stop. My heart was racing, and I didn't know how it was possible to breathe without pulling apart, but somehow, we were.

His toes tangled with mine, and I had the absurd thought that our feet were holding hands.

"Oh god, Rose," he whispered, his breath tickling my neck.

It was like every nerve ending in my body had gathered in my spine, tensed and waiting. We rolled over until I was sitting on top of him. He stared up at me, his eyes wide. His hair was a mess, and I ruffled my fingers through it, laughing. And then, very slowly, I reached for the hem of my shirt.

Jamie tugged off his own shirt, and then, as if checking that it was okay, unbuttoned the top of his jeans. They were tight to begin with, and far too tight now.

I'd never touched a boy there, but I reached for it, curious, and Jamie breathed in sharply.

"Wow," he said, laughing.

"Sorry," I apologized.

"Don't be," Jamie shook his head. "I just wasn't expecting it."

"I'm here, aren't I?" I asked.

And then I reached for the button on my own jeans.

Hold me close and make all my dreams come true, the record warbled.

And so we did.

We climbed under the covers, making our own warm little cave, tracing our fingers over each other's skin in fascination. His fingers were over my bra, and then under it, and then some other places that I'd never been touched before. I reached for him, and it was as though I held his heartbeat in my hand.

And then, out of nowhere, someone shouted in surprise.

Jamie and I sat up, shocked.

Logan hovered above the end of the bed, gaping down at us in horror.

"What the hell?!" he yelled. "That's my little sister!"

Oh my god.

"Logan!" I gasped, clutching the covers to my chest. "Get out!"

But Logan paid me no attention. He glared at Jamie, his chest heaving.

"Get away from her!" he demanded. "Now!"

The ceiling fan sped up, whirling so fast that it was like a miniature storm had taken over the room. The papers on Jamie's desk rippled madly, then took flight. "Logan, stop!" I said.

But he didn't. Instead, he let out a miserable wail.

The bookshelf on the wall trembled, and, one by one, the books shot out, banging against the opposite wall.

"Watch out!" Jamie said, pressing me close, like he needed to protect me.

"I can't *believe* you!" Logan shouted. "I can't believe *both* of you!"

"Logan, calm down," Jamie said.

"Calm down?!" Logan yelped. "You're in bed with my little sister!"

"I'm *not* your little sister!" I said. I pulled on my shirt. "Logan. Hallway. Now."

Logan glared at me but went. I folded my arms across my chest and glared.

"You are so out of line!" I accused.

"Me?" Logan shot back. "*You're* the one going to *parties* and drinking *beer* and having *sex*—"

"Oh my god, we weren't having *sex*," I cut in. "And even if we were, it's none of your business! You can't spy on me like this! It's super creepy to barge into someone's house!"

"*I'm* creepy?" Logan said, his chest heaving. "*I'm* creepy for worrying about my little sister?"

"I'm not your little sister anymore!" I snarled. Logan's face fell, and instantly I wished I could take it back.

"You are too!" Logan insisted, his jaw trembling. "Little sister isn't an age, it's a relationship. And it means I'm supposed to look out for you."

"That's what you've been doing?" I asked incredulously. "Crashing Sam's party and following me around, that's looking out for me?"

Logan didn't answer me for a moment. Instead, he bit his lip and stared at the floor.

"It never used to be like this," he said, sounding defeated. "You've been pushing me away ever since you met *him*."

"That's not true!"

"You'd rather be with him. I bet that's why you're losing the ability to see me," Logan accused.

"That's ridiculous," I said.

Even though it wasn't.

Even though it made a horrible kind of sense.

I hadn't been able to see Logan right after Jamie's

and my first kiss. What if there was an actual correlation between falling for Jamie and my losing the ability to see Logan?

"You're ridiculous," Logan accused, sulking. "You're a ridiculous butt made of ridiculous butts."

It was the most brothery thing he could have said. And just like that, everything was okay between us again.

"At least I don't moon people," I said, giving him a playful shove.

Wrong move. My hands hit some kind of invisible barrier, and I bounced backward, my shoulders hitting the wall.

"Are you okay?" Logan asked, worried.

Jamie banged open the door. His jeans were unzipped, and his shirt was unbuttoned, and he looked panicked.

"What happened?"

"Nothing," I said, rolling my shoulders. "I'm fine."

Jamie rounded on Logan.

"I didn't do anything," Logan swore.

"Except break into my house, and spy on us, and destroy my room," Jamie retorted.

"You slept with my kid sister!" Logan accused.

"At least one of us won't die a virgin," Jamie snapped.

Logan's eyes darkened, suddenly more holes than actual eyes. Everything about him blurred, shifted, and writhed.

"Say that again," he growled. *"I dare you."*

I stepped between the two of them.

"Stop it!" I begged. "Both of you! Please!"

My shoulders were stiff and sore, and I belatedly realized that I wasn't wearing any pants.

"*Booooooo,*" Logan moaned sarcastically, feinting a lunge.

Jamie jerked back, and Logan laughed.

"Scared of me, huh?" Logan asked, looked pleased. "Good. Now stay away from my sister."

"*Logan,*" I warned, but he was already gone.

Above us, the hall light flickered and then went out.

Jamie sighed. Raked a hand through his hair. Gave me a small smile that was meant to be reassuring but mostly just looked tired.

"I'm sorry," I said as we got dressed. "I can't believe Logan did this."

His room really was a mess. I bent down and started picking up a stack of books.

"Leave it," Jamie said, sounding exhausted. "It's fine."

"I'll talk to him," I promised. "Make sure he knows he crossed the line."

I expected Jamie to smile and say that sounded like a plan, but he didn't. Instead he turned toward me, his expression serious.

"I'm worried about him, Rose," Jamie confessed. "A couple of months ago he couldn't even use the remote. Now he came all the way here and did this."

"I don't think he was expecting to find us, um, together," I said, coming to Logan's defense. "Plenty of people would have yelled or thrown things or whatever."

"But not plenty of ghosts," Jamie said.

"He threw a tantrum," I insisted. "That was it. He'd never hurt anyone."

Jamie nodded, but I could tell he wasn't convinced.

21

HALLOWEEN WAS ON Saturday. The Donovans had tickets to some charity costume ball and were fine if Sam had a few friends over. Apparently, they'd said, "If you're going to drink, we'd prefer you do it at home," which made them miles cooler than my parents, who had finally agreed to let me stay out past eleven.

I baked sugar cookies and decorated them with what was possibly my greatest Pinterest fail of all time, homemade royal icing. Mostly, it meant that I paved our entire kitchen with runny frosting and ran out of time to clean it up.

Mom sighed when she saw the mess.

"When's Jamie coming over?" she asked.

"Twenty minutes," I said, with a pleading expression. I was still in my sweatpants.

"Get dressed. I'll take care of it," Mom said, and I stared at her incredulously. "Just this one time. And only because of that A you brought home in precalc."

"Yes! You're amazing!" I said, giving her an icing-covered hug. And then I raced upstairs to shower and change.

I wanted to surprise Jamie with my costume. I'd found it in the rentals department at Harbor Playhouse while I was pulling pieces for *Dracula*. It was a Cleopatra gown, complete with gold edging and a beaded headband.

Seeing it all put together with my hair and makeup was surreal. The costume was even better than I'd hoped. The creamy chiffon fell in soft folds to the floor. There was a train of sky-blue polyester, and a wide gold belt, and metallic embroidery along the hem. I'd pinned my hair under, following a YouTube tutorial for a faux bob, and the shorter length made my eyes look huge. I kind of loved it.

I'd been expecting Logan to show up that afternoon, begging to tag along. But he'd stayed away, almost like he knew I'd tell him not to come. Still, I wished he'd gotten to see my Halloween costume.

"Rose!" my dad called. "There's someone here to see you."

"Coming!" I yelled, grabbing my phone.

I burst out laughing when I saw Jamie. He was dressed as a Roman gladiator, in one of those cheap, terrible Halloween store costumes, complete with a bulky plastic breastplate and wrinkled cape.

"Wow," he said, staring at me. "Did you cut your hair?"

"I tucked it under," I explained, still giggling over his costume.

"Stop laughing," he said miserably. "It looked better in the package."

"You two are adorable!" my mom exclaimed, coming out of the kitchen. "Rose, you didn't tell me you were planning to match!"

I suddenly realized who Jamie was supposed to be, and I wondered how I'd ever thought he was wearing a silly store-bought gladiator costume. I'd expected him to come as King Tut, but he hadn't. Instead, he'd come as Cleopatra's ill-fated lover, the one I'd read about in Shakespeare's play.

"Antony and Cleopatra!" my dad exclaimed. "I get it now."

"Didn't want to ruin the surprise," Jamie said, winking at me.

"Dad, no," I said, noticing the way he was clutching his iPad. "No photos."

"I don't know," Jamie said, grinning. "I was hoping I could send some to my mom."

"See!" My mom was triumphant. "Jamie wants photos."

There was no use explaining that he'd only agreed to pictures to antagonize me. So we stood there and posed together while my dad held up his gigantic tablet and kept exclaiming, "That one's a keeper!"

He must have taken at least fifty pictures before my parents finally let us go.

"What?" Jamie asked as we walked down the front steps. "You keep staring at me funny."

"How did you know what I'd wear?" I asked.

"I had a hunch."

"What if you'd been wrong?" I teased. "And I'd dressed as a sexy bunny?"

"Then I would have looked ridiculous, but at least I'd have a sexy bunny on my arm," he joked.

I whacked him, and he twisted away laughing. And then he leaned in and pressed his lips softly against mine.

"Happy Halloween, Cleopatra," he said.

And for once, I felt like that stupid nickname fit.

When we got to Sam's house, the party had already started. Claudia met us at the front door dressed as Mary Poppins, which suited her perfectly.

"Finally!" she said. "What took you so long?"

"My mom wanted pictures," I said miserably.

"Well, come on," Claudia said, ushering us inside. "Heads up, Nima invited Abby. And whatever you do, don't make fun of her costume," she advised.

"Why on earth would they do that?" Max asked. He was dressed as Waldo from the children's books, but somehow still managed to sound dignified.

Claudia scowled at him.

"Be nice," she warned. "For Nima."

"I'm never nice," Max said, frowning. "It's a mystery why you'd think I'd start now."

"Should have gone with the Oscar Wilde costume," Jamie told him, and Claudia made a strangled sound like she was trying not to laugh.

Our friends were putting the finishing touches on the decorations when we walked into the living room. Nima was Spider-Man, and Darren had tied on a terrible vinyl cape that wasn't a costume at all.

We set the cookies down on the counter, where Abby was poking gummy worms into a bowl of popcorn. She was dressed as a sexy wizard in a Hogwarts bustier, hot pants, and stripper heels.

"Ooooh, Rose, those look amazing," she said, beaming at my plate of B-minus cookies.

"Thanks," I said, and then, because Claudia had told me to, "I like your costume."

"I'm such a Harry Potter nerd!" she proclaimed. "I even took an online quiz to find out which house I'm in!"

I smiled politely, Max's gleeful warning echoing inside my head.

Sam bustled in from the garage, carrying a huge bottle of rum and wearing a Thor costume.

"This drink. I like it," he said, pouring the rum into a plastic cauldron.

"Spooky accurate, right?" Claudia said, beaming at him.

Sam passed around the drinks, which tasted suspiciously like flat vanilla Coke.

"Careful with these," he warned, mostly for Jamie's benefit, since he was the only one driving. "They're stronger than Polyjuice."

"Stronger than what?" Abby asked, wrinkling her nose.

Max clapped a hand over his mouth, trying to muffle his cackling. Claudia's lips disappeared into a thin line.

We all crowded into the living room, balancing greasy paper plates of pizza on our laps while we watched *The Evil Dead*. There were four of us squeezed onto the couch, and Jamie's shoulder pressed into mine. We kept glancing at each other, exchanging these little smirks over the movie. Meanwhile, on the carpet in front of us, Abby was clutching Nima's hand and couldn't stop squealing over the fake blood.

After the movie ended, Claudia held up a Ouija board, grinning.

"Who wants to contact the dead?" she asked.

"Yaaasss!" Max exclaimed. "A séance!"

"I don't know," Jamie said, trying to sound disinterested, even though I could tell he hated the idea. "Sam's just going to push the indicator around."

"Hey!" Sam yelped. "I respect the spirit world. Max is the one without a sense of honor."

"Take that back!" Max insisted, reaching for a spatula. He held it like a dagger, daring Sam to reach for one of his own, but Sam just gave him a look.

"I'm not really feeling a séance, either," I said, since Jamie seemed so against it. "Let's watch another movie."

"Come on, Rose," Claudia whined. "Where's your Halloween spirit?"

Everyone was staring at Jamie and me, clearly wanting to have the séance. And I didn't know what to do. Usually I just went along with what everyone else wanted. Besides, I had no idea why Jamie was being so sensitive about it. What was the worst that could happen?

"Fine," I said, giving in.

Claudia lit a few candles, which made the room feel instantly spookier. Suddenly, in their flickering light, Sam's house felt so far from a silly costume party with a pile of pizza boxes on the counter.

She led the séance, asking us all to hold hands. Jamie squeezed mine, and I squeezed back, my heart hammering.

I didn't know why I was so nervous. But with all of us sitting there in the flickering candlelight, with the curtains drawn and Claudia's old Ouija board on the table, the night felt suddenly ominous. Even Claudia, dressed as a cheery British nanny, looked mysterious and shadowed, the candle flames dancing in her dark eyes.

"Spirits of the past," Claudia intoned, "you are free to move among us. Be guided by our light and honor us with a visit."

I glanced at Jamie. Claudia was taking this far more seriously than I would have liked. His mouth was in a tight, nervous line.

"Everyone, close your eyes and repeat after me," Claudia said. "Dear spirit, we summon you."

"Dear spirit, we summon you," everyone chanted.

I mouthed it.

"Rose," Claudia whispered, raising her eyebrows.

Feeling utterly defeated, I joined in, chanting along with the rest. I could hear the rumble of Jamie's voice on my right, the purr of Darren's on my left as we chanted the phrase again and again in our candlelit circle.

Something bad is going to happen, I thought. And then, *nothing is going to happen.*

"This isn't working," Nima complained. "Maybe we need to sacrifice a chicken or something."

"I think there are some nuggets in the freezer," Sam told him, keeping a straight face.

"Oh my god, you can't sacrifice frozen chicken nuggets," Abby said.

And then the ghost showed up.

One moment we were bent over Claudia's Ouija board discussing chicken nuggets, and the next, an angry old lady was hovering next to the kitchen sink.

She was solid everywhere except for her hands and feet, which were too blurred to make out. Her nightgown was filthy and worn.

"WHAT HAVE YOU DONE TO ME?" she screamed, her eyes like holes.

Oh my god. We'd really summoned a ghost. And she was terrifying.

I glanced over at Jamie. He looked horrified, and I didn't blame him.

Everyone else was strangely calm, and that was when I realized: Jamie and I were the only ones who could see her.

"Is there a spirit here?" Claudia asked, totally unaware.

Suddenly, the candle flames jumped wildly, licking toward the ceiling in a violent dance of blues and golds.

"Holy shit," Sam said, gawking at the candles like they were the most interesting thing happening. "This séance is actually working."

"I know." Claudia beamed.

Jamie squeezed my hand, and I squeezed back, grateful that I wasn't the only one seeing this—seeing *her*.

"YOU MONSTERS!" the ghost screeched, whirling around. "HOW DARE YOU?!"

The room felt far too warm all of a sudden. My heart was hammering in my chest, and my rented costume was glued to my back. The ghost was so close that, if I reached out, I'd be able to touch her.

"O Spirit," Claudia intoned. "We mean you no harm. You are welcome here."

"YOU'VE BEEN PLANNING THIS!" the ghost accused. "TRAITORS! HARPIES!"

The kitchen cabinets rattled, and then all flew open at once with a loud bang.

Abby shrieked, and I didn't blame her.

"Claudia, make it stop!" Darren yelled.

"I don't know how!" Claudia said, sounding panicked.

Jamie let go of my hand and leaned forward, grabbed the Ouija board indicator.

"Be gone! Leave us alone!" he demanded, pushing the planchette to GOODBYE.

But the ghost didn't go anywhere.

"YOU WON'T GET A CENT FROM ME!" she screamed, her mouth contorting into an angry howl.

LEAVE, I thought desperately. *PLEASE, PLEASE LEAVE.*

Finally, the ghost darted through the sliding door and into the yard.

All at once, the candles blew out, plunging us into darkness.

Out in the yard, Sam's dog started barking frantically.

And just like that, it was over.

"Is everyone okay?" Claudia asked, holding up her cell phone as a light.

Everyone's faces looked pale and nervous in the glow of her screen, Jamie's most of all. Because the ghost hadn't gone back to wherever she'd come from; she'd gone out into our neighborhood.

I could feel the tension radiating off Jamie, and I wondered why he'd grabbed for the planchette, what he'd thought he could do.

"We shouldn't have done that," Darren said.

"Oh, whatever." Max shrugged. "I mean, it was all a joke, right?"

I stared at him in surprise, wondering how he could possibly think that.

"Totally," Nima agreed.

And suddenly the spell broke, everyone talking at once about the stage effects and tricks that could have been used. Trick candles. The cabinets on a timer. A magnet in the planchette. Only Jamie and I were silent.

"Ugh," Jamie said, glancing at his phone. "My dad's pissed. Says he wants me home right now."

"What? Why?" Sam asked.

"Long story," Jamie said with a convincing sigh. But I knew the excuse about his dad wasn't true. There was no way Jamie was going home with that ghost on the loose.

"I'll come with you," I said.

"No, you should stay here," he insisted, but I just shot him a look and grabbed my purse.

The street was silent, punctuated only by the occasional flicker of a jack-o'-lantern. Trick-or-treaters rarely ventured this high into the canyon, and those who did had gone home hours ago.

"We shouldn't have done the séance," Jamie said as we walked down Sam's driveway.

"It's not like we knew that would happen," I pointed out.

"Still," Jamie said, his shoulders tense. "Rose, you should go home."

"Why?" I narrowed my eyes. "What are you going to do?"

We passed beneath a streetlamp, and it flickered on, the way streetlamps do sometimes, as if promising that nothing bad will happen. But too late for that.

"Rose—"

"I'm not leaving," I said. "So whatever it is, you should tell me now."

Jamie sighed, scrubbing a hand through his hair. He looked silly in his store-bought costume, but I'd never seen him so serious.

"I'm going to help her move on," he said.

"What?" I didn't think I'd heard him correctly.

"You know. To exorcise her, or whatever," Jamie continued. "I've done it before."

I hadn't known it was possible. That we could do anything more than see ghosts. But Jamie had. And he'd kept it from me.

"How many ghosts have you exorcised?" I asked, my throat dry.

"Two," he admitted.

He couldn't be telling me this. Not now.

The streetlamp was too bright, and the fog was too thick. The walls of the canyon felt like they rose up forever, like we were trapped here and I'd only just noticed.

"Rose?" he asked, looking concerned. "You okay?"

Of course I wasn't. My heart was hammering so hard that it hurt to breathe.

"Fine," I lied.

Jamie's eyes were dark and brimming with concern, and he seemed to be holding his breath, waiting for me to ask him about Logan.

But I couldn't. I wouldn't even let myself think it.

"I'm sorry," he said. "I should have told you."

"Yeah, you should have," I said, and then something occurred to me. "Can I exorcise ghosts too?"

"I don't know," Jamie admitted. "But I think we're about to find out."

WE CLIMBED INTO Jamie's car, and he turned on the high beams. They lit up the fog like a stage effect as we drove up and down the canyon, looking for the ghost.

"This isn't working," Jamie muttered after the fifth street.

He pulled over, digging out his phone. After frowning over our local paper's obituary section for a few minutes, he nodded slightly, as if he'd solved a homework problem. And then, wordlessly, he passed me an obituary featuring a photo of the old woman we'd just seen.

Her name was Amelia Lee. She'd died two months ago, at the age of eighty-seven. She'd been a schoolteacher, and a WAC in Vietnam.

An estate sale listing showed she'd lived at 9228 North Canyon View Drive.

"So how does it work, exactly?" I asked as we drove over. "Do we need a Bible? Holy water?"

"Aren't you Jewish?"

"Well, I assume you don't exorcise a ghost with matzoh," I shot back.

Jamie snorted.

"They're people, Rose. You mostly just talk to them."

"Wait, so exorcism is therapy for ghosts?"

"Yep," Jamie deadpanned. "We literally talk them to death."

He stepped out of the car, adjusting his ridiculous gladiator costume. And then he ducked his head back inside.

"You coming?"

The ghost was hovering in front of an expansive Spanish-style house, staring at the *SOLD* sign that had been staked into the lawn.

Her face was more solid now, covered with lines and age spots. Her anger was gone, replaced with confusion. It was as though she'd gotten turned around and couldn't figure out which way led home.

"Um, excuse me," Jamie called.

The ghost turned around, glaring at us, the darkness in her eyes returning.

"GET OFF MY LAWNNN!" she shrieked, rushing toward us.

I twisted aside, narrowly avoiding the collision.

"Stop it! Mrs. Lee? We came to talk to you," Jamie said.

The old woman was taken aback. She spluttered a moment, and then the crazed expression in her eyes faded a little, replaced with curiosity.

"You can see me?" she asked, peering at us.

Jamie and I nodded uneasily.

"Well, then," she said, pleased. She smoothed the front of her nightie, as though trying to make herself more presentable. And then she glared. "You're not moving into my house, are you?"

"Um, no," I said.

The ghost drifted closer to us, and next to me, I felt Jamie go stiff.

"They were waiting for me to die," she confessed. "My children. They were after the money all along. They locked me up and sold my house."

"That's awful," Jamie said.

"I'm really sorry," I added quietly.

"My husband's waiting for me," the ghost said, her shoulders sagging. "I just can't get to him."

"Tell me about your husband," Jamie said.

"Oh, he was wonderful," she said. "He used to come by my father's mechanic shop every few weeks, his hair all combed, looking nervous. There was always something the matter with his car. Turned out he was having all of that car trouble on purpose. Finally got up the courage to ask me to the drive-in."

"Do you have a favorite memory of him?" Jamie asked.

"The way we used to dance around the kitchen," she said. "He'd ask what I was making for dinner, and then he'd put on a record, and we'd dance until our dinner was ready."

"This is great," Jamie said. "Keep going."

She stared dreamily off into the distance, describing the

different types of dancing they used to do.

"Okay," Jamie said, turning to me. "I need you to concentrate. Count of three, we're in her kitchen watching them dance. Got it?"

I nodded. It sounded absurd, but I tried to do what he said. To see Amelia Lee, much younger, in a frilly apron, her head on her husband's shoulder as a chicken roasted in the oven.

I was just about to say it wasn't working when, miraculously, it was. We were moving, and yet we weren't. I felt dizzy and a little sick. But there we were, in a tiny kitchen, watching an older couple sway together, their eyes closed.

"Got it," I whispered.

"Me too," Jamie said.

At first, the ghost was stuck tight, tethered to her house, to this canyon, but the bonds began to loosen. And then break. And I realized we were causing it, somehow.

The ghost was so pale now she was practically transparent. She let out a sigh of relief.

"Thank you," she whispered. "I can see him now. I can hear the music."

And so could we, a faint, quick jazz song, all saxophone.

The ground lurched, and everything slid sideways again until we were back on her lawn in our Halloween costumes, just the two of us.

My head was pounding, like someone had pressed their hands to my temples and squeezed. Judging from the look on Jamie's face, he felt even worse.

I sunk down to the ground, overwhelmed by the enormity of what we'd just done.

I didn't know that ghosts could move on. That they'd want to. Or that it was so easy to do.

"Rose?" Jamie said, laying a hand on my shoulder. "You okay?"

"Fine," I said, giving him a shaky smile. "But we can't tell Logan about this. Not ever."

Jamie nodded.

And then my phone started buzzing.

Oh no. My curfew.

"Hello?" I said. "Mom?"

"It's 12:19," she said, sounding upset. "Where are you?"

"I'm still at Sam's," I said. "Sorry."

"That wasn't the deal. You have four minutes to get home or I'm taking your phone away."

"Crap," I muttered, hanging up. "I missed my curfew. I have to get home, like, now."

"Shit," Jamie said, digging out his keys. "Come on."

Even as he ran toward the car, somehow I knew we wouldn't make it.

22

MY MOM WAS furious. I'd missed my curfew by almost half an hour, and she didn't believe for a second that I'd lost track of time at Sam's.

"I saw you pull up in his car," she fumed, arms folded across the front of her bathrobe. "He better not have had *one* drink."

"Mom, of course not," I promised, even though it wasn't true.

"I said you could go to Sam's," she went on. "With your friends. Not driving around god knows where until after midnight."

"We *were* at Sam's," I insisted. But I could tell she didn't believe me. And I didn't blame her. I knew what it looked like.

I wished I could tell her the truth, because I knew that whatever she was picturing was far worse than what had really happened.

But she just shook her head, disappointed, and held out her hand.

"Phone," she demanded.

"Mom," I pleaded. "No."

I needed my phone. It was my lifeline to Jamie, but my mom's hand was still outstretched, waiting. And I didn't have a choice. So I powered it down and passed it over.

"I'll take care of this until I feel you've earned it back," Mom said.

And then, because that wasn't bad enough, she grounded me for two weeks for lying that we'd been at Sam's.

IT WAS A disaster not having my phone. Plus, when I woke up, I discovered my mom had changed all my passwords, so I couldn't even use my laptop to DM.

I sent Jamie an email, but it felt as futile as stuffing a message into a bottle and tying it to a balloon. I wished Logan would turn up, so I'd have someone to hang out with, but he stayed away entirely, leaving me to my homework and an entirely unsatisfying string of *Friends* episodes on Netflix.

Even in school, I felt detached. Gardner was on a rampage about everyone being off book, and my friends spent lunch frantically running lines. Abby joined us, and Nima slung his arm around her, looking thrilled.

When she showed up again on Tuesday, it was clear that she'd become a permanent fixture. Max rolled his eyes over it, but Nima was so excited that I knew no one really minded. And every afternoon, when everyone else stayed behind for rehearsal, I was the one who stuck out, not Abby.

The doorbell rang on Wednesday afternoon while I was finishing up my precalc homework at the kitchen table.

It was Jamie, in his glasses and sweatshirt. He was carrying two cups of frozen yogurt.

"Sorry, I forgot to get spoons," he said.

"What about rehearsal?" I asked.

"Gardner let everyone who's off book leave early," Jamie explained. "I would have texted, but . . ."

"Yeah," I said. "Not sure how long my parents are going to keep this up. I'm going stir-crazy."

"I thought you were hanging out with Logan," Jamie said, following me into the kitchen.

I took out two plastic spoons from the drawer where my mom saved all of the take-out condiments.

"Nope," I said.

"Then we should go somewhere," Jamie said.

"Grounded," I reminded him.

"Who's going to know?" he asked through a mouthful of frozen yogurt. "We don't have to go far. Claudia told me she passed by our old tree fort the other day, and it's still there."

Jamie stared at me, his expression pleading. He looked so hopeful about our childhood fort. And it really was one of the last warm days. I could feel the weather changing, the Santa Anas changing into a sharp winter wind.

Besides, the end of the block wasn't really going anywhere.

"Okay," I relented. "We can go to the preserve."

JAMIE ENTERTAINED ME with stories about rehearsal as we walked over. He seemed so excited to be in the play, and so pleased that Gardner had dismissed him early.

"Abby's a disaster," he confided. "Claudia's convinced she's one of those bad-rehearsal-great-performance types, but I'm not so sure. And Max is having a hard time remembering his lines."

"Max?" I said, surprised.

"He's taking even more APs than I am," Jamie said. "I think he's going to implode."

"Either that, or he'll get into Yale drama," I pointed out.

Jamie let out an enormous sneeze.

I stared at him in shock, and his lips twitched, unable to hold back a smile.

"You totally bought that prophesneeze," he accused.

"Oh my god, you're the worst!" I said, laughing.

We'd reached the end of the street. The sun was just starting to set, making the limestone take on a soft orange glow. We walked past the fork in the trail, then cut past the honeysuckle bushes to the tree fort.

It was still there, weathered but intact. The platform was lower than I remembered, only eight or nine feet high, if I had to guess. Jamie scrambled up the rope ladder first and then reached down for our frozen yogurts.

"Was it always this small?" he asked as I climbed up.

"Memory makes things shrink," I joked, squeezing next to him. There was barely enough room for the two of us to sit down.

"God, I remember when Sam's dad built this place," Jamie said. "I have so many good memories here."

I didn't say anything. Just stirred the yogurt on my lap and stared down at my dangling feet. I'd worn my Birkenstocks, stupidly, and the left one kept threatening to fall off.

"I was here the day Logan died," I admitted.

Jamie looked appalled.

"Rose, you should have *said* something."

"It's okay," I said, shrugging. "I mean, he's not really gone. We'll probably hang out tomorrow."

"Yeah, and I'll see my dad in a few hours. But it's not the same as when he used to cut the crusts off my sandwiches," Jamie pointed out.

"Do you remember how Sam used to eat all of our pizza crusts?" I asked.

"Yes," Jamie said. "Claudia used to ask if she could eat my cheese, and it drove me nuts. She didn't want any other part, just the cheese."

"The cheese is the whole thing," I argued. "Crust is expendable."

"Exactly."

I smiled and stirred my yogurt. It was coffee-chocolate

swirl with mochi and coconut, a combination that seemed very Jamie.

"Thanks for this, by the way," I said.

"It's apology yogurt," Jamie explained. "I should have told you about the other ghosts. The ones I got rid of. I swear to god, I tried that first day in your kitchen. Except Logan seemed so different, and I didn't want to scare you."

"That old lady we exorcised," I said. "Are the other ghosts you've seen like her?"

Jamie's mouth tightened.

"Worse," he said, reaching for my hand.

The electricity was back, flowing between us, and for the first time, I wondered if I wasn't making it up. If maybe we were connected by an invisible bond, like the ones we'd broken to exorcise that ghost. Or maybe it was the ghosts that were connecting us.

My sandal chose that moment to fall off and drop to the ground.

I sighed.

"Back in a sec," I promised, climbing down the rope ladder.

When I got to the ground, I stiffened, because we weren't alone.

"Logan," I said. "What are you doing here?"

My voice sounded fake and upbeat, exactly like Delia's had whenever she got caught bad-mouthing someone.

"Don't," Logan said coldly. "I overheard everything!"

Oh my god. This couldn't be happening. My heart sped up as I tried to remember everything Jamie and I had said.

"It's not what you think," I began, but Logan cut me off.

"No, it's worse," he insisted, floating up to the tree fort.

"Hey, buddy," Jamie said. I'd never heard him sound like that before. He sounded scared.

"I can't believe you," Logan accused. "You hooked up with my sister, and now you're getting rid of ghosts?"

"Logan, come down from there!" I shouted.

But Logan ignored me. He was in Jamie's face, hovering above the platform.

Jamie winced and took a step back.

"You ruined everything!" Logan accused. "I wish you'd never come!"

"Stop it!" I cried.

There was a cracking sound as the branches holding our tree fort started to break. One of the nails flew out, embedding itself in the dirt.

"Let's get down from here and talk about it, okay?" he asked.

Logan shook his head, hysterical.

"No, you're going to exorcise me!" he said, sobbing.

"I promise I'm not going to exorcise you," Jamie said.

Overhead, a tree branch snapped in half.

"Logan, please!" I cried. "You're going to hurt him!"

The platform cracked ominously.

"Good!" Logan sobbed, his whole body blurring.

Jamie took another step back, but there wasn't anywhere to go. His foot hit a branch, and he wobbled for a second, his arms pinwheeling.

There was a terrible thud as he hit the ground.

I must have screamed, because my ears were ringing, and it seemed too quiet all of a sudden.

"Jamie!" I cried, rushing over.

No, please, no.

I couldn't breathe. I felt like I'd gone back to the day when I'd found Logan's body, covered in beestings, already cold.

And then, miraculously, Jamie twitched.

"Ughhhh," he groaned.

My shoulders sagged with relief, and I didn't know whether to laugh or to cry.

"Jamie," I said. "I thought—I thought you were dead."

My voice sounded wrong, far too high, like it belonged to someone else.

Jamie winced. His face was pale, and there were leaves and bits of twig in his hair.

"So did I," he said, clearing his throat. He glanced around nervously. "Where's Logan?"

"Not here," I said.

"Good. Because the next time I see him . . ." Jamie sat up cautiously, then gasped, clutching his arm.

His shoulder was jutting out at an odd angle. It was too sharp, and all wrong.

242

"I think it's dislocated," he said, gritting his teeth.

"What do we do?" I asked.

"Google 'dislocated arm'?" Jamie suggested, his voice tight with pain.

I could do that. I reached into my back pocket and stopped. No phone.

"Um," I said. "Slight problem."

"Mine's in my car," he said.

I grabbed his key lanyard and ran. By the time I got back, carrying Jamie's schoolbag, he wasn't alone.

Nima's dad was helping Jamie to his feet. His running shirt was soaked through with sweat, and a pair of earbuds dangled around his neck.

"Hi, Mr. Shirazi," I said.

He insisted on giving Jamie a lift to the ER. I hovered uselessly as he helped Jamie into his car. Jamie's face was white with pain, and his arm hung limply at his side.

"Rose? You coming?" Mr. Shirazi asked.

"Um," I said, hesitating. I was still grounded, and my parents would be home any minute.

And then, as if I'd summoned her, I watched as my mom's car pulled into the driveway.

Crap. Jamie's Prius was still parked outside our house. My mom stared at it, and then shaded her eyes, squinting at us.

"Rose?" she called. "That you?"

Jamie let out a hiss of pain, clutching his arm.

"Yeah, Mom," I shouted back from Nima's driveway. I didn't know what to do.

"I'll see you tomorrow, okay?" Jamie said.

"Yeah, tomorrow," I promised, although it was possible my mom would kill me before then.

SHE VERY NEARLY did. Jamie had come over while I was grounded, and not only had I left the house, I'd been reckless. That was what she called it—"reckless"—which is a terrible word because it sounds as though nothing at all has been wrecked.

"You *know* that fort is old and unstable," she said, shaking her head. "What if he'd pulled you down when he fell?"

"But he *didn't*," I said.

"Rose, honestly. I have no idea what's going on with you these days," Mom said. "You used to tell me everything."

She was so wrong. I couldn't help it, I burst into tears.

"I'm sorry, okay?" I shouted. "I'm sorry I'm the worst one and you got stuck with me!"

And then I ran upstairs to my room, slamming the door and crying until I fell asleep.

23

"WHAT THE FUCK, dude?" Sam asked, gawking at Jamie's arm. It was immobilized in a sling, the kind that fastened around his waist for extra support.

I was carrying his lunch, and I laid it on the grass, watching as Jamie sat down clumsily. We hadn't gotten a moment to talk, and I'd naively thought that we'd have a chance at lunch. But clearly I'd thought wrong.

"Holy shit," Max said, looking up from his script. "Please tell me that's a prop."

"I broke the tree fort," Jamie lied. "I guess those things have an expiration date."

"It's all my fault," Claudia said, looking miserable. "I was the one who told you to go there."

Jamie shook his head. "That wood is ancient, and the nails were rusted through. You couldn't have known."

I felt even worse than Claudia, watching Jamie lie about what had happened. And watching Claudia blame herself for something that definitely wasn't her fault.

Abby joined us then, carrying a hot lunch.

"Oh my god, how long?" she gasped, peering at his arm.

"Three weeks," Jamie said. There was a bitter edge to his voice that I didn't understand. I couldn't figure out what I was missing.

"Gardner's never going to let you do the play like that," Abby went on.

Everyone stared at her, horrified.

"Like you weren't all thinking it," Max pointed out.

I hadn't been. But I certainly was now. I felt so awful that I wished I could disappear.

"Maybe Gardner will say it's okay," Jamie mumbled hopefully.

HE DIDN'T.

I fiddled with the costume rack, watching as Jamie pleaded with our drama teacher. But Gardner just shook his head, his expression grim. I watched as Jamie's face crumpled, as he fought a battle he would never win. And then I watched as Gardner pulled aside Seth Bostwick, giving him the role.

My friends were all frozen onstage, trying to pretend they weren't spying.

"Okay," Gardner said, clapping his hands. "We're going to run act two again, subbing in Seth."

Jamie didn't even stay to watch. He pushed out of there,

and I heard the stage door slam shut.

"Am I supposed to know the blocking?" Seth asked nervously.

Max let out a sigh.

"You're the one who begged to be an understudy," he accused.

I went to find Jamie.

He was sitting on the ground outside the door, looking miserable.

"Hey," I said, sliding down next to him.

"Gardner cut me," he said, marveling at it.

"I know," I said. "I'm really sorry. It got so out of hand yesterday, with Logan, and then you fell—"

"I didn't *fall*," Jamie said, sounding shocked that he had to spell it out. "Logan *broke* the platform."

"He didn't mean to," I said.

"Yes, he did," Jamie insisted. "He absolutely meant to hurt me. He even said so. I could have *died*. And now I'm stuck in this stupid sling, and Gardner kicked me out of the play, which is just *perfect*, because it was, like, the one thing I was really excited about."

Jamie shook his head, turning away.

"I'm sorry," I said, feeling like a broken record. "But at least, if you don't have rehearsal anymore, that means we'll have more time together."

"With Logan turning up every five seconds to threaten me."

"He won't," I promised.

Jamie scrubbed a hand through his hair and looked over at me, like he had something important to say. He bit his lip, briefly debating.

"I think we need to do something," he said, "about Logan."

"What?" I scoffed. "Like exorcise him?"

I meant it to sound ridiculous, but Jamie didn't deny it.

"No," I said, still convinced I'd misunderstood.

"He's not stable anymore," Jamie accused. "He *attacked* me, Rose."

"And your solution is to get rid of him? I can't believe you'd even suggest that!"

My throat was tight, and I could feel the tears welling up inside of me, hot and boiling.

"Gardner gave my part to *Seth Bostwick*," Jamie said, and I'd never heard him sound so bitter. "I have to get *physical therapy*, and my dad is freaking out about insurance premiums. My mom is on the other side of the world losing her shit. And now my *girlfriend* is defending the asshole who did this to me."

"I'm not defending him, I'm saying a shoulder injury and killing someone aren't the same thing."

"He's already *dead*, Rose!" Jamie fumed. "And you seriously need help if you can't accept that."

"Wow," I said, dripping sarcasm. "Tell me how you really feel."

"You should have tried out for the play," Jamie went on. "But you let him bully you into sitting at home. It sucks that he died, and I'm sorry, but he's ruining your life from beyond the fucking grave, and now he's ruined mine, too."

It was the worst thing anyone had ever said to me, a patchwork of half-truths that sounded even uglier as a group. And I couldn't believe Jamie was saying any of it.

"If you feel that way, then maybe we shouldn't be together," I whispered, feeling the tears well up.

"Maybe we shouldn't," Jamie said, his voice tight.

"Great." I climbed to my feet. It hurt to swallow, and I knew I was going to lose it any second and start sobbing. "So I guess we're done."

"Rose, come on," Jamie pleaded. "I can't watch you do this to yourself anymore."

"Then don't," I snapped. I was furious all of a sudden. Jamie had no right to say such terrible things about me or about Logan. And he'd made no move to apologize.

"He's going to hurt you," Jamie warned. "You can't tell him no. And why is that, Rose? Because you know, deep down, that he's dangerous."

"You're wrong," I said.

My chest hurt, and my throat was too tight, and my eyes were burning, and I wanted to scream and cry simultaneously. The bell wasn't going to ring for another fifteen minutes, but I didn't care.

I picked up my things and walked away from the theater.

The universe had warned me, on the first day of school, but I hadn't listened. I'd ignored all the good-hair days, thinking maybe I'd been wrong about them, but it turned out I'd been wrong about Jamie. The universe always expected payment, and this time, it was my heart.

MY MOM WAS at home, banging around the kitchen with a cookbook and an entire raw chicken, which couldn't be right.

She didn't even look up from her cutting board when I came in.

"Hi, honey," she said. "My root canal canceled, so I thought we could make coq au vin."

"Mom," I said. Cooking some ridiculous Julia Child recipe was the last thing I wanted to do right now.

"Rose," she said, matching my tone. "This isn't negotiable. Unless you have something more important going on that I should know about."

"As a matter of fact, I do," I snapped.

"Honey?" Mom said, finally realizing something was wrong.

"Jamie and I just broke up," I announced. "So please don't make me cook dinner."

And then I went up to my room and closed the door.

I curled up on my bed, hugging a pillow to my chest, unsure whether I wanted to sob into it or to scream.

24

MY MOM FORCED me to go to school the next morning. She even drove, letting me eat a Pop-Tart wrapped in a paper towel in the passenger seat. I told her I didn't want to talk about it, but she kept glancing at me, concerned, as though I should want to tell her everything.

Except I couldn't. Not unless I wanted her to think I'd gone crazy, raving about ghosts and exorcisms. So I told her to please, please just give me some space, or else I'd start crying and would have to go to school with a puffy strawberry face.

We pulled into the drop-off lane, along with all the underclassmen in their parents' minivans. And something occurred to me.

"Am I supposed to walk home?" I asked.

Mom scrunched her mouth to the side, as though it hadn't occurred to her.

"Can you get a ride with your friends?" she asked.

I looked at her like she was crazy.

"They have rehearsal," I reminded her.

"Maybe I can move my crown this afternoon," Mom said doubtfully.

"It's not that far, I'll just walk," I told her.

"Sorry," Mom said.

"It's whatever, I don't care," I said, and then I climbed out of her SUV, joining a sea of fourteen-year-olds who were hugging their algebra textbooks.

DARREN WAS WAITING for me in homeroom. He grinned when he saw me and flicked his hair out of his eyes.

"You won't believe who posted a butt selfie on Instagram," he told me.

His phone was already out.

"Darren—" I started.

"It's Nima's sister," he said gleefully, tilting the phone in my direction.

It was definitely a butt. With a lower-back tattoo of the Deathly Hallows symbol. And a black-and-white filter that wasn't succeeding at making it any classier.

"Nima's parents are freaking out," Darren went on. "It's amazing."

I managed a weak smile, and then I took out my precalc and pretended I had an exam, just so I wouldn't have to keep talking.

At lunch, I went back to my table in the library, the one

where Jamie had found me running lines all those weeks ago, after he'd chosen me as his partner in drama.

I hated that I was sitting there, staring at homework I'd already done, but joining my friends on the grass was totally out of the question. This was why I'd liked being invisible. Because my disasters were mine and mine alone. This breakup felt publicly catastrophic. I didn't want to be the train wreck that everyone was watching in real time, and I didn't want to see Jamie, his arm in a sling, watching Seth Bostwick stumble through the lines he'd already memorized.

I wished we'd never had that séance. That Jamie had never told me we could exorcise ghosts. But most of all, I wished that the tiny, perfect world I'd created could have gone on forever. A world where I hung out with Logan and Jamie after school.

Except nothing lasts forever. I knew that more than anyone, but how easily I'd forgotten. So I slid down in the hard plastic chair and watched everyone else, who didn't believe in ghosts, who had never encountered the dead, who didn't have to give up anything to play at being ordinary. I watched as they copied homework and snuck sandwiches out of their backpacks and scrolled through their phones. They were happy. Carefree. Normal.

I wondered what it was like.

WHEN THE BELL rang, I would have given anything not to go to art history. But I didn't have it in me to skip.

Of course Jamie got to the classroom before I did. I knew he would. I could picture him waiting there, his parka draped over the back of his chair—another thing no one else wore—his notebook and pen already out.

I'd gotten it exactly, and I hated that I knew him so well, that I could conjure him in my head like that.

"How was the library?" he asked.

I hated that he knew me, too.

"Fine," I said, sliding into my seat and taking out my notebook. I'd switched to pen sometime in the past few months, so it would match when we had to share a handout, and it looked so wrong on my desk now, this thing that you couldn't erase.

The bell rang, and still neither of us dared to say anything else.

The silence between us screamed.

"Rose—" Jamie began, but Mr. Ferrara started class then.

"You're going to be partnering up for the next few classes," he said, handing out instruction sheets. "And selecting two works of art that have symbolic or allegorical images. I want you to discuss how the works use these to convey meaning."

It sounded like nonsense. Like he was just making up words for the sake of teaching, not like those were actual instructions for an assignment.

"You can choose your partners now," he said.

I could feel Jamie straining for us to work together. But I knew that would be the worst idea ever. So I turned around and caught Preston's attention.

"Partners?" I asked.

"Sure," he said, shocked.

Jamie stared at me as though I'd betrayed him. I doubted he knew Preston had asked me to prom last year, but it was my theory of closed friend groups once again, how you're always supposed to pair up with the same people.

I switched seats with the tall red-haired boy who'd been sitting next to Preston, who became Jamie's de facto partner.

Up close, Preston had more acne than I remembered. He smelled faintly of fast food, and I realized that he'd gone off campus for lunch.

"This is unexpected." Preston raised his eyebrows. "You didn't want to work with your boyfriend?"

"Not today," I said.

Preston glanced down at the instructions sheet, his brow wrinkling.

"So, any ideas?" he asked helplessly.

"Me?" I said, surprised.

"I'm totally lost in this class," he confessed.

I resisted the urge to groan.

LOGAN WAS WAITING for me by the front door when I got home. Same shorts. Same hoodie. Same ridiculous socks with the hole in the toe. Everything had felt so off balance

255

in school that day. So ruined. But here Logan was, the same as always, waiting for me so we could hang out, just the two of us.

"Logan!" I said.

"You can see me?" He sounded overjoyed, which seemed strange.

"Of course. Why?" I asked.

"You couldn't the other day," he said. "I kept screaming your name, but you were in bed crying. Did Jamie do something? Is that why you were upset?"

I set down my bag with a sigh.

"Jamie's not coming over, is he?" Logan asked, his eyes narrowing.

"No," I confirmed. "We, um, aren't seeing each other anymore."

"Good," Logan said, grinning happily. "Now I get you all to myself."

Logan looked so glad to see me that I wondered if he knew how much I was hurting. But of course he didn't. Because he hadn't seen Jamie and me break up. Hadn't witnessed my lunch in the library or my shameful partner switch in art history.

"I feel like we should rewatch *Star Trek*," he said, and then amended, "The originals. I have no ulterior motive . . . other than exploring *space, the final frontier.*"

"Sounds good," I said, pasting on a smile. Because this was what I'd wanted, after all. Not just yesterday, but back in those first few months after I'd lost him.

One more day, just the two of us, just sitting around and watching TV in the living room after school, I'd wished.

Funny how wishes can twist into unrecognizable shapes when your back is turned.

25

WHEN I GOT to school on Monday, Claudia was standing next to the bike rack with two cups of fancy coffee from Bean & Bond. She was wearing a velvet coat and boots that laced up to her knees, and she looked impossibly cool.

"Rose," she said, smiling when she saw me.

I was a mess compared to her. My hair was scraped into a knot, and my leggings had a hole in the back of the knee, and there was a pimple on my chin.

"Hey." I bent down and U-locked my bike. "Is everyone ready for tech week?"

Claudia gave me a look.

"You owe me, like, fifteen texts," she said. "And an explanation. Jamie says *you* broke up with *him*?"

She handed me the coffee and I took a sip. Milk, no sugar, vanilla syrup. I was touched that she'd remembered.

"I didn't see your texts," I apologized. "My mom took my phone."

It wasn't an answer, and Claudia seemed to realize the same thing. But then, I couldn't exactly tell her the truth about why we'd broken up. Whatever I said would sound absurd and fake, because it would be a lie. And Claudia would know I was lying. She'd think I didn't trust her enough to tell her what had really happened, and the rift that had split me from Jamie would widen until I was cut off from everyone.

"It's—complicated," I told her.

"Well, you both look sick over it," she said. "You guys should talk. Work it out."

"I don't think we can," I confessed.

Claudia bit her lip, wishing I would just tell her. And I wanted to. I wanted to sit down on a bench and tell her everything, and have her fold me into a hug and tell me what I should do. But that could never, ever happen.

"Listen," she said. "Did something happen at the tree house? He wasn't pressuring you or anything. . . ."

"No." I shook my head. "Nothing like that."

"You can tell me, whatever it is," Claudia said. "Just so you know."

"Thanks," I said. "But I need some more time."

Wrong. It wasn't time I needed, it was a different love story. Before, when I was the only one who knew about Logan, the secret was contained. Manageable.

But I was starting to realize that sometimes, keeping a secret means losing the freedom to be yourself.

LOGAN WAS WAITING for me after school, hovering impatiently around the edge of the hiking trail. As I walked my bike down our street, he chattered about the cleaning lady, who had come that morning.

"I kept moving her bucket over," Logan said. "Whenever she wasn't looking. It drove her crazy."

"That's mean," I said, unlocking the front door.

I always felt like I had to tiptoe around after the cleaning lady came, like I was trying not to disturb a patch of unmarked snow. The house smelled of pine-scented cleaner, and the pillows on the sofa had been fluffed and placed in perfect rows.

"It was funny," Logan insisted. "She really freaked out toward the end. Crossed herself and everything."

"What did you do?" I asked suspiciously.

Logan shrugged.

"I maybe moved the mop."

"Logan!" I said. "If she quits, Mom will start up with the chore wheel again."

"Fine, okay," Logan said, pouting.

He flung himself onto the sofa, and I went into the kitchen to make a sandwich.

I watched as he scrolled through my Netflix queue.

"There's gelato in the freezer," he said without looking up. "Vanilla."

Ugh. Mom always chose the worst flavors.

I took a bowl of it anyway and brought my food over

to the living room. Logan turned on an episode of *Buffy*, grinning as he punched the buttons on the remote. I'd never really related to Cordelia before, but I understood her now. She was lonely and unsure, and learning that there were supernatural creatures in the world had ruined high school for her, splitting her off from her friends.

"One more?" Logan asked after the episode ended.

"Sure," I said, digging my art history packet out of my backpack.

I read the instructions for our group assignment, then started leafing through the textbook. Working with Preston was going to be a nightmare. He was the worst type of nerd—the kind who wasn't actually smart. I was going to have to do the whole assignment myself.

"Rose," Logan whined. "You're not watching."

"I'm listening," I promised. "I'm just doing homework."

"Do it later," Logan insisted.

"I can't," I snapped. "Because I have a lot *more* home-work, which I'm *already* putting off until later."

"One episode," Logan pleaded. "And then you can take out your homework."

I sighed.

"I can't. I already told you."

"You mean won't!" Logan accused. He was so angry that he was shaking. All of a sudden, his eyes were too big for his face, and his mouth was trembling, and he scared me, just a little bit.

The coffee table flipped over without warning. My meal

went flying, splattering the just-cleaned rug with orange juice and melted gelato.

"Logan!" I scolded, running to the kitchen for a roll of paper towels.

"I didn't mean to," he said, looking panicked. "I don't even know what happened!"

"It's fine," I said. "Accidents happen."

Logan hovered over my shoulder while I sopped up the mess. He kept repeating that it had been an accident, that he hadn't meant to. And I told him not to worry. I didn't tell him that I was already worried. That he'd lost control, just like he had at the tree fort. That, for a few seconds, I hadn't recognized him, and it had terrified me.

MY DAD BROUGHT home a pizza that night, so I knew my parents had been talking about me. That was how it worked: pizza always came with a cross-examination. Because when the universe provided something nice, it had to balance the scale somehow.

"You know you can tell us everything," Mom said over dinner.

It was almost exactly what Claudia had told me, and it made me feel twice as awful. Because I couldn't tell them anything. Not about Jamie or Logan. I'd been keeping my parents at arm's length for years, shielding them with a stitched-together blanket of half-truths and omissions. And I was starting to realize how much damage that had done.

So I mumbled something about how Jamie and I were better as friends, but I could tell they didn't quite believe me.

And then my mom put my phone down on the table.

"I think this punishment has gone on long enough," she said.

"Thanks," I said dully, reaching for it. Because of course I would finally get my phone back when there was no one I wanted to talk to.

"We might have changed all of the passwords," Dad admitted.

"To what?" I asked.

"'Make smart choices,'" Mom said, and I resisted the urge to groan.

AFTER DINNER, I turned on my phone, watching the old messages pop up, like a rerun of my former life.

Everything was broken now. Maybe it had been for a while, and I'd been the only one who hadn't noticed. Or maybe the brokenness was my fault. Logan had died of a beesting, and I'd gotten the ability to see ghosts, and it just wasn't fair, any of it.

But then, life had never promised to be fair.

Later that night, after I got out of the shower, I heard the TV on downstairs. I hoped it wasn't Logan.

As I came down the stairs, I realized it was a ball game.

"Hey," my dad said, glancing up at me. "Look who came to join her dear old dad."

"I couldn't stay away," I told him, sitting down.

Watching baseball was boring, no matter how much I tried to enjoy it. They kept pausing the game and replaying it, which made me want to scream at the announcers to just keep going.

After a while, a commercial break came on, and Dad fast-forwarded through. But then he paused.

"Kiddo, what happened?" he asked.

"Nothing," I said. "Jamie was too busy with the play. Honestly. I don't want to talk about it."

"You know," Dad said, "your mom never had problems fitting in at school. I was the nerd, and then you kids got it from me. Remember all of that *Star Trek* and *Doctor Who* we watched when you were little?"

I stared at him in surprise. I'd forgotten how it had started. But very faintly, I remembered all of us in matching pajamas on Christmas morning, watching the specials together.

"You kids were so into that stuff," he continued. "It was like you forgot the rest of the world existed. But I want you to promise me something, okay?"

I nodded.

"I don't want you to stop putting yourself out there just because it didn't work out with Jamie. You're wonderful, and smart, and beautiful, and the world is lucky to have you in it."

Dad winked at me and tapped a finger to the side of his nose.

And I wrapped my arms around him, breathing in the familiar scents of him: eyeglass cleaner and peppermint tea and aftershave.

"I love you," I said.

"Love you too, Rosebud," Dad said. "Now don't tell your mother I went and fixed everything. She probably has a self-help book all picked out for you."

26

AS IT TURNED out, Mom *did* have a self-help book for me. One that she'd secretly stashed in my backpack, and which I found during advisement the next morning. I read it in the library at lunch, trying not to snort as it suggested ways to improve communication with the opposite sex.

By the end of it, I wished I'd read her book about joyful sock folding instead. But at least it gave me something to do other than staring out the window at my friends, who were sprawled in the grass looking like the front page of a fall catalogue, laughing and joking.

That is, all of them except for Jamie, who was hunched over, his arm still in the sling, trying to read a novel one-handed.

LOGAN'S BIRTHDAY WAS that Saturday. He would have been twenty.

My dad didn't go into work, and the three of us smiled

thinly at one another over toast and coffee that morning, tiptoeing around a conversation, because we all knew what was coming.

A trip to Logan's grave.

I hated going. Hated seeing the gravestone, with the date of his death etched into it. Hated watching Mom press a hand over her mouth, her shoulders trembling. Hated watching Dad take off his glasses and pinch his nose. But most of all, I hated thinking, *He's not really gone*. Or, *I'll see him tomorrow*.

After we got home, I took the world's longest shower, as though it would rinse away the dust from Logan's grave. Except I could still feel the wrongness all over me, no matter how hard I scrubbed. I was out of Q-tips, so I went down the hall to steal one from my parents.

And that's when I saw the light on in Logan's room.

It was Mom.

She was sitting on his bed, staring at his dresser. The top drawer open and full of clothes. On her lap was that self-help book about how magical it is to tidy up.

"Mom?" I said, pausing in the doorway. I was still in my towel, and I could feel the water from my hair dripping down my back, making me shiver.

"Everything in here sparks joy," she said softly, half to herself. "Even after all these years."

She looked up at me, as though asking for my permission.

"I can't do it," she said. "I can't throw anything out."

"That's okay." I sat down next to her. "I don't think you need to. If you leave someone's Facebook page up, you can probably leave their sock drawer alone."

Mom laughed.

"When did you get so wise?" she asked me.

"It's one of my secret powers," I said.

Mom leaned over and folded me into a hug. We stayed like that for a while, my hair dripping onto Logan's old blue duvet, the two of us staring at his untouched room like it was another tombstone we didn't know what to do with.

PRESTON AND I got a B on our presentation in art history.

I expected more from you, Rose, Mr. Ferrara wrote on the top of our evaluation sheet.

It was Monday, and I was back in my assigned seat, next to Jamie, who had a big red A on his evaluation. He looked over at mine and made an apologetic face. But I didn't want his pity.

When the bell rang, Jamie took his time. Or maybe he was just slow packing up one-handed.

"Rose?" he said.

I was standing over my chair, putting my binder into my backpack.

I glanced up at him. At his hair, which really did need to be trimmed. At the glasses he was still wearing, with a small smudge on the left lens. At his button-down shirt, one of my favorites, with the little dots on it. At the canvas sling he was wearing over it, and the scrape on the side of his face, fading fast.

I miss you, I thought suddenly. *I miss you, and you're right here, and Logan is dead, and permanently fifteen, and a secret that's becoming harder and harder to keep.*

"What?" I said instead.

"A bunch of people are going to Duke's tonight," Jamie told me. "After tech rehearsal. If you want to come."

"Oh," I said.

"Claudia asked me to invite you, since she knew we have class together," he added, ruining the whole thing.

"I'm still grounded," I lied, and I'm not sure which of us was more relieved.

I DIDN'T WANT to go home, so I wound up biking over to Plaza Island, just to do something. I thought maybe I'd wander around the shops by myself, but then I remembered the public library was just across the street.

It had been a long time since I'd come here, since mostly I just used the website to check out e-books. But there was something reassuring about the burgundy carpet and the dusty smell of the library stacks.

The children's section was in the back, and I wound up there, running my fingers over the familiar spines of stories I'd checked out when I was a kid. Here was Narnia, and there was Hogwarts, and Camp Half-Blood, and Howl's Castle.

I kept going until I reached the children's nonfiction section. The books were slimmer than I remembered, and the print was much larger. But they were all still here. The ancient Egypt books.

I pulled out a stack of them and sat down with my back against the shelf, leafing through the familiar pictures of pyramids and pharaohs and papyrus scrolls. Except they reminded me too much of Jamie. Of our stupid fight over these books, and of our accidentally matching Halloween costumes, and of ringing each other's doorbells on Saturday mornings back in elementary school.

The books were still here, unchanged, ready to be checked out at any time. But we'd outgrown them now.

I was putting the books back when I spotted a familiar rolling backpack parked at one of the tables in the teen section. Sure enough, Kate was there, reading a stack of graphic novels with a blue-haired boy from our school's marching band. His instrument case was next to her backpack, bulky and oversized and somehow perfect.

She looked up and saw me.

I felt so self-conscious, standing there by myself in the children's section. But I took a deep breath and forced myself to smile and wave.

Kate looked surprised, but then she smiled and waved back. It was such a small thing, but it felt good. Right.

I was on my way out of the library when a display of books made me stop short. *Self-Help Starts Here!* a sign read.

Most of the books were my mom's greatest hits. But there was one book with a tag announcing *Just arrived!* that I hadn't seen before. It was about *hygge*, the magic of finding happiness in warmth, sharing, and coziness. The summary was all about how Denmark is the happiest country in the world, and everyone there is constantly drinking cocoa by candlelight and cuddling on a sofa.

I took it to the checkout and dug my ancient library card out of my wallet.

This was it. My chance to give Mom a self-help book. Because I was pretty sure this was the one she'd been searching for. The one that would convince her, once and for all, that it was okay to clean out Logan's sock drawer.

A FEW DAYS later, I got an email that my PSAT score was available online. Logan and I were sitting in the living room watching TV, and I told him I'd be right back.

I ran upstairs and closed the door to my bedroom, taking some deep breaths. *Whatever it is*, I told myself, *you'll be okay.*

I got out my laptop and logged in to the portal. For the few seconds it took the score to load, it felt like my heart was going to escape from my chest. And then, there it was, in black-and-white: 1400.

"Yes!" I said.

"What is that?" Logan asked, peering over my shoulder.

I hadn't realized he'd followed me.

"Rose?" Logan asked. "What *is* that?"

"It's my PSAT score," I said, relieved. I'd done well enough for most of the UC schools.

Logan had a strange look on his face.

"You're going away," he accused. "I knew it!"

"Logan," I said, "we have plenty of time."

But it was too late. He was livid, his eyes dark and terrifying, his mouth stretched wide and angry in his face. He didn't look like my brother anymore. He looked like a monster.

"YOU'RE GOING TO LEAVE ME HERE!" he screamed. "ALONE!"

My dresser drawers all flew open at once, the contents spraying out.

"Stop," I begged him.

My alarm clock rose off the table, its plug straining like a kite string. And then the plug came out of the wall, and the clock flew at my head.

I didn't duck. Maybe I didn't really believe it would hit me. It connected with my cheek, hard, and I yelped at the sudden burst of pain.

I stared disbelievingly at Logan, waiting for him to snap out of it. But all the clothes that were on the ground funneled into the air, creating a tornado. Logan rose up to the ceiling, howling. No, not Logan. His ghost.

"Get out," I snarled.

I didn't realize I was sobbing until the clothes dropped

to the ground and I was left all alone, a purple bruise rising on my cheek.

Of course my mom was horrified when she got home and saw me.

I felt awful that I couldn't tell her the truth. So I made up a lie that I'd done it backstage in Gardner's class.

"I was trying to get down a bolt of fabric. I didn't realize it was attached to a curtain rod."

My mom grabbed my chin, inspecting the bruise for the second time in as many minutes.

"I want you to keep icing it," she said. And then she went to the freezer and got out another bag of vegetables, because apparently the one I already had wasn't enough.

That night, as I lay in bed with my cheek throbbing, I couldn't deny it anymore: Jamie had been right about Logan. He wasn't holding me together anymore; he was holding me back. And it was time for both of us to let go.

27

THE PLAY WENT up on Friday. I put on about a million pounds of concealer, trying to hide my bruise, but it didn't really matter, because we were on assembly schedule.

Mrs. Yoon led us over to the theater to watch the performance. Even though I'd seen the programs before, I still flipped through mine, looking at all the smiling photos and reading everyone's bios. Sam's crowd never took them seriously, and this year was no exception. Max's bio read: *Call me, Edward Cullen, and we'll go for drinks.* But I lingered over Jamie's the longest:

Jamie Aldridge makes his Laguna Canyon High theater debut in his dream role of Grumpy Male Buffy. He regrets to inform you that the tagline of tonight's performance is not "someone's getting the wrong end of the stick."

The programs had been printed too early, and a little piece of paper had been stuck in, announcing that the role of Van Helsing would now be played by Seth Bostwick.

I stared down at that slip of paper, and at Jamie's bio, feeling terrible. It was all my fault. I knew that now. I'd refused to accept the truth about Logan, even after it had become impossible to ignore.

Jamie had lost his chance to do the play after he'd worked so hard for it. And then I'd broken up with him, because running away was easier than facing my problems head-on.

I wished I'd done so many things differently. I could feel Logan's bruise on my cheek, throbbing and painful, and I wondered how I could have ever thought his ghost was a figment of my imagination, because this wasn't at all how I would have imagined my brother.

The theater went dark, and the curtain opened, and the play began. I watched as Van Helsing recognized the marks on Lucy's neck as vampire bites. As he kept the information to himself, convinced no one else would believe in vampires or supernatural illnesses. I watched as things went from bad to worse, as Dracula grew younger and more powerful. I watched as Van Helsing killed Dracula, freeing him from his vampiric illness. And I watched as, at the end of the play, everyone tried to go back to life as usual but found themselves haunted by the knowledge of the supernatural. In the last moment, Seth, as Van Helsing, stepped forward, urging the audience to remain vigilant for evil in the world around us, and to be ready to defeat it.

He dropped a line in the middle, and I saw him wince, stumbling to get back into character. It had never been more obvious than in that moment that it was supposed to be Jamie up there, not Seth. And it had nothing to do with flubbed lines. Jamie could have made as many mistakes as Seth did, or more, not that it was possible. Seth was playing a role that he didn't fit, and I knew all too well what that was like.

I'd done it back in middle school, when I'd become part of Delia's clique. I'd done it for the past few years, hanging around the edges of the school plays without ever pitching myself into the heart of them. And I was doing it now, because I was too scared to go back to the people I cared about and say the words out loud.

But not for much longer.

THERE WAS ANOTHER performance that evening. And afterward, the cast and crew party. I hadn't been planning to go, since it was at Abby's house. But now I realized I had to.

Because I had to see a boy about a ghost.

My parents weren't exactly thrilled that I wanted to borrow a car to drive to the cast party, but Dad stuck up for me.

"Julie, we should let her go see her friends," he said, winking.

"Really?" I stared at him, shocked. "Thank you. Thank you thank you thank you."

"Just one thing—" Dad said.

"I know, I know. Watch out for poles," I said.

"I was going to say, have fun," Dad said. "But now that you mention it . . ."

I groaned and grabbed the keys.

Abby lived in the mansions down by the pier, and her house was ridiculous. It was all glass, with one of those modern staircases that seemed to float in midair. When she flung open the front door, she was wearing a tight gold dress and her stage makeup.

"Rose!" she squealed, throwing her arms around me. "Ohmygosh, you came! Everyone's going to be thrilled. We've missed hanging out with you!"

She leaned in.

"Can you tell I'm drunk?" she asked.

"Not at all," I promised, although I probably wasn't the best judge. "Your house is amazing."

"My dad's a plastic surgeon," she said, a little too loudly. "So my nose was free."

She stared at me, clearly waiting for me to say something.

"It looks awesome," I told her, and she beamed.

"Totally natural, right? I was paranoid people would be able to tell, and I'd be 'that girl who got a nose job.'"

"I promise, no one even noticed," I said.

She led me through endless white hallways with marble floors, past a few pieces of art that probably weren't prints, and into an enormous yard that seemed to stretch on forever.

This definitely wasn't a kickback. It was a real party, messy and loud and full of people. There was a grill area covered with booze and a pool chair stacked with pizza boxes. Most of our drama class was already there, along with a surprisingly large crowd of kids I recognized from school.

I spotted Adam from my art history class playing flip cup with some guys from the Mock Trial team, and a bunch of beanie-wearing jocks clustered furtively around a vape pen.

Leo was DJing some kind of retro hip-hop. He was still wearing the lab coat from his costume, which he'd unbuttoned over an Adidas tracksuit. He bent over his equipment, totally blissed out as the Renaissance Faire girls danced nearby, trying to catch his attention.

"Holy shit," I said, and Abby laughed.

"My parents couldn't make it to the play." She rolled her eyes. "So this is how they made up for it. Enjoy."

Suddenly, Abby was gone. And I was alone. In the middle of a genuine house party. Except I didn't feel self-conscious, or nervous, or like I didn't belong. Instead, I knew exactly what I needed to do.

I turned around and bumped into Claudia. She was still wearing her stage makeup, her hair teased into an old-fashioned updo. But she'd changed into her own clothes. She looked ridiculous, and I knew it didn't bother her in the slightest.

"Claudia!" I said.

"Rose, you came," she said, sounding surprised. But she wrapped me into a hug anyway, and I found myself hugging back, hard.

"You were great," I told her. "The play was amazing."

"I flubbed a line," she said. "In the scene with the blood transfusion."

"I couldn't tell," I promised.

"You're just saying that." Claudia sighed. "Also, can we all please agree that Abby was terrible and one-note?"

"I kind of like Abby now?" I said. It came out as a question.

"Ugh, I do too." Claudia made a face. "I wish Jamie had gotten to do the play. He would have been way better than Seth, even wearing a sling. This morning, in the third act? I swear to god, it was like watching Kramer kill Dracula."

I couldn't help it, I snorted.

"Can you and Jamie please make up already?" Claudia pressed. "Or can you just sit with us again anyway?"

"I will," I promised. "But I want to fix things with Jamie first. Have you seen him?"

I twisted around, looking for him.

"He's not here," Claudia said.

My face fell.

"He's not here," I repeated in disbelief.

"Well, it *is* the cast party," Claudia said. "I don't really blame him for bailing."

"Oh," I said, feeling like an idiot, because if I'd thought about it for two seconds, I would have realized Jamie had stayed home.

"Look who I found!" Claudia said, beaming. For a moment, I thought she meant Sam, but then I realized she was talking about me.

"The Queen of the Costumes returns!" Sam said,

wrapping me in a hug. He smelled like dried sweat, and his neck was streaked with stage makeup, but I didn't mind at all. I'd missed him.

"Everyone's on the tennis courts," Claudia said.

"There are *tennis courts*?" I asked, impressed.

"Just one," Sam said, grabbing a couple of beers. He offered one to me, and I shook my head.

"No thanks," I said. "They taste like if the ocean could sweat."

Claudia threw her head back and cackled, making a scene.

"Oh my god! Yes! Armpit Sweat of the Sea," she announced.

Sam glared.

"You better not call me that," he warned.

"I'll get bored of it soon," Claudia assured him.

"But *I* won't," I said, smiling sweetly.

Sam let out a frustrated growl.

"You two are deadly together, you know that?" he asked.

"We are well aware." Claudia slung her arm around my shoulder, and Sam held open a chain-link gate.

Sure enough, there was a tennis court back here, green and white, with a net flapping in the ocean breeze. Nima, Max, and Darren were seated in one of the squares, passing a bag of barbeque chips back and forth. Judging from the empty cans, they'd already gone through a couple of beers each.

Max was wearing his Dracula cape, and it flapped behind him, looking polyester and fake now that there was no stage magic to transform it.

"We're friends with Abby Shah now," he announced, a little too loudly. "It's a thing that happened."

"I like Abby," I said, because it was true. There were layers to her, and the more of them I peeled away, the more I realized she was just as insecure and weird as the rest of us.

"God help me, I like her, too," Darren said.

"Everyone likes Abby," Nima said happily. "And next year, she's promised to run for spirit chair, so I don't have to."

Claudia groaned.

"You mean to tell me," she said, "that we have to look forward to *another* year of pretending to be psyched to spin the spirit wheel?"

Everyone laughed, and I sat down, realizing that Jamie may have guided me back here, but this was where I belonged.

28

I RODE MY bike over to Jamie's house early the next morning. Jamie's dad opened the front door. He was dressed for the gym, or maybe jogging, in a matching tracksuit that was accidentally cool.

"Rosie!" he said.

I hadn't seen him in years. His hair was thinner and more gray than blond, and a pair of wire-framed glasses was sliding down his nose. Even in track pants, he still looked like a rumpled professor. He also looked nothing like Jamie.

"Hi, Mr. Aldridge," I said.

We stared at each other, and I wondered what, if anything, Jamie had told him about us.

"I'll let Jamie know he has a visitor," he said.

Before he could, Jamie appeared in the hallway, looking surprised to see me.

"I've got it, Dad," Jamie said.

He tilted slightly to the side, as though he was studying me, and he frowned. Even though the bruise on my cheek was covered with makeup, I knew he still noticed it.

"Um, hi," I said awkwardly. "You busy right now?"

"Let me grab my keys," he said, and then hesitated.

I knew that pause. That hundred-questions silence. That holdback he did. It made my entire chest ache with the weight of all those unsaid words.

He returned a minute later, wearing the loafers I'd noticed on the first day of school, so distinct amid a sea of sandals and sneakers.

I stared down at them, and Jamie made a face, as though he could read my mind.

"Sam gave me shit for them too, but they don't have laces," he said.

"Oh," I said, feeling awful. "Right."

"Dad, we're leaving," he called.

Without waiting for an answer, he shut the door behind us.

"We don't have to go anywhere," he said, holding up his keys. "I just—I thought—so we could have privacy."

"No, it's perfect," I said, hating that he was so nervous around me, and that I'd made him so unsure of what I wanted.

I smiled, and Jamie relaxed a little. I could feel the electricity flowing between us, tentative at first and then stronger.

His car had been parked outside overnight and was covered in droplets of moisture. Climbing inside was like ducking into a freezing cave. If a freezing cave smelled like stale coffee and was full of library books.

"Sorry," Jamie said, reaching for the heater. "Give me a minute."

He glanced sideways at me, and it killed me, seeing how much I'd hurt him.

"Rose—" he began.

"No, me first," I said, cutting him off. "I'm so sorry. I never should have reacted like that when you said we should exorcise Logan."

"I'm not taking it back," Jamie said. "I just want that to be clear. I still think . . ."

"I know," I said. "So do I."

Jamie stared at me, surprised. I could see him wondering what had changed.

"He hurt you, didn't he?" Jamie said. It wasn't a question. Slowly and carefully, he reached for my cheek, inspecting the bruise.

"It was an alarm clock," I said, and Jamie winced. "He freaked out when he saw me checking my PSAT score. Which was awesome, by the way."

"Now who's always trying to change the subject to the PSAT?" Jamie teased.

"Still you," I accused. "Nerd."

Jamie shook his head, smiling.

"I'm not the one who eats lunch in the library," he shot back.

"At least I don't wear loafers without socks," I returned.

"It's a look," Jamie insisted.

"There were at least fifty people at the cast party last night and not a single one of them was wearing it," I informed him.

"You went to the cast party?" Jamie frowned. "Why?"

Wasn't it obvious?

"I was looking for you," I said.

"I didn't really feel like partying," he said.

"You would have loved it. No one could shut up about how Seth made a lousy Van Helsing."

"Really?" he asked, brightening.

"Definitely," I promised. "You make a far more believable . . . old man."

"And here I thought you were going to say vampire slayer." Jamie grinned.

"Whatever, there's no such thing as vampires."

"Bet you twenty bucks there are some high school students on the other side of the country saying the exact same thing about ghosts," Jamie joked, raising an eyebrow.

"I miss you so much," I said, before I could think about it. "I miss hanging out with you, and talking to you and—"

"Cleo?" Jamie said.

"Yeah?"

"Me too," he said, and then he kissed me.

It was soft and tentative, a question mark of a kiss, asking, *Can I? Can we?* And then I kissed him back, and it wasn't a question anymore, it was a definitive *yes, oh please, yes.*

When we broke apart, I rested my forehead against

Jamie's for a moment, so we could stay connected just a little longer.

"Um," he said nervously. "Not that this isn't amazing. Which it is. But your brother isn't going to show up and . . ."

"No," I promised. "At least, he better not."

It hit me all of a sudden how wonderful it was, to be alone with Jamie. To be sixteen together and growing older the same amount each day. To have so much history behind us and so much future ahead. There would be parties and movie nights and road trips and plays, and I could have all of those things. I just couldn't have Logan, too.

"What are you thinking?" Jamie asked. He was tracing circles over my palm, slow and deliberate, as though drawing an invisible lifeline of us.

"That it's going to be okay," I said.

Jamie's face broke into a grin.

"Who ever heard of a ghost story with a happy ending?" he teased.

"This isn't a ghost story," I told him. "It's a love story with a ghost in it."

And then I thought: *But not for much longer.*

29

I WAS LATER than I realized coming home. When I opened the front door, my mom was in the living room, curled up with a mug of coffee and a book.

"Morning," she said. "I thought you were still asleep."

"Nope, that's my stunt double. There have been two of us this whole time," I joked, and then apologized, "Sorry I didn't text."

"I'll let it slide," Mom said. "Since if you're up this early, at least I know you're not hungover."

My jaw dropped, and Mom laughed.

"Make smart choices," she reminded me, and I somehow resisted the urge to roll my eyes.

"What are you reading?" I asked.

Mom held up the book. It was the one I'd gotten from the library and left on her bedside table. The *hygge* book.

"Good book?" I asked innocently.

"I'm really enjoying it," Mom said. "You know, it's so easy to forget to treat yourself. But deciding that a blanket gives you joy isn't the same thing as actually *feeling* joy every time you use it."

"Mom, seriously, I'm glad you like the book, but enough with the self-help already," I insisted, sitting down next to her on the couch. "You don't need a stranger telling you how to live your life, one size fits all."

I reached for her coffee and took a sip.

"Ew," I said, making a face. "Is there cinnamon in this?"

"I figured I'd try something new," Mom said. She shifted a little on the sofa and sighed. "Although these throw pillows have got to go. I don't know what I was thinking with all of these sequins. We need something cozier."

"Really?" I asked hopefully.

"Don't tell your father, he'll be thrilled," Mom said with a wry smile. "Which means we'll have to find another way to torture him so he doesn't sit here all night watching baseball."

"Is that what the pillows were about?" I asked.

Mom's guilty expression was all the answer I needed.

"If you're changing the pillows, I think this room would look great in different shades of blue," I went on. "With a fish tank in the corner, there."

"A fish tank?"

"Little fish," I said. "Practice koi."

Mom lit up at the idea.

"We could have a mother-daughter redecorating project," she said. "Breathe some life into this space before you go off to college."

It felt so natural, her saying that, in a way it never had before. And so inevitable. I was leaving. Not tomorrow, or next month, but soon enough.

We stared out at the living room, imagining how it could change. A fish tank here, a throw blanket there. And I realized that, in the four and a half years since Logan's death, my parents hadn't shut out what had happened. They'd simply found ways to move forward in spite of it.

And maybe that was why ghosts were invisible, or why they were supposed to be: so they didn't cast a shadow over the people they'd left behind.

"You seem happy today," Mom said, breaking the silence.

"I am," I said. And for the first time, I really meant it.

"Is Jamie coming by later?" she asked, too clever by half.

"Mom," I complained.

"I'll order pizza," she threatened.

"You better not!" I told her. "I know how you operate."

"Well, you might," Mom said, laughing. "But Jamie doesn't."

LOGAN STAYED AWAY for the rest of the weekend, and by the time Monday morning rolled around, I had the impression that he was purposefully giving me space.

Mom had already left for work, and Dad was pouring his coffee into a travel mug when there was a knock at the front door.

"If it's Girl Scout cookies, buy five boxes of Thin Mints and don't tell your mother," Dad advised.

I laughed.

"Deal," I promised.

It wasn't Girl Scouts. It was Jamie. He was wearing his glasses, and his hair was still wet from the shower, making little droplets on his sling. I started thinking some very non–7:30 a.m. thoughts.

"You do realize it's a school day," I told him.

"Well, if you don't want a ride . . ." he said, grinning.

"I'm completely out of the way," I protested. "I can't believe you drove here just to drive back down again."

"One handed," Jamie boasted. "At least, for another week. You ready to go?"

I grabbed my schoolbag and told my dad I was heading out.

"Thin Mints?" he asked.

"Sorry." I shook my head. "They have an app now that tells you where to buy cookies."

Dad stared at me as though I'd revealed one of the secrets of the universe.

"Can I get it on my iPad?" he asked, and I tried not to laugh.

"I DEFINITELY DON'T miss having helmet hair," I told Jamie as we pulled into the school parking lot.

"You're not nervous what will happen if you have a good-hair day?" Jamie teased.

"Eh, someone told me that was a spurious correlation."

I tried to keep a straight face.

"You don't say." Jamie frowned. "Next thing you know prophesneezes will be debunked."

"Never."

"Well, if you don't mind chancing it, then I can drive you every day," Jamie promised. "But advance warning that I'm trying out for the spring play."

"Good, 'cause I am too," I said.

Jamie stared at me in surprise.

"Really?" he asked.

"You guys *have* to stop hanging out without me," I said. "I can't handle all of the inside jokes."

"Technically, if you're not there, that makes them outside jokes," he said.

"Oh my god," I said. "No."

"You're welcome." Jamie grinned.

The song we were listening to ended, and some familiar bars came through the speakers.

"Hold on," I said, narrowing my eyes at the little cable I'd thought was a charger. "This is *Hamilton*. Since when do *you* like show tunes?"

Jamie looked guilty.

"Claudia maybe got me into it," he admitted. "What? I didn't know it was about the American Revolution! They actually rap about the constitution! I wish my History Day team had thought of that."

"History nerd," I teased.

"Theater geek," he shot back.

◄◄━►►

OF COURSE OUR friends were overjoyed when I joined them at lunch, sitting down on the little slope of grass and taking a bagel out of my backpack. Jamie sat next to me, and everyone stared at the two of us. For a moment, no one said anything. And then Darren pantomimed applause.

"Next time you guys fight, Jamie's the one who has to leave," Sam announced, grinning.

"I still think we all should have moved into the library," Claudia said.

"That close to all of those books?" Max shuddered. "I often think hell must be some kind of school library."

We all laughed.

I watched as Jamie struggled to unzip his parka one-handed. He kicked off his loafers, even though it was, like, sixty degrees out, and tilted his face toward the sun.

"Can someone tell NorCal that we actually *do* have seasons down here?" Sam joked.

"'In the depths of winter, I found within me an invincible summer,'" Jamie shot back.

"That's Albert Camus," Abby said, and we all stared at her in shock. "What? I totally have that quote on my Pinterest."

JAMIE DROVE ME home from school that day, and when I asked if he wanted to come in, he shook his head.

"You should spend some time with Logan," he told me.

I promised I would, and then I went into the living room

and turned on an old episode of *Doctor Who*.

Logan showed up halfway through the opening credits.

"You're home early," he said.

"Got a ride."

"From Jamie." It wasn't a question.

I glanced over at Logan. He was upset, but trying to stay calm.

"He's not going away," I said. "And I don't want him to."

I needed Logan to understand. The two of us had spent so long together in our private version of Narnia. But I'd grown up, and I couldn't stay here much longer. And that's the part the children's stories never tell you. They never explain that it's okay to let go of things you once needed and find others to take their place.

Logan sighed.

"I get it," he muttered. "He's the Harry Potter to your Ginny Weasley."

"Wait," I said. "How am I Ginny?"

Logan shrugged, grinning.

"No, you have to tell me," I insisted. "How am I *Ginny*?"

Logan just shook his head and unpaused the TV.

We sat back and watched the episode, and he laughed at all the jokes he already knew, not because they were funny, but because they were familiar. I stayed quiet, because I kept finding far too many familiar things here, hidden in this show I'd seen a million times.

There were memories tucked between the scenes, and

I didn't realize I'd put them there. Memories of my older brother tapping on my door on Saturday mornings, before our parents were awake. Memories of us sneaking down to the living room in our matching footy pajamas, pretending we had the house to ourselves. Of Mom bringing us waffles on plastic plates. Of Dad popping his head in, pointing his teaspoon in our direction, and yelling "Exterminate!" in his terrible Dalek voice.

I remembered wishing that we really *did* live in a world like the one on our screen. A world where an oddly dressed time traveler would show up in the backyard, promising adventures, and staying the same age as I grew older. That my magical companion would be there whenever I needed it, offering me a chance to escape the real world and explore somewhere wonderful.

Except Logan wasn't a time lord with a magical spaceship. He was a ghost, and had been for years, and as long as I hung around with him, I was stuck in my own rerun instead of having new adventures with new companions.

Jamie was my new companion. My new adventure. It just hadn't started yet.

The show was almost over, but I couldn't wait any longer.

"Hey, Logan? Can I ask you something?"

Logan's eyes stayed glued to the TV.

"Uh-huh."

"Why did you come back?"

Logan turned toward me in surprise, and I realized I'd

never asked him this. Not once.

There was a long stretch of silence.

"Mom and Dad told us to watch out for each other," he said. I thought he wasn't going to say anything else, but then he added, "And then I messed it up and ruined everything."

"What are you talking about?" I asked, confused. If anything, I'd been the one to mess it up.

"That day you ran out to the preserve," Logan went on. "You were so upset about the play, and I should have gone after you right away. But I'd just started watching a new episode, and I didn't want to pause it. So I waited until it was over to come find you."

I stared at him in surprise.

"I thought you were waiting for me to come back on my own," I said.

Logan shook his head, looking ashamed of himself.

"I was on the sofa watching TV," he admitted. "And then I realized Mom and Dad would kill me if anything happened to you, so I ran out there to make sure you were okay. And I was too lazy to go upstairs and grab my EpiPen, even though Rule Number One of having a life-threatening allergy is Always Remember Your EpiPen. So."

Logan shrugged, leaning back on the sofa, despite the presence of a particularly spiky throw pillow. I sat there processing what he'd just said, because it was so different from how I remembered that day.

"But I said you had no friends," I sputtered. "I was an unforgivable brat."

"You were twelve," Logan reminded me. "I was fifteen. That's old enough not to lose it over a stupid insult. And old enough to remember a fucking EpiPen."

I closed my eyes and took a deep breath, realizing Logan was right. I'd always blamed myself for how he'd died. But he was the one who'd gone out into the preserve without his meds. He hadn't died of a beesting; he'd died because he'd forgotten to bring the antidote. And that wasn't even a little bit my fault.

When I opened my eyes, Logan was peering at me, looking concerned.

"Rose, say something," he said.

"You're such a dumbass," I told him.

"And you're such a bummer," Logan shot back. "'Woe is me, the mean theater lady wouldn't cast me in the play, now I can never act again.'"

"Shut up!" I said, threatening him with a throw pillow.

I meant it as a joke, but Logan's eyes went dark, and his face contorted, and the coffee table flipped onto its side.

Logan stared at it, horrified, his eyes returning to normal.

"I keep losing control," he said, his voice small. "I don't know why."

"It's because I grew up," I said. "I'm sure of it. You can't keep being a big brother if I'm the older sibling."

"This mess started when Jamie turned up," Logan accused.

"No, it didn't," I pointed out. "That's a spurious correlation."

"A what?"

"Nothing," I said, shaking my head. "It's not important."

I fixed the coffee table while Logan hovered, embarrassed.

"Are you guys going to exorcise me?" Logan blurted.

I bit my lip, hating that he'd guessed.

"Only if you want us to," I promised.

"You're going away to college, aren't you?" Logan mumbled, half to himself.

"That's the plan," I said. "Oh, and I'm trying out for the play next semester. Plus a bunch of us might take that SAT course Max did at the university."

"So we're running out of time," Logan said. "Either I go, or you leave me behind."

I nodded, facing the truth of it head-on. I owed Logan at least that much.

"I think it's better if I go," he said.

I let out a breath I didn't know I'd been holding.

"Okay," I said. "We can do that."

"We should do it soon," Logan said. "Before I go all Hulk on you again. Because it might not be the coffee table next time."

"It's a deal," I promised.

"There's just one thing," Logan said, his voice small. "I want to see Mom and Dad one last time."

I DON'T KNOW how Logan managed to do it, but he stuck around all afternoon, until our parents got home from work. Dad had picked up Chinese food again and was stubbornly trying to make Mom use chopsticks.

"Not this again," I groaned, shaking my head.

Logan hovered near the stove, watching. I expected him to pipe up with some comment, distracting me, but he stayed out of it. I glanced over at him a few times, expecting an eye roll or a snarky comment, but he pretended not to notice.

"Roger," Mom said, laughing, "you know I'm terrible with these."

"You just need practice," Dad insisted, setting them on her place mat.

Mom frowned.

"How about this," I bargained. "You try the chopsticks for five minutes, and then you can have a fork."

Everyone stared at me in surprise.

"How did you get so clever?" Dad asked as Mom doubtfully picked up the chopsticks.

"It's all that TV I watch," I said, and Logan snorted.

We dished out the egg rolls and rice, and Mom made good on our bargain, trying to use the chopsticks. Dad and I watched, laughing, as she struggled to pick up the egg roll.

"I heard someone came by the house this morning to give

you a ride," she said, stabbing a single chopstick through her egg roll and eating it like a skewer.

"Dad!" I accused.

He shrugged guiltily.

"Only for the rest of the semester," I said. "Since he won't have to stay late for rehearsal. Although I was thinking maybe I could try out for the spring play."

"That's wonderful!" Mom said. "I used to love seeing you in all of those plays when you were little. You and Claudia, with those adorable braids in your hair."

"I'm sure we have photos somewhere," Dad said.

"You made the cutest pirate," Mom went on, beaming.

"Stop, I haven't even auditioned yet," I said, making a face.

But my parents were smiling at each other across the dinner table, and for once, it wasn't because I'd lied and said what they wanted to hear. It was because I'd told them the truth.

I glanced over at Logan's empty chair and then at where he was hovering in the doorway, watching us. He nodded, happy. And I realized I didn't have to be enough to fill both of our chairs. I just had to be me. And that was all anyone had ever asked for.

30

THAT WEEKEND, I said good-bye to Logan in his bedroom.

It seemed right, somehow. In all the times Logan had turned up after school, sprawling onto the sofa, or across the foot of my bed, I'd never once seen him there.

Jamie came, because I wasn't sure I could do it alone, and because he said I shouldn't have to.

"You're sure it's okay Jamie's here?" I asked Logan for what had to be the fifth time. Logan sighed.

"Well I don't want you messing it up and splinching me in half," he shot back.

"I'd never do that!"

"You backed Dad's car into a pole," he pointed out.

"One time!" I insisted. "It was the one time! And there's a super-creepy ghost in that parking lot!"

Jamie coughed, looking guilty.

"You didn't!" I accused.

"He wanted to move on," Jamie said. "And besides, I couldn't take it anymore. I had to pick up groceries."

"Oh my god, I hate you guys." Logan sulked. "How can you talk about Trader Joe's at a time like this?"

"You started it," I pointed out. "And besides, we can always do this tomorrow."

"No way," Logan said. "Tomorrow's a full moon!"

He looked so horrified that I couldn't help it—I started laughing.

"You don't honestly still believe in that stuff?" I asked. "You're dead."

"Exactly! That's gotta be bad luck!" Logan said.

"He has a point," Jamie said, adjusting his sling. "Everyone ready?"

Logan stood very still, squeezing his eyes shut, like we were about to inject him with an EpiPen.

"I'm afraid it's going to hurt," he said, his voice small.

"Nothing's even going to touch you," I said.

"Not the exorcising part," Logan explained. "The saying good-bye."

"I'll give you a minute," Jamie said, closing the door behind him.

Logan opened his eyes and grinned, dropping the act.

"You did that on purpose," I accused.

"Well, yeah," he said. "But now we get some alone time, so I can impart my great wisdom."

I snorted.

"You're fifteen," I said. "How much wisdom can you possibly have?"

"Depends. How many *Buffy* quotes do you have time for?"

"One," I said firmly. "So choose wisely."

Logan nodded, taking a moment to think.

"Got it," he said. "'The hardest thing in this world is to live in it. Be brave. Live. For me.'"

"That's one of my favorites," I said. "I'll remember it."

"You better," Logan said. "And you'll have to remember to set a timer from now on, because I won't be around to tell you when the cookies are done."

"You don't," I complained. "You only tell me after they're already burning."

"And Rose?"

"Yeah?"

"Take care of Mom and Dad, okay?"

I pretty much lost it at this point.

"I promise," I said, feeling a tear slide down my cheek.

"And go somewhere really great for college. Even if it's five thousand miles away," he insisted. "And make friends, and go to parties, and see the world."

I nodded.

"And when you're alone in your room, and no one is around, pretend I'm there and tell me about all of it."

"I will," I promised, sniffling.

"Okay, I think you can get Jamie now," Logan said.

I went out into the hall, and Jamie wrapped his good arm around my shoulder, and together we walked back into Logan's room.

Jamie opened the window, and the chatter of little kids playing in the next yard drifted in, along with a blast of cold air. Summer was long gone, and the Santa Ana winds had finally made their retreat.

"So, Logan," Jamie said. "Tell me about your favorite memory."

"That time I made you fall out of a tree." Logan grinned, floating upward.

"Can you please take this seriously?" I asked.

"Jeez, okay." Logan went quiet a moment, thinking. "Um, I guess it's when I was twelve, and Rose was eight. It was Christmas break, and we woke up early one morning to watch the *Doctor Who* special. And Rose complained that it never snows here, so we covered the entire living room with powdered sugar to pretend that it had."

I'd completely forgotten about that. But it all came rushing back to me. The way Logan had yanked the blankets off my bed because he knew it was the only way I'd get up while it was still dark outside. How he'd stubbed his toe as we ran down the stairs. His terrible bedhead. The embarrassing decorations Mom used to put up, paper dreidels I'd scribbled on in preschool, the menorah made out of Logan's tiny handprints.

"Logan, keep going," Jamie said. "This is great."

"Okay," Logan said, "um, we made snow angels on the carpet. Mom came down to see what was going on and had a fit about the mess. There was sugar in our hair for days, and one of those guys had to come out with a giant carpet vacuum. He asked what had happened, and when Rose told him we made it snow sugar, he laughed like he was crying."

I closed my eyes, listening to Logan tell the story. And when I opened them again, Jamie and I were watching from a distance as the three of us stood in Logan's old bedroom.

"Count of three, we're in the living room on Christmas morning," Jamie whispered.

I counted down, and suddenly everything shifted. There I was, watching a tiny me and a tiny Logan making snow angels in our matching pajamas.

I watched as we reached into the bag, throwing handfuls of sugar into the air. Logan picked me up and swung me around, laughing. I was so much smaller than him. So much younger. His hair was dusted with white powder, and the rubber bands in his braces were neon blue, and he was so vividly alive.

Logan was stuck more tightly to this place than I could have imagined. There were so many layers, so many years of things that bonded him here, to this house, this room. And to me.

I hadn't realized how tightly he was bonded to me.

I could feel the places where some of the bonds had come loose, where I had begun to sever our connection. I just hadn't done it all the way. I'd been afraid Jamie was the reason I hadn't been able to see Logan sometimes, but he wasn't.

It was so many things: My first kiss. Falling in love. Experiencing the pain of a broken heart. I'd grown up. I'd become someone who didn't need to be looked out for, because I could look out for myself.

Gradually, Logan began to come unstuck. And I felt myself coming unstuck as well.

"Rose," Jamie whispered. "Look."

I opened my eyes.

Logan had become soft around the edges and was fading fast.

"Good-bye, Rose," he said.

"Logan—" I choked.

But he was gone. And all that responded was the particular emptiness of a bedroom no one has slept in for years. Only moments before, a vital part of me had been here, but Logan's ghost had disappeared without a trace. I stared at the wall as though it might contain one last message, some final piece of my brother. But it was just paint and sunlight and emptiness.

"No," I cried, sliding down to the floor. "No."

This couldn't be it. Except it was. Logan was no longer a part of this world. I'd known that for a long time, but this was the first moment I truly felt it.

Suddenly, I understood why people lit candles on the

High Holy Days. Why they stayed behind in synagogue to recite silent prayers that were only for mourners. Why they visited graves on cold November nights. It wasn't because we needed tangible things to find our way back to the ones we'd lost. It was because the dead were invisible, and it was up to us to mark the places they'd left behind.

I felt Jamie's hand on my back, soft and warm. And I realized that the connection I felt between us, the electricity, was real. It was what Logan had meant about the universe not being able to tear us apart. Because we'd torn apart the universe, and rearranged the pieces, and making a connection like that was rare.

"You going to be okay?" he asked.

I nodded, wiping away my tears.

"I think so," I said, glancing out the window at the crisp slant of late afternoon sunlight. "Come on, there's something I need to do."

I pulled open the door of Logan's nightstand and removed the little blue box that contained his EpiPen.

Jamie shot me a confused look.

"You'll see," I promised, and then I took his hand and we walked out into the preserve.

We didn't stop until we reached the cluster of honeysuckle bushes that had haunted me for so many years, the ones I'd stopped to look for on so many bike rides. The breeze was cold, and the trees moved with a slow whisper, as though guessing at what we were about to do.

"Hey, Cleo?" Jamie asked with a frown.

"So I had this idea," I said. "Remember how, in ancient Egypt, they buried things the dead might need to bring with them?"

Jamie's face lit up with understanding. We knelt down, and he passed me a rock, and together, we dug into the earth. I popped open the smooth plastic case, staring at the EpiPen that Logan had forgotten all those years ago.

It felt right to leave this here, in the preserve, a place that was designed to look after things, to keep them safe.

I pressed dirt on top of it until you couldn't tell anything was buried here at all. And then I took a step back, crying with an intensity that surprised me. Logan was gone, and I'd never truly mourned him. But I'd never truly lost him, either.

For some reason, I thought about the phrase "giving up the ghost," which means the opposite of what you'd think. It has nothing to do with letting go of someone you've lost. Instead, it's a euphemism for dying. But maybe that's not so strange, because losing someone can feel a lot like becoming lost yourself.

We read into fortune cookies and found pennies, looking for a sign that we're on the right path, that the road ahead of us isn't about to crumble away. Except no one ever tells you that, if the path does crumble, and you get lost in the wilderness, you can sometimes find your way back again.

It isn't easy, but it's possible.

307

I knew that as I sat with my friends at lunch, on our grassy slope where we never had to worry about having enough seats for everyone. As we carpooled to SAT prep over Christmas break, laughing because we couldn't ever agree on the music. As we tested each other at rehearsal, making sure we'd be okay when we had to know our lines from memory. And I knew it as Jamie drove us through the dark canyon, hoping we wouldn't see anyone else's ghosts, but knowing that we'd handle it together when we inevitably did.

I'd made so many spurious correlations, and I saw that now. I'd started to doubt myself and question where I belonged even before Logan's death. It was only after that I'd tried to find meaning in the mess of it all. I'd scrutinized my worst days, looking for some tangible thing that connected them, some omen I could use to recognize impending disaster. But the past doesn't tell you all that much about the future, no matter how hard you wish it did.

Sometimes you look around at your life and you see a ghost of a different one. It watches from the wings like an understudy that knows it won't go on. The play unfolds, and eventually, when you glance backstage, that life you knew is gone, and no one watching ever knew it was there at all.

Acknowledgments

When I was twenty-four, I found a time machine in Brooklyn. Technically it was the bathroom in a bar, and it had been decorated to look like the TARDIS from *Doctor Who*. To this day, I remain utterly convinced that I wouldn't have a writing career without that bar, that bathroom, or its owner. So here's to Andy Heidel and the Way Station. Without his glowing recommendation, I never would have found my incomparable agent, Merrilee Heifetz, who has been a mentor and friend for the past six years. And without my agent, I never would have found my incredible editor, Katherine Tegen, or my home at HarperCollins. And without my publisher, I never would have been on that flight to BookExpo America where I met Daniel, the boy I would eventually marry. And without Daniel, I never would have written this book. You're probably not supposed to thank a toilet in your acknowledgments, but thanking a television show or an online fan community is probably worse, so I'm going with the toilet. And now, a few additional side dishes of thank you: To my parents, always. To Julie Buxbaum, for joining me in the trenches. To Nadia Banteka, for letting me borrow some superstitions, and for luring me all the way to Greece to finish writing this novel. To Ari and Jenna Lubet, without whom this book would have been finished two months earlier. To Yvonne Tam, who brought me scientific ghost stories and spare pieces of philosophy. And to Yulin Kuang, who asked if I had any ideas for low-budget kissing scenes, a question that eventually led to this book.